"Don't Sara," Devo...

"Don't what?" Sara moved closer, drawn by his eyes. "Don't ask questions? Don't disagree with you? Don't get close?" A gentle plea entered her voice. "Fantasy is a part of growing up." She touched his face. "Maybe it wouldn't hurt you to fantasize a little."

He slowly raised her hand to his lips. "I already do," he said quietly. He drew her close. "You make me imagine totally impossible things."

Leaves rustled with the soft, sea-scented breeze. He smoothed flyaway strands of hair from her face. "I remember the first time I saw you. You were drinking from the stream. Something about you reminded me of the doe in the legend you were telling Mickey about. I think I was about his age the first time I heard it."

"Did you believe it, then?" she asked.

"No." He carried his touch along her jaw. "You make me want to believe in magic now, though."

She felt her heart bump against her ribs. "Maybe if you'd stop being such a cynic, you *would* believe. Even if it's just for a little while. . . ."

Dear Reader,

In a world of constant dizzying change, some things, fortunately, remain the same. One of those things is the Silhouette **Special Edition** commitment to our readers—a commitment, renewed each month, to bring you six stimulating, sensitive, substantial novels of living and loving in today's world, novels blending deep, vivid emotions with high romance.

This month, six fabulous authors step up to fulfill that commitment: Terese Ramin brings you the uproarious, unforgettable and decidedly adult *Accompanying Alice;* Jo Ann Algermissen lends her unique voice—and heart—to fond family feuding in *Would You Marry Me Anyway?;* Judi Edwards stirs our deepest hunger for love and healing in *Step from a Dream;* Christine Flynn enchants the senses with a tale of legendary love in *Out of the Mist;* Pat Warren deftly balances both the fears and the courage intimacy generates in *Till I Loved You;* and Dee Holmes delivers a mature, perceptive novel of the true nature of loving and heroism in *The Return of Slade Garner*. All six novels are sterling examples of the Silhouette **Special Edition** experience: romance you can believe in.

Next month also features a sensational array of talent, including two tantalizing volumes many of you have been clamoring for, by bestselling authors Ginna Gray and Debbie Macomber.

So don't miss a moment of the Silhouette **Special Edition** experience!

From all the authors and editors of Silhouette **Special Edition**—warmest wishes.

CHRISTINE FLYNN
Out of
the Mist

Silhouette Special Edition

Published by Silhouette Books New York

America's Publisher of Contemporary Romance

SILHOUETTE BOOKS
300 East 42nd St., New York, N.Y. 10017

OUT OF THE MIST

ISBN: 0-373-09657-7

First Silhouette Books printing March 1991

Books by Christine Flynn

Silhouette Romance

Stolen Promise #435
Courtney's Conspiracy #623

Silhouette Special Edition

Remember the Dreams #254
Silence the Shadows #465
Renegade #566
Walk Upon the Wind #612
Out of the Mist #657

Silhouette Desire

When Snow Meets Fire #254
The Myth and the Magic #296
A Place to Belong #352
Meet Me at Midnight #377

CHRISTINE FLYNN

is formerly from Oregon and currently resides in the Southwest with her husband, teenage daughter and two very spoiled dogs.

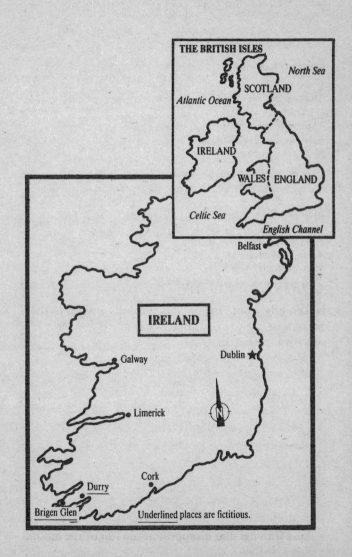

THE BRITISH ISLES

North Sea

SCOTLAND

Atlantic Ocean

IRELAND

WALES ENGLAND

Celtic Sea

English Channel

Belfast

IRELAND

Galway

Dublin ★

Limerick

N

Cork

Durry

Brigen Glen

Underlined places are fictitious.

Chapter One

Back in the days when Ireland was young, the most incredible tales sprang from the mist that clung to her coasts. It was said that a banshee could not wail without that fog, nor could elves turn their coal into gold. More importantly, the ethereal mist was necessary for the mysterious enchantments that lured men's hearts.

One such legend told of a golden doe who returned to Brigen Glen once every hundred years in search of the love that would make her real. She appeared as a beautiful woman, bewitching the first eligible bachelor she encountered into a grand obsession with the unusual sound of her voice. She came with the first light of day, when the fog was its thickest, and if the man failed to win her heart, she would take his happiness with her and disappear at the full of the moon.

* * *

The morning fog seemed heavier than usual to Devon
O'Donaugh. The mist curled ahead of him, swirling and
silvery in the weak morning light, as he followed the moss-
covered path through the woods beyond his cottage. The
path skirted a wide glen—lush and verdant when the sun
shone, shrouded in gray on mornings such as this. Beyond
the glen half a mile away sat the linen mill Devon managed
for his family. On a clearer day, the mill's massive chimneys would be visible over the rise. Today he'd be lucky to
see the building before he bumped into it.

The fog—that soft Irish weather as it was affectionately
called by those who lived with it—was as familiar as rain.
Normally he gave it no thought. The mist was simply there,
obscuring the view and softening the edges of his world,
until it lifted. Yet this particular morning, the damp air felt
peculiar...expectant, if that were possible, or ominous
somehow. The feeling did little to ease his already agitated
mood.

Devon stooped to walk under a low-hanging branch,
leaves rustling dully as his broad shoulders failed to completely clear it. He barely noticed the scattering leaves or the
perturbed admonishments of the birds he'd disturbed. As
usual, he was too preoccupied to pay more than a moment's attention to his surroundings.

As the oldest able-bodied male member of the O'Donaugh family, Devon's thoughts were nearly always on his
responsibilities. For the most part, he accepted his role
without question, though sometimes, especially when it
came to dealing with his Aunt Kathleen, he found the du-
ties thrust upon him frustrating. Yet, even frustrations had
their place. They helped fill the empty spaces in his life and
kept him from thinking too much. As for his aunt, he supposed she felt obligated to remind him of his failings.
Heaven knew he gave her enough material to work with.

This morning, however, it wasn't his aunt's incessant nagging that put the tension into his powerful strides. It was the prospect of arriving at the mill to find more of the vandalism that had befallen it over the past week.

He broke through the trees, automatically glancing in the direction of the mill. The fog erased the ancient stone chimneys from view, but directly ahead of him the mist had lifted enough for him to see along the stream that meandered through his narrow little valley.

His stride, purposeful and unhesitating until now, suddenly slowed. Narrowing his glance to sharpen his focus, he drew to a halt where the purple heather met a copse of oak trees. Though it was still hazy, he could see a woman crouched at the bank of the stream.

Her head was bent and her fawn-colored hair fell forward, hiding her face as she cupped her hands to drink the cool water. The veiling mist made it difficult to see clearly, so he moved closer, curious to know who would be out so early. Villages, like families, had habits. While people were certainly out and about, it was unusual to see anyone in the glen at this hour.

A twig snapped beneath his boot. The sound, sharp in the fragile silence, caused her to jerk around like a startled doe.

Though he was less than twenty feet away, Devon knew she didn't see him. Dressed in a dark sweater and pants, he blended with the trees behind him. He started to call out, to let her know it was a man not a beast that had frightened her. But she looked neither frightened nor especially curious as to the cause of the noise. In the next instant, he found the assurance of her safety unnecessary. Tall and lithe, she moved with agile grace as she rose, then turned to run along the edge of the stream. Within seconds, she was swallowed up in the fog.

Devon, bemused, watched her go. He had only caught a glimpse of her warm brown eyes and golden skin, but something about her had reminded him of the deer that came down from the hills to drink at the stream. His next thought as the mist swirled in to cover the ground where she'd stood was that it felt as if he'd only imagined her.

"You're going daft, man," he muttered to himself and turned his thoughts in a more practical direction. It wasn't like him to engage in fancy. The old men did that, usually after a pint too many. He knew what he'd seen.

What he had seen was an outsider, a stranger to Brigen Glen. Certainly *he* had never seen the woman before. He'd lived in the remote little village all of his thirty-six years, so he knew every one of its two hundred and eight inhabitants. The woman who'd just disappeared into the mist was not one of them.

That being the case, he couldn't help but wonder who she was—and as he took off after her, what she was doing so near his mill.

Sara Madigan slowed her pace as she followed the stream around the curve of a hill. The fog wasn't as dense as it had been when she'd started out, and she was fairly sure that the dirt road ahead of her was the one that had led her here. She didn't remember the fork in the road several yards ahead, though, or the long stone fence running parallel to it. Beyond the fence was a dew-drenched meadow. Out of it rose the misty shape of a gray building with four massive chimneys. The fog must have obscured it all earlier.

Not in the least concerned that she might be lost, she gave the knees of her beige sweatpants a tug and sat down on the three-foot-high wall. Going for a run in the fog wasn't particularly smart since she was unfamiliar with the terrain, but she'd lacked the patience to stay quietly in her room and wait for the weather to clear. She'd never been one to sit around when she could be doing something.

Now she wanted to do nothing more than quietly absorb the fact that she was actually here. In the three weeks since her grandmother had died, she'd pushed herself mercilessly to accomplish that goal. She had promised, after all. And she'd done it as fast as humanly possible. As a buyer for a specialty importer, Sara had rushed through twelve trade shows in half a dozen cities to conclude her current buying trip. She'd finished up in London yesterday, landed in Shannon last evening, taken a bus as far as Glengariff and arrived by horse-drawn trap in Brigen Glen late last night.

She set those thoughts aside. Now that she had a chance to catch her breath, she didn't want to think of why she was here, or even of what she'd promised her grandmother. There would be time for that later. At the moment, she needed to orient herself. She felt as if she'd taken a turn in a time tunnel. She'd left the twentieth century behind and stepped back three hundred years.

There were no cars here, few telephones and the nearest fax machine was more than fifty miles away. The roads were dirt, narrow and rutted. Stone cottages with thatched roofs dotted the incredibly green rolling hills and the rich, loamy smell of burning peat from the home fires scented the morning air. The only sounds she heard were of wakening birds and the distant rush of the stream. A sense of peace hung over the village, much like its protective, concealing mist.

Yes, Sara sighed to herself, hugging her arms as she breathed in the damp, clean air. It was just as her grandmother had told her it would be. All it lacked was the sound of laughter from the leprechauns purported to inhabit the stumps of fallen trees.

Blessed with a fertile, fanciful imagination, she knew that if she tried hard enough, she might be able to hear such a sound. She could even imagine, if she really concentrated, that the butterflies hovering over a nearby clump of pale yellow flowers were actually faeries dancing on the morning mist. She had often been told about the faeries and so many other tales—wonderful, delightful, mysterious tales—about the place of her grandmother's birth.

Those thoughts made her smile. They also made her sad. She missed her grandmother very much. Compounding that ache was a sense of guilt that she should have spent more time with her these past few years. *Made* the time. Her grandmother had worried so about Sara being "out in the world," as she'd put it, and asked often to see her. Whenever Sara spoke with her on the phone, she'd offered the assurance that she was fine. But always, too, there had been some reason she couldn't get away just then; trouble with some account, or an upcoming trip that couldn't be postponed. Then she'd received the call that her grandmother was dying.

Right now she couldn't hear leprechauns, but pulling her from the memory of the woman who had raised her was the distant laughter of a child. Looking up from the gossamer-winged butterflies, she could see a young boy coming through the light mist that hovered over the rutted road.

He wore knickers and knee socks and his corduroy coat had patches at the elbows. A puppy, spotted white and brown, tumbled around his feet. The dog was after the sack the boy carried, and the child seemed torn between scolding the dog for its behavior and giggling at its antics.

The puppy darted forward and back, jumping for the sack. The way he wove in and out of the boy's legs made it nearly impossible for the child to watch where he was going—especially when the boy held the sack higher to keep it from reach. That was why, still giggling, he didn't see the pothole in front of him.

Sara didn't have time to call out a warning. One second the boy was upright. The next he was on his hands and knees. Then with the speed and nonchalance peculiar to young children, he scrambled to his feet and was running after the dog.

The tweed cap that covered his curly, cinnamon-colored hair had fallen off and lay forgotten in the damp dirt. The playful little mongrel had the bottom edge of the sack clamped between his jaws and was spilling its contents in a trail behind him, seeming inordinately pleased with the chase.

Sara headed the little thief off at the fence. Scooping up the five-pound ball of fur, she turned to the boy.

Seeing her, he went stock-still.

The moment she'd picked up the dog, it had let go of its prize. Now it had its paws planted on her chest and was trying to lick her chin. "Quite a handful, aren't you?" she said to the puppy, then smiling, held the squirming animal out to the boy. "Does he have a name?"

The child stared up at her and said nothing. He just reached out and took the dog.

With a shrug for his reluctance, she retrieved the abandoned sack and retraced the path the dog had taken. An apple was dropped into the bag. Two steps ahead lay what appeared to be a paper-wrapped sandwich. Depositing that in the sack, she glanced back to the little boy. He was watching her closely, the puppy hugged tight to his chest.

"If he were mine, I think I'd call him Mischief. I can't have a puppy, though," she went on, wanting to put the boy at ease. "I'm away from home too much. Do you live near here?"

No response was forthcoming, so she turned back to her task. A small napkin-wrapped packet had come open and three cookies lay in a clump of damp grass crowning the hump in the road. They had been crushed to crumbs when the boy ran over them.

Taking a granola bar from the pocket of her jogging suit, she surreptitiously dropped it into the sack to replace his dessert and proceeded on to his hat. A couple of whacks against the side of her thigh as she walked to him and the cap was free of whatever dirt had clung to it.

She held the sack out to him. Slowly, his soulful eyes never leaving her face, he reached out and took it. It occurred to Sara as he did that he wasn't frightened of her. He was just terribly shy.

"My name is Sara," she told him, her voice hushed and gentle. "Do you have a name?"

The little boy nodded, then cocked his head to one side and frowned.

That made Sara frown, too. "Is something wrong?"

He nodded again.

"Can you tell me what it is?"

His gesture was hesitant, but he raised his hand and very slowly extended his index finger toward her.

"Did you hurt your finger?" she asked, thinking that the only logical conclusion to his action.

He shook his head as he moved his finger closer to her. He was pointing to her mouth.

For a moment, she thought he might be mute, that he couldn't say what it was that had his little brow so furrowed. Then she remembered what had first made her notice him—the sound of his laughter as he'd scolded the puppy.

"I'm sorry, but I don't know what you're trying to tell me." Genuinely at a loss, she could do nothing but offer him an apologetic smile. How was it possible, she wondered, that a child so young could look so solemn?

He didn't want to speak. That was apparent. Even as she started to move away, she could see his reluctance. Yet his curiosity over whatever had him so puzzled outweighed his reticence. After another moment's hesitation, he quietly said, "You talk funny."

The look on his face was so serious that she couldn't help but smile. To him, she probably did sound different. They both spoke English, but his pronunciation of the language was accentuated with the Gaelic lilt of the Irish. Hers was a more prosaic American.

She hunched down in front of him and placed the cap on his head at a jaunty angle. The kid had the longest eyelashes and the biggest brown eyes she'd ever seen. Given about fifteen years, he'd be breaking hearts all over County Cork. "That's because I come from a place very far away and this is how we speak there. Do you know where America is?"

He slowly shook his head.

"Have you ever heard of it?"

Again the slow, negative shake.

He was only five or six, so she wasn't particularly surprised at his reply. No doubt few children his age back home knew where Ireland was, either. But oddly, he didn't seem in any hurry to end their one-sided conversation. He seemed to want to keep *her* talking—intrigued as he was by her accent—but he was too shy to reply.

With the puppy placing wet and generous kisses along his neck, the tickling making him giggle, he asked where America was.

Thinking it simpler to show than explain, she sat down by the side of the road. With the end of a stick, she drew a map of sorts in the damp dirt while the boy—Mickey, he finally told her his name was—did his best to keep the puppy from messing up her lines. The puppy, she learned when it started pulling on the end of her stick, was called Tug. He'd earned the name because of a game he liked to play with his uncle's socks.

Sara was fascinated with children. Their honesty and innocence were as yet untainted, and though she seldom found herself around them, she enjoyed their company immensely. The world through a child's eyes was a wonderous place, filled with all manner of excitement and discovery.

That was how Sara saw the world, too. She kept herself constantly on the go, always wanting to discover new places. But her enthusiasm wasn't what it had once been, and now she seemed more caught up in the movement than in the purpose. Her grandmother had pointed that out more than once in the past year.

Sara shook off that errant thought, finding that it had no place in this land of leprechauns and legends, and tried not to laugh at Mickey's determined but futile efforts to control his puppy. Her laughter must have encouraged another smile from Mickey, but when she glanced up her own smile faltered. A moment later, it died completely.

A man had emerged out of the mist. Brooding and silent, he stood with his hands on his hips, his brow knit in a frown as he watched her and the boy.

Sara felt her breath catch. She'd been startled, but it wasn't fear that rooted her to the ground. It was fascination.

In this place out of time, he fit perfectly. He was a big man, tall and commanding. Primitive. Powerful. Strength and purpose were revealed in his face; his lean, angular features more rugged than classic. Thick and black, his hair curled over the collar of his heavy knit sweater. He wore it long, a style that much of the civilized world would look upon as a subtle form of defiance. And his eyes, a blue so deep the color rivaled the Kerry Sea, revealed absolutely nothing.

He reminded her of a Celtic warrior, one of that great lot whose love of liberty had led to such bravery in battle. As she shivered at that thought, it occurred to her that this man might rightfully claim such ancestry. He had the look of a man not easily disposed to compromise or understanding.

"Mickey. Are you all right, lad?" Even his voice hinted at an unyielding strength. Deep and smoky, it carried more than a hint of a brogue.

Suddenly subdued, the boy rose, batting at the dust on his seat, and looked up with his great, solemn eyes. His head dipped in a nod.

"Then you'd best be getting on to school, hadn't you? You don't want Miss Cavanaugh to worry that you're late." He glanced toward Sara, then back to the boy as he picked up his sack. The deep voice gentled further. "You're sure you're all right?"

After another nod, more vigorous this time, Mickey was off. The puppy, which had darted toward the man as if certain of his welcome, immediately altered its course to scramble after its young master.

Children shouldn't talk to strangers. Sara assumed the rule to be universal. Ready to assure the child's rescuer that she'd meant the boy no harm, she stood and pushed her long hair from her face. She had no more opened her mouth, than she closed it again. The man was walking toward her, each step measured and deliberate. His glance moved with that same aggression over the pale, silken hair tumbling past her shoulders and down her willowy frame. The look in his eyes was unmistakably male, his appreciation of her feminine attributes quite evident in his slow perusal. Yet distrust clearly marked his expression when his scrutiny returned to her face.

"Good morning to you."

The simple, civil greeting threw her. She'd anticipated challenge. "Good morning," she returned, and saw him hesitate.

His glance narrowed, caution shadowing his features. The sound of her voice had seemed to catch him off guard. Perhaps, as with Mickey, she thought, it was her lack of a brogue that he found curious. Whatever the reason, he seemed more suspicious of her presence than he had a moment before.

"This is my property." His glance swung beyond her shoulder to the large stone building across the meadow. Rows of weathered wood-paned windows marked its two floors and he seemed to visually check each of them before he returned his attention to her. "May I ask what you're doing here?"

The tone of his question was specific. He wanted to know what she was doing in this particular spot, not what she was doing in Brigen Glen. That would take more of an explanation than she felt inclined to give him anyway—even though he might have been able to help her locate the man she'd come here to find.

She turned to the clump of heather where the butterflies still hovered. If he wanted to know what she had been doing, she'd be happy to tell him. After all, if it was his property, he had a right to know. "I'd gone for a run and stopped here to rest," she explained. "I was waiting for the faeries when Mickey came along. His puppy was after..."

"The faeries?"

She smiled easily, her eyes reflecting the fondness of a memory. "I wanted to see if they really danced on the mist in the morning. My grandmother always told me that they did, but I think they must be somewhere else today."

"I hope you weren't sharing such nonsense with the boy."

He'd asked a question and she'd answered it with complete honesty. In turn, she'd thought he would have accepted the explanation in the congenial spirit with which it was offered. The terseness of his response made it clear that she'd been mistaken. He was obviously not open to amicable references to the local lore, nor was he particularly receptive to a friendly smile. All he did was scowl at her.

He'd been protective of the child, though. That redeemed his present manner enough for her to indulge a little of her natural curiosity.

"Is Mickey yours?"

"He's my responsibility," he cryptically replied. "And I'd prefer that strangers didn't fill his head with impossibilities. The boy has troubles enough as it is."

"I wasn't filling his head with impossibilities. I never even mentioned the faeries."

She wasn't given a chance to mention what they had been discussing, either. Impatience entered the man's voice, along with a definite trace of sarcasm. "I'm most relieved to hear that. Now I'd appreciate learning what you're really doing here. I saw you not long ago. By the stream. You were just there, weren't you?"

He seemed determined to put her on the defensive. It wasn't a position she often took, but she wasn't allowed a choice at the moment. She never lied. Even shading the truth made her uncomfortable. Yet he obviously didn't believe her. Still, she maintained her calm.

"I was by the stream," she admitted, though she certainly hadn't seen him. Except for Mickey, she hadn't seen anyone this morning. "I just came from there. If I was trespassing, I'm sorry. I didn't see any signs to indicate that it was private property."

"There are none. We've never found a need for postings in Brigen Glen." There was an implication in his words that he might be reconsidering that need—and that she could very well have something to do with that circumstance. She couldn't imagine why, though, or why his eyes narrowed in accusation. "You weren't by any chance on your way to the mill, were you?"

She assumed he must be talking about the large building beyond the stone fence. The stream flowed past it, its clear, cold water captured in a pond beside the gray structure. A wooden waterwheel turned slowly at the dammed-off end of a pond. Nestled amid a stand of oak trees, the setting was picturesque, serene. He clearly didn't like the idea that she may have intended to trespass there, too.

As she met his cool-eyed scrutiny, it occurred to her that he thought her guilty of something other than unintentionally breaching the boundaries of his property.

"I wasn't going to the mill," she told him, because until the fog had begun to lift she hadn't even known it was there. The place was starting to intrigue her, though, seeming a little forbidden because of his concern about it. "I already told you what I was doing."

Exasperation now joined his impatience. "You don't really expect me to believe that a grown woman was sitting here waiting for an apparition, do you?"

"All I expect," she returned gently, "is that you believe what I say."

His heavy dark eyebrows rose fractionally. "Am I to assume that you actually believe such ridiculousness?"

He had already indirectly called her a liar. Now he was calling her ridiculous. In the process, he also attacked the basis of memories she held very dear. Common sense told her that faeries and elves and such weren't real, but she saw no harm at all in indulging imagination. It expanded the soul, her grandmother had said. Aside from that, what mortal knew for certain what was truly real and what wasn't?

Silently labeling him both opinionated and pompous, she gave him an angelic smile. "I'm sure what I believe doesn't matter to you in the least. And you may believe whatever you wish."

With the toss of her head, she took off at a trot, her long hair swaying against her back. Devon didn't know if it was the touch of insolence in her dismissal or the athletic grace of her movements that intrigued him most.

She was obviously a tourist. They didn't get many visitors here—scarcely a handful a year—but occasionally one or two would find their way down the rocky peninsula and stick around for a day to photograph the countryside. She didn't have a camera, though, and tourists, like quail, tended to travel in pairs.

That thought resurrected the initial reason for his less than hospitable behavior. She was a stranger and with all the strange happenings at the mill—all of them having taken place when no one was about—he'd had every right to question her presence.

What wasn't so easy to justify was the wariness he'd felt when he heard her softly accented voice. It was seductive, like her laugh, and it had done something odd to his senses. He'd had the strangest urge to reach out and touch her, to see if her skin was really as soft as it looked. She was a beautiful woman, her face fine boned and delicate. As she had spoken, his attention had been drawn to the lovely shape of her mouth. For a fleeting moment, he hadn't been able to keep from wondering how it would feel against his own.

A knot of need formed at that thought. The ache was deep and strong, its swiftness startling. She was lovely, but he'd be better off forgetting he'd ever seen her. He had learned to live without the comfort of a woman. Yet something about her demanded that he remember what he was denying himself.

The path his thoughts were taking could lead him nowhere. He swung his leg over the fence to cross the meadow to the mill. It did little good to tell himself to dismiss the encounter. There was another inexplicable phenomenon to consider. Specifically, the effect of the woman on Mickey. Now that he thought about it, when Devon came upon them they'd been engaged in conversation.

That fact hadn't registered at first because he'd been too far away to hear their voices. Then he'd been too busy fighting the lure of her smile to consider it. But Mickey had actually been *talking* with the woman. Devon had rarely heard the child speak.

Mickey was his cousin Molly's son. The middle of three boys, he was the quietest and the least likely of his many young cousins to cause any trouble. He'd always seemed painfully shy and not at all inclined to deal with anyone outside his family. Even with them he was so quiet one would scarcely realize he was there. His reticence had become even more acute in the past year. Yet he'd been chattering away to a stranger. It was almost as if she'd charmed him.

Were Devon inclined to admit it, he supposed that he had felt her charm, too. Though certainly on a much more elemental level.

How did that old legend go? he wondered, lengthening his purposeful strides. Did the deer only have to speak to put the spell in place?

For the second time that morning, he shook his head at his own foolishness and dismissed his thoughts as absurd. Devon was a dyed-in-the-wool realist. Over the years, he'd learned that the less a man believed in, the less were his chances of being disappointed with what life handed him— or with what he chose to take from it. The old myths were utter nonsense, nothing more than entertainment for small children and something for old women to pin their warnings on. The woman he'd just met was simply a flesh-and-blood woman. Beautiful flesh, he had to admit, and probably very warm blood judging from the awareness he'd seen in her eyes, but human nonetheless.

He reached that conclusion about the time he reached the mill's heavy wooden door. It groaned on its hinges when he opened it with one of the long keys tied with a leather thong to his belt. Silence greeted him, a silence that would be replaced within the hour by the clank of machinery and the chatter of voices. Throwing switches to add light, he made his way to his office, quickly checked it to see that all was in order, then hurried on through the hackling area to the room housing the looms.

Everything seemed to be as it had been left last night. The large hand looms with their interweaving warp and woof of flax threads sat quietly in the glare of the bare overhead bulbs. In the next area, the ungainly steam-driven looms waited for the ancient generator to jolt them to life. Beyond them, bolts of finished linen lay in neat rows by the side service door. Wrapped and ready for shipment, that lot had been contracted for enough to provide the remainder of the down payment on the new power looms Devon wanted to order. The shipment was due to go out this morning.

He hadn't realized how tense he'd been until he felt his breath slowly release. Pushing him this morning had been the vague fear that something had happened to the fabric—that the vandals might have gone from merely inconveniencing him to incapacitating him. But nothing had happened. Kevin would be here within the hour and the lot would be loaded on a cart and safely on its way.

Consciously relaxing his shoulder muscles, kneading at the knotted one in his neck, he turned his thoughts to the day ahead. He'd been in such a hurry to get here that he hadn't bothered to make himself coffee. The first thing he needed to do was start a pot.

He was nearly back to his office when a scraping sound, slight and muffled, froze him in his tracks. The noise was followed by a thud and the sound of tumbling boxes. The commotion came from behind the door of the storage room he'd just passed.

Two weeks ago someone had broken into that room and stolen the new chemicals he wanted to try, a new additive to keep the flax from rotting in the retting pools. Aside from increasing the quantity of usable flax, the chemical would speed up the process of freeing the fibers from their woody stalks. It had taken him until two days ago to replace the supply.

His powerful body instantly alert, he jerked around and threw open the door. It slammed into the wall, wobbled on its hinges and bounced back. Empty boxes that had been stored near the ceiling lay scattered over the floor and the top of a nearby table. No one appeared to be in the room. It was as if a phantom had swept through the place, upending the boxes as it passed.

Unbidden, the sweetly innocent face of the woman he'd encountered just a short while ago flashed through his mind.

He took another step into the room. When he spoke, his voice was low, menacing. "I know you're in here."

A head of brown curls immediately emerged from the other side of the table. The woman's eyes were huge behind her wire-rimmed glasses, startled as she obviously was by the racket he'd made with his entry.

"Lord a mercy," she muttered and let out her breath. "You scared the daylights out of me, Devon O'Donaugh."

Mary McMurtry lifted her short, round frame from the wood-slat floor, adjusting her shawl as she did, and pointed an accusing finger at the top shelf. "You don't suppose it'd be asking too much to put the bobbins back on a low shelf, would you? Not all of us can reach so far up."

Barely five feet tall, she didn't have a prayer of reaching the eight-foot shelf. She'd obviously tried . . . and the stool she'd used to stand on had come right out from under her.

"How did you get in here?"

"I walked through the door. Just like I always do." She frowned. "Are you feeling all right?"

She'd come in after him—after he'd unlocked the door and while he was checking to make sure that all was as it should be. Realizing from the questioning look on Mary's weathered face that she thought both his question and his behavior puzzling, Devon closed his eyes and drew a deep, stabilizing breath.

If anyone should be expressing concern, it should be him. He always preached safety to the people who worked for him, insisting that nothing was more important. He'd even been accused of being fanatical about it at times. It galled him to think that his own neglect could have caused someone harm.

Devon had put the bobbins on the top shelf himself while rearranging supplies to make room for the plastic bottles containing his newly replaced additives. He'd meant to put the bobbins in a more convenient place, but he'd been interrupted before he'd had the chance.

He explained that to Mary and asked if she had hurt herself when she'd fallen.

Mary brushed off his concern with the wave of her hand. "I caught myself on the table. Broke my fall before I ever hit the floor. Now if you'll reach me the bobbins, I'll be getting out of your way."

Satisfied that Mary was as unscathed as she insisted, he moved three boxes of the tall, flax-wound spindles to a shelf at waist height. Mary was the fastest weaver in all of Cork County, though she modestly denied such talent, and she went through more bobbins in a week than the other women who worked the looms did in two. Her speed and proficiency had come from forty years' experience. She'd started on the looms as a young girl, as had the other twenty women in his employ.

He turned to make sure she had everything she needed and caught her frowning at the foreign-looking plastic bottles with their complicated, scientific names. The way her lips thinned spoke volumes.

Changes of any kind weren't tolerated well in Brigen Glen. It didn't matter if the change involved an attitude, a method or a style. If something was approached in a manner much different than what was already accepted, the new way was immediately suspect. At best, it was an affront. At worst, it was a threat.

Mary's silent commentary now made it apparent that she didn't think much of his attempts to update production methods. Just as obvious was Devon's refusal to acknowledge her disapproval. Mary had worked for his father and for his father's father and she was as dedicated to the old ways as the rest of the villagers. That was why Devon didn't discuss his plans with anyone anymore. He simply did what he knew he had to do.

So far, that approach had worked well. With his uncle away on holiday, the only person in Brigen Glen who still vocalized opposition was his Aunt Kathleen.

His groan met Mary's fading footsteps. He'd just remembered that he was expected at his aunt's cottage for dinner tonight.

Chapter Two

Sara couldn't put it off any longer. She was lousy at procrastination anyway.

Pocketing the thick gold ring she'd worried between her fingers for the better part of half an hour, she came to a halt by her bed, pivoted and headed for the door of her comfortable but very tiny room. When she had returned to Mrs. Carrigan's Inn and Pub this morning, she'd bathed and changed, then proceeded to pace. She always paced when she was agitated.

This morning, though, she wasn't exactly sure what she was agitated about. It didn't matter that the alien and compelling peace she'd experienced when she'd arrived had been so rudely snatched away. And there was certainly no point in being upset with the lummox of a man who'd taken it upon himself to deprive her of it. She didn't have to deal with him anyway. What she *did* have to do was find the man her grandmother had told her about. That was why she was here, after all.

Another trip across the room and she decided that was why she'd nearly worn the pattern through the carpet. Until she'd arrived in Brigen Glen, she hadn't had time to really think about how uneasy she felt about this task.

Uneasy or not, she had promised she would do it.

It was well after noon and the fog had burned away to let a pale sun peek through the scattered clouds. Without its concealing veil, the whole of Brigen Glen could be seen stretching out along the gently rolling emerald land. The village didn't appear to have a center, at least not one marked by commercial buildings. The church, a squat, whitewashed structure with heavy wooden doors and topped by a spire and cross, seemed to serve that purpose. It occupied a small rise along with a single oak tree.

Once she passed the hill with its church and a cemetery on the farthest side, she followed the narrow dirt road past beehive-shaped straw huts and small fields of grazing sheep. Between those fields sat thatch-roofed cottages made of the gray stones that were as prevalent as blades of grass on the Bere Peninsula. Each cottage sat in a yard enclosed by a hip-high stone wall. For as far as the eye could see, everything seemed to be separated, joined or delineated by that continuous line of three-foot-high stone fence.

Sara had no trouble finding the cottage she'd set out to locate.

"It's the third on the left past the church and two pastures from the back of the mill," the kindly woman who owned the inn had told her.

Now approaching the freshly whitewashed front door, she wished that her search hadn't been quite so easy. Everyone in Brigen Glen, small as it was, knew everyone else, so finding the home of a person who'd lived there all of his life hadn't been difficult. She couldn't help thinking that it would have been nice if Thomas O'Donaugh's cottage had been a little more difficult to locate. Running into an obstacle or two would have given her an excuse to stay longer in this strange and wonderful place.

Since no one had answered her knock, she stuffed her hands into the pockets of her tailored slacks and walked around the side of the neat little structure. Lace curtains hung on all the paned windows, a small table holding a bowl of marigolds visible through one of them. Two of the windows were open to let in the breeze. The flowers had no doubt come from the garden lining the rock wall. Except for a patch of incredibly green grass with a birdbath in its center, the entire space was filled with blooms of every imaginable shade.

At the far side of the yard, an elderly woman wearing a bright blue scarf knelt over a pot of deep-pink blossoms. She was carrying on an animated dialogue with a fuchsia, her tone soothing as she told the plant how much better it would feel in a larger pot.

A smile crept across Sara's face when the woman paused as if to allow the plant time to reply. Her grandmother had always talked to her plants, and her geraniums had been the biggest and brightest in all of upstate New York. Sara herself had never acquired the knack for growing things. All she'd developed was a taste for the blooms—especially nasturtiums and peppery carnations. She never had understood all the fuss when, a few years ago, chefs began to incorporate them into salads and labeled the addition nouvelle cuisine. She could hardly think of edible flowers as new when she'd been eating them most of her life.

"Excuse me," Sara said, apology in her smile for the interruption.

The woman's head bobbed up. From beneath her scarf, a wisp of silvering red hair fell over her forehead. She blew it away with a puff.

Seeing a stranger in her yard didn't seem to concern her. She greeted Sara like a neighbor—with a smile and a twinkle of welcome in her bright blue eyes.

"Good day to you. Good to see the sun. Been hiding from us for days it seems. Devil of a fog this morning, wasn't it?"

Sara apparently wasn't expected to do anything more than agree.

The weather. The subject was universal enough to open a conversation anywhere and in Ireland it was discussed as zealously as the stock market was on Wall Street. Speculating what the weather might do next was a form of national sport. In thirty minutes' time, it could go from sun to rain to hail and back again.

The woman rose, knocking the dirt from her trowel as she did. The trowel then disappeared into the pocket of the blue canvas apron she wore over her print housedress. "What can I do for you, miss?"

"I'm looking for Thomas O'Donaugh. This is his house, isn't it?"

"It is. And who'd be looking for him?"

"My name is Sara. I'm Fiona Madigan's granddaughter."

A wing of cinnamon-colored eyebrow arched in quiet surprise. "Fiona Madigan." The woman said the name slowly, drawing it out as if to recall every syllable. She made the words sound like an incantation. "Now there's a name I haven't heard in a good while."

The woman brushed the dirt from her hands, the motion as efficient as the careful once-over she gave Sara. Her eyes were as clear as a summer sky and unapologetically shrewd. "You're her granddaughter, you say?"

Sara nodded.

"And you're looking for Thomas?"

Another nod, this one a little less certain. Sara felt her fingers close protectively over the cool metal in her pocket.

A twinge of reluctance made itself felt as she caressed the familiar shape. "My grandmother asked me to give him something shortly before she died."

Puzzlement—then caution—flitted over the woman's face. It was difficult for Sara to determine what that caution meant. Especially since the woman was so quick to cover it.

After saying she was sorry to hear that her grandmother had passed on, and quickly crossing herself in an automatic prayer for the repose of her soul, the diminutive woman slipped off her apron. "My manners are suffering today, I'm afraid. I'm Kathleen O'Donaugh," she offered by way of introduction. "Thomas's sister. He's been living with me since his wife passed on a few years ago. Said he couldn't stand being by himself, but I suspect that what he couldn't stand was his own cooking. Takes a remarkable talent to make a good piece of mutton taste like lamb's wool, but Thomas has the knack. Be that as it may, he gave his house over to one of our nieces and her family and I've been putting up with him ever since."

Her tone was conversational, but etched over her wrinkles was a faintly martyred expression. That stoicism would have been convincing if not for the twinkle in her eyes. "No need me boring you with my troubles," she continued, looking as if she were trying to figure out what to do with her unexpected guest. "Please. Come inside and I'll fix us some tea. It's not often that we get visitors here."

Under any other circumstances, Sara would have been most eager to accompany the outspoken old woman. There was a certain irreverence about Kathleen that appealed to Sara, an attitude that said she didn't take herself too seriously, though she probably expected her family to do so. Sara didn't get a chance to really appreciate all of that, though.

Thinking that perhaps the man she'd come to see was inside, she hesitated. She wanted very much to do as her
grandmother had asked. Yet part of her held back, the part
that protected all the memories she had of the woman who
had been the only family she had ever known. Suddenly it
felt as if by fulfilling her promise, those memories would be
threatened, that everything she'd known would never be the
same.

She shook off the disquieting thought. Logic told her that
nothing could change the way she remembered her grandmother. No one could change what had been. Still, the
vague apprehension lingered.

"I don't want to impose."

Kathleen waved off the concern. "You're not. I could use
the company. Come now. And watch where you put your
feet." She pointed to the ground as she started around the
corner of the cottage. Stepping stones formed a line between flower and vegetable garden. "The mud's particularly bad along here."

For all practical purposes, Kathleen appeared most gracious as she set about her tiny kitchen preparing tea and
setting out a plate of shortbread. But Sara was aware of a
certain reserve in her manner—the caution she'd first seen,
perhaps—along with a definite curiosity. Sara took no offense. She would have been curious, too, had a stranger
from a distant country arrived with a bequest from a near-
forgotten acquaintance. Still, Thomas's sister made an effort to keep her inquires polite—and to keep any prejudice
she may have felt toward Fiona to herself.

"I never knew much about your grandmother," the older
woman told Sara as she set a porcelain pot and cups on the
lace-covered table between two comfortable wing chairs. She
invited Sara to sit, managing to appear occupied with the
ritual of pouring tea when what she was really doing was

studying Sara. "She rarely came into town and we weren't allowed back in the woods where she lived."

"You weren't allowed?"

Kathleen smiled and handed her a cup. "It was for our own protection. It had been that way ever since we were children. Especially then we never dared go into the forest. Our parents would tell us the most dreadful tales of what fate met the boy or girl who did. Of course," she continued, finding nothing unusual in her revelations, "most of those tales were a bit embellished, designed to put the fear of God into the child so he'd stay close to home. But you can be sure there was some truth to the stories. It was dangerous in the woods for those who weren't familiar with them."

Sara's brow furrowed as she watched the sweetly scented steam curl over her cup. She was confused. Her grandmother had never mentioned living in a forest. "Is it still that way?"

"It might be if most of the forest hadn't been cut down. Now it's not near so dense as it once was." A look of regret touched her face, as if she truly missed what had once frightened her. Sighing, she added, "The woods aren't the same at all."

The melancholy departed as quickly as it had appeared. Daintily lifting her cup, the woman took an idle sip of tea. Her unhurried motions were deceptive. Sara knew that Kathleen was gauging her reaction. The woman had to know that much of what she'd said had raised questions in Sara's mind.

She eyed Sara over the top of her cup. "You said you've come with a bequest for my brother. Where is it exactly that you've come from? Your accent is American, isn't it?"

Sara told her that it was and, for lack of a better place, said that she was from a small town in upstate New York. She actually hadn't lived there in ages. But that was where her grandmother had raised her and that was where her grandmother had died. For the past several years, Sara herself had maintained a small apartment in Hartford because the company she worked for was based there. She was rarely in Hartford, though, and it had never been "home."

As Kathleen systematically persevered in her questions, Sara began to realize that the man she'd come to see either wasn't in the house or Kathleen wasn't going to get him until she'd satisfied her own curiosity about Sara's visit. Sara couldn't imagine where he could be hidden, though. The cottage with its worn but comfortable furniture was quite cozy—and far too small to provide any real privacy. If anyone else were there, behind the one closed door off the kitchen, perhaps, surely he would have heard voices and come to inquire by now.

"Are you at liberty to say what it is that she left him?"

Pulled from her pondering by the very direct question, Sara reached into her pocket.

They were sitting by a window, the one through which she'd seen the bowl of flowers earlier. Now she reached past the marigolds, her palm out, and offered an old, worn ring. After staring at it for a moment, as if trying to decide whether or not she wanted to touch it, Kathleen picked it up between her thumb and index finger. She turned it this way and that.

"It's a Claddagh," she said, then looked to Sara as if waiting for further explanation.

The small gold circle was formed by two hands holding a heart which was topped by a crown. The symbol was an old one and not unfamiliar to anyone in the British Isles. The hands represented friendship; the heart, love; and the crown, loyalty. Both women knew that much. What Sara didn't know, and apparently Kathleen didn't either, was the significance of the ring to Thomas.

The sunlight streaming past the fluttering curtains flashed against the ring as Kathleen handed it back to her. Sara cradled it in her palm again, and with the delicate touch of her fingers she traced its intricate shape. "My grandmother always wore this."

"Do you know why she wanted my brother to have it?"

Sara sighed. She didn't know and that bothered her. "I was hoping he could tell me. She'd never spoken of him before she asked me to give it to him. She never mentioned anyone here by name, actually. She talked only of the place."

The uneasiness she'd felt earlier took a stronger hold. It seemed there were a few other things her grandmother hadn't mentioned.

Along with that unsettling realization came a tug of possessiveness. The feeling wasn't a comfortable one, to be sure. Though the thought hadn't consciously crossed her mind until her grandmother had brought up the subject, Sara had hoped that the ring would someday be hers.

"I'd really thought she'd leave it to me," she said, though she hadn't intended to speak the words aloud.

The sound of her own voice, soft and a little too wistful, brought her out of her musing. She slipped the ring back into her pocket. When it was safely tucked away, she met her hostess's guarded smile.

"I'm sure Fiona had her reasons for asking you to give it to him, dear. Must be that Thomas knows something that he never mentioned to me. Not," she added in a tone teetering between affection and disgust, "that a man that stubborn confides much, you understand. Seems every male in the O'Donaugh family comes by that trait too easily."

Thinking that Kathleen might possess a fair portion of stubbornness herself, Sara politely glanced toward the door. It seemed pointless to put off the inevitable. "May I ask when you expect your brother?"

"Along about the end of next week. Or first of the week after." Kathleen must have realized that her response had caught Sara unawares. She looked genuinely surprised when Sara hesitated. "Surely whoever told you how to get here would have mentioned that he's in County Clare."

The lady who owned the inn had said nothing of Thomas's present whereabouts. But then Sara couldn't fault her for that. Sara had asked if she knew Thomas O'Donaugh and where he lived and the woman had said, indeed, she did know him and promptly told Sara how to get to his house. Sara had asked a question and received a literal answer.

"Mrs. Carrigan was kind enough to give me directions. But she didn't mention that he was traveling."

A knowing nod accompanied a quiet, "Ah, yes. If that's who you asked, then you got only what you asked for. Appalling lack of curiosity that woman has. And her owning the pub, too," she added, making it sound unpardonable that someone uninclined to gossip should be in such a position.

"You really don't expect him until next week?" she asked, as if somehow Kathleen might change her mind and alter that schedule.

"No, dear. He's visiting. We've a sister there with five of her own and a dozen grandchildren to boot. He's to see all of them before looking up a cousin or two and seeing a mate in Kilkishen."

She appeared willing to continue, not nearly so reticent as the owner of the inn with her information, but the consternation in Sara's expression abruptly ended a recitation of her brother's rather loose itinerary. Concern made her tone softer. "I can see you weren't expecting to find him gone. If you'd care to leave it with me, I'd be certain to see that he gets the ring."

The cup and saucer barely made a sound as Sara carefully placed them on the little table. Rising to stand in front of the window, she looked out to the green and rolling land. The shadow of a cloud moved slowly over, turning the top of one distant hill from the bright color of new buds to a deep emerald.

"Thank you, but I can't do that. She had me promise to deliver it to him myself."

The moments leading up to that promise would be with Sara forever. She had sat by her grandmother's bed, holding her hand. She remembered how frail it had felt, the skin papery and dry, and how little strength had been left in her grip. The once spirited woman had lay thin and pale against the sheets, refusing to let go of that last breath until Sara had told her she would do as she asked. A smile had come over her grandmother's face then, a beautiful smile that spoke of internal peace, and she had told Sara not to cry. *It is as I promised,* her grandmother had whispered. *When you give him this ring, all will be as it should.*

Fingering the plain gold chain at her throat, Sara drew a slightly shaky breath. She had to know what that meant. And only Thomas O'Donaugh could tell her.

The decision she made filled her with a certain relief. She hadn't wanted to leave here just yet. Now it appeared that she couldn't. "I guess I'll just have to wait for him."

A chair spring squeaked as Kathleen stood. "You'll be staying at the inn?"

Sara said that she would, somewhat absently, because her thoughts were still occupied.

"That being the case, you might as well stay for supper."

Sara thought she detected a slight reluctance in the invitation. Maybe because she'd heard her hesitation herself, Kathleen hurried to assure Sara that her staying would not be an imposition at all. In fact, her nephew was coming for supper, too, she said, and that reminded her that she needed to start thinking of what she would prepare. As long as Sara was here, she could keep her company while she picked some vegetables from the garden.

* * *

He shouldn't have agreed to this, Devon thought, his heavy footfall absorbed by the pasture's damp grass. Evening was rapidly descending, hastened by the cover of clouds rolling in over the hills. He should have told his aunt that he had paperwork to do at the mill tonight, or that he needed to finish the trundle bed he was building for his cousin Anna's two girls. He could have come up with *some* excuse. In the mood he was in this evening, he couldn't help thinking that it would have been better if he had.

The load of linen he'd sent off to Cork this morning—the lot that was to have given him the rest of the down payment for a new power loom—had somehow come off the cart and landed in a bog. Now all the fabric was gone.

It was bad enough that his plans had met another delay, that today's "accident" appeared to have been deliberate only added anger to his frustration. There was no reason the lashings should have come loose, not even when the cart tipped. He'd tied the ropes himself.

Devon drew his hand over the back of his neck, the muscles there knotted and tense. Kevin Connor had been driving the cart, and Kevin swore he didn't know what had spooked his horse into bolting as it had done.

Kevin had left with the load right on schedule this morning. But instead of returning tomorrow after having delivered the lot to the broker, he'd returned to the mill about noon, catching a ride back on a milk cart with one of the Healy boys.

The way he'd told it, he was five miles out of Brigen Glen, trotting along at a decent clip, when all of a sudden the horse reared, then took off as if the hounds of hell were nipping at its heels. Kevin threw himself off just as the cart's tongue snapped. The horse, trailing its bridle, disappeared into the fog, the cart came to a halt with its nose in the bog and Kevin, supposedly, landed a ways back in the grass and muck at the edge of the road. He'd said there wasn't a thing he could do but watch the whole load roll off the cart.

To Devon, he'd looked awfully clean for a man who'd gone face first into the mud. He hadn't said anything about that. He'd simply sent Kevin home to take care of the blisters he'd rubbed on his heels before the Healys had given him a ride. After leaving one of the other men in charge at the mill, Devon then took the Stanton brothers with another cart to see if they could rescue the cloth. Kevin had been very specific about where the "accident" had occurred and they'd had no trouble finding the tree with two trunks. Legend had it that two men had met at that spot in the road and neither had wanted to move his cart to let the other pass. A wood sprite, annoyed with their arguing, had turned them into the tree, rooted forever in the spot neither would give up.

It was a familiar landmark on the road to Durry. But the cart wasn't visible in the bog beyond the tree as Kevin had said it was when he'd left it. The water was only knee-deep, but the bog had a bottom like quicksand. It had apparently swallowed its prize, cart and all. There had been no hope of recovering a single bolt.

Devon wanted to believe what Kevin had told him. So much had ridden on the sale of that lot and to think that someone who had been such a good friend would sabotage him in such a way...

Had been. The words overrode his other thoughts, making Devon realize that quite a while had passed since he and Kevin had shared anything more than necessary conversation. Devon justified that circumstance by blaming it on the responsibilities that had encroached on their time. Kevin had a wife and family now. A son, Devon's namesake, and a daughter of just a few months. Devon himself had been gone off and on for the past year, touring other manufacturing facilities in Cork, Dublin and Belfast, seeking better ways to run his own mill.

Granted, Kevin wasn't too keen on Devon's ideas as far as the mill was concerned, but just because they didn't see eye to eye on a few things didn't mean he shouldn't be able to rely on Kevin's integrity. He was a good man. Proud of his work and loyal to his friends. Devon couldn't accept that he would deliberately destroy a shipment.

Whether he wanted to accept it or not, the thought nagged at him—along with the question of whether Kevin might also be responsible for some of the other incidents at the mill. Or maybe it was one of the other men in his hire. The boisterous John Tully, perhaps.

With a disgusted sigh, he cut off his speculation. Until today he'd thought the acts of vandalism to be those of a stranger. Suspecting someone in the village felt traitorous. Suspecting someone he'd once considered his closest friend made him feel like a louse.

He also felt betrayed.

The creak of the garden gate grated through the early-evening sounds. The crickets living under the broken plant crates by the fence alternated calls to one another and, off in the distance, the whinny of a horse met the bark of a dog. The atmosphere was one of peace, but peace was a sense that had always eluded Devon. All he felt as he followed the stones through his aunt's garden was a profound determination to accomplish what he'd set out to do and an escalating resentment toward whoever it was that was making the task more difficult than it needed to be.

"Here comes my nephew," Kathleen announced when she saw Devon move through her garden. "Oh, dear."

At that ominous-sounding comment, Sara glanced up from the pile of vegetables she'd help gather for a salad and saw Kathleen quickly wipe her hands on her apron. A pinched frown settled between the woman's faded red eyebrows, a distinct contrast to the curiosity that had been on her face most of the afternoon.

The time Sara had spent with Kathleen had been pleasant, despite the woman's not-so-subtle interrogation. Sara wasn't accustomed to talking about herself. Even as a child she had much preferred listening, watching. But with Kathleen, she hadn't been allowed to let the other person talk. Kathleen had pointedly asked about her job and her travels, wanting her impressions of the places she'd visited. But she'd seemed most interested in her family. She'd found it most interesting that Sara had never known any family other than her grandmother. It was always just the two of us, Sara had said, and Kathleen had found that very odd.

Sara chalked that attitude up to the social differences of a small village where most of your neighbors were relatives and the more mobile society she'd been born into. As for Kathleen's curiosity, Sara only wished it had been a little less intense. Because of it, she hadn't had a chance to learn anything about the rest of Kathleen's family. At the very least, she'd have liked to know something about the nephew joining them now. Other than to say that he'd be here for supper, she'd made no reference to the man.

What she said now didn't make Sara particularly eager to meet him, either.

"Oh, dear," she heard Kathleen repeat, taking another glance out of the window. "He's got a look of foreboding about him, he does. Leave that salad to me and visit with him, Sara. Lord knows he'll be looking at your company as a gift, so the sooner he knows he doesn't have to put up with me for the whole evening, the happier he's likely to be."

There was no time for Sara to consider whether or not she wanted to serve as appeasement for someone's moody nephew. Kathleen opened the oven to take out a golden pastry-covered casserole just as the back door banged shut.

Sara looked up, then went stock-still.

Staring back at her was the man she'd met by the mill this morning. He'd stopped inside the door, his gaze riveted to her face. He looked very much as she remembered him: disapproving, brooding, big. Only here, in the intimate interior of the cottage, he seemed even more imposing—and much more intimidating—than he had with the outdoors surrounding him. He seemed to fill the room, making the furnishings look too small, too delicate, for his large frame.

"Hi," she said, offering a tentative smile.

Devon's only response was a tight nod. For several seconds, he simply stared at her, not quite believing what he knew he saw. So many times today the image of this woman had flashed through his mind, the recollection of the same gentle smile he saw now. And her eyes, cautious, yet somehow trusting. Dark and huge, they held his, shying away only when his own glance took a bolder approach and moved down the elegant line of her throat.

When he'd seen her this morning, her hair had been unbound, spilling past her shoulders. Now it was held in a loose knot at the top of her head and a few stray tendrils curved about her face. She had the look of a gamine, a young mischievous street urchin who could steal your wallet along with your heart.

What was she doing here? he finally asked himself.

Aunt Kathleen walked past him, carrying a steaming lamb pie between two thick towels. "Evenin', Devon," he heard her say. "We've company tonight. Sara Madigan, this is my nephew Devon O'Donaugh," she continued, bustling about her kitchen setting dishes out. "Devon, take Sara into the living room and visit with her until supper is ready. While you're in there, you might add more peat to the fire. The evening's chill is setting in."

Kathleen was too preoccupied with her preparations to notice the scowl that settled like a shadow over her nephew's darkly attractive features. Sara caught it, however, and its effect was immediate.

"I'd be glad to set the table," she offered, but Kathleen wouldn't allow the reprieve. Insisting that she'd done enough already, the older woman coaxed Sara out of the kitchen and into the living room. She tried to usher Devon out, too, but he wasn't having any part of it.

The kitchen door closed behind Sara with a solid thump. Finding herself alone, and not particularly enamored with the idea of eavesdropping, she cast a wary glance toward the door and wandered across the room. It was apparent enough that Kathleen's nephew wasn't overly pleased with her presence. It was just as apparent that Sara, like it or not, was going to hear about it. As she'd suspected before, the cottage was much too small for any real privacy.

"What is she doing here?" she heard him demand.

"Now, Devon," came Kathleen's placating reply. "It's not what you think. I didn't invite her here for you. After that disaster of an evening with you and Margaret O'Day's daughter, I've given up trying to find you a wife. Though now that we're discussing it, it wouldn't hurt if you looked up one of the McMurtry granddaughters the next time you're in Cork. I understand from Mary..."

"Aunt Kathleen," Devon cut in, his voice tight. "The woman in the other room. Who is she and why is she here?"

"I'll be getting to that in a minute, if you'll not interrupt. I was just going to say that Mary's granddaughters are both lovely young..."

"I'm not interested in Mary's granddaughters. What about *her*?"

Sara could easily imagine Devon scowling at his aunt, his arm outstretched and finger pointed toward the kitchen door. She could also picture the totally nonplussed blink of Kathleen's shrewd blue eyes as she looked up at her strapping nephew.

"Really, Devon. Lower your voice. Sara is here because she came looking for Thomas. Seems her grandmother died and left him a ring and she's not leaving until she gives it to him. I asked her to supper because it would have been rude not to. That and I'm not wanting to take any chances."

"Any chances with what?"

Kathleen's voice dropped another notch. "Her grandmother was one of the woods people."

Sara hadn't realized she was pacing until she stopped. Now, hearing nothing but silence, she unabashedly waited for Devon or Kathleen to say something else.

It was Devon who finally spoke. "What difference does that make?"

"Now don't be acting like you never heard about them."

"Please," Sara heard him say, suddenly sounding very weary. "It's been a long day. And not too much about it has gone right. All I ever heard about the woods people was a bunch of nonsense based on silly superstition. I have no idea what any of this has to do with the woman out there. She's an American, for God's sake."

"Don't be irreverent. She's related," came the questionably logical reply. "Surely you've heard that they weren't like we are. They weren't quite..."

Her voice had grown so hushed that Sara could barely hear her. It sounded as if Kathleen had said "normal," but Sara wasn't sure. Her grandmother had been every bit as normal as she was. And what was all this business about superstition?

There were drawbacks to eavesdropping. The biggest was that hearing what you weren't intended to hear left you with questions you couldn't ask.

She wasn't given a chance to ponder Kathleen's puzzling remarks any further. Devon had dismissed whatever it was that Sara hadn't heard anyway and his irascible aunt was telling him that one of these days he was going to regret his impudence. A cabinet door bumped shut. A moment later came the sound of a drawer being closed. "Let's not leave our company waiting out there alone," Sara heard Kathleen say. "And Devon," she added, "do try to behave yourself."

Hearing the door open, Sara sank into the nearest chair and tried to look absorbed in the magazine she hurriedly grabbed from the table next to it. She didn't think it would set well if Devon realized that she'd been privy to his conversation, though she really didn't know what to expect when moments later his long strides carried him right past her.

He headed straight to the sideboard across from where she sat. His back to her, he uncapped a decanter of amber liquid that he took from one of its shelves and splashed some into a glass. "Care for a drink?" he asked without turning. "We've whiskey or ale."

Sara didn't handle alcohol well. One drink for her was the equivalent of two for anyone else. She blamed that unfortunate consequence on a fast metabolism, and usually stuck to what was safe. Right now, especially, she wanted to keep her wits about her. "Water would be fine."

She was absolutely sure he wasn't pleased with his assignment to entertain her. Yet none of his motions betrayed the tension she could see bunching the muscle in his nicely sculpted jaw. He acknowledged her request with little more than a nod, and a few moments later he crossed the handsome hand-loomed rug to stop in front of her. He held out her drink.

"I've been told to behave."

"Does that mean you're not going to dump that on me?"

He looked from her to the glass and back again. A hint of a smile, unexpected and remarkably wry, touched his mouth. "I believe my aunt would think that inhospitable. But no sense pressing your luck, is there?"

At the subtle taunt, she reached for the glass. His smile took the harder edges from his austere expression, but it never reached his eyes. There she saw only the same distrust she'd encountered this morning.

She expected him to move. He didn't. He didn't even glance away. There was nothing extraordinary about his casual stance, yet Sara found his proximity disturbing. She couldn't quite determine why, although it might have had to do with the tension she felt radiating from him, a raw energy that electrified her nerves and made her uncomfortably aware of how very male he was. Or maybe it was simply because they had gotten off to such a bad start this morning and they had yet to overcome it.

Whatever it was, she needed very badly to break the silence.

"The mill by the stream," she began, grasping the first thought that occurred to her. "What do they make there?"

To her relief, he turned from her and hunched down in front of the round-bellied stove. Its door opened with a groan. "We make linen, twine, thread." He pushed a bar of peat into glowing coals. "It's a flax mill."

"What grades of linen?" Staring at his back, she watched the way the muscles moved beneath his flat knit sweater. "I buy textiles sometimes," she'd hurried to add, wanting to explain her interest—and to focus on something other than his very compelling physique. "For the company I work for."

"Everything from fine to... lost." Sparks flew as he put a brick in. "I have a load that took a bath in a bog today. If you can get to it, I could guarantee a decent price."

The door of the stove groaned shut. Rising, Devon brushed his hands against his thighs and picked up the glass he'd set on the floor. He tipped it back and took a healthy swallow. Sara had the feeling there was nothing personal behind his cynicism. Whatever put the edge in his tone had been there for a very long time. She also had the impression that he was intimately familiar with the quick anger that had slipped into his expression when he'd mentioned the lost load—and just as accustomed to suppressing that feeling.

She understood what it was like to bury feelings. She'd had to do it all her life. Her question came softly. "How did that happen?"

For a moment Devon simply looked at her. Her inquiry wasn't appreciated. He didn't want to discuss what had happened today, even if he had been the one to bring it up. At least, he hadn't thought he wanted to talk about it, but something in her tone made him think she wasn't merely trying to make conversation.

Inexorably drawn by the sincerity in her expression, he felt some of the tumult filling him slowly seep out. It was a strange sensation, almost a healing one.

"You really want to know?" he heard himself ask.

She gave the merest of nods as she looked into his eyes. "Yes," she said quietly. "I do."

The pull of her soft smile was seductive, the promise of gentleness and ease a potent lure for his battered soul. He hadn't even realized how battered he'd felt until just then. She actually wanted to listen.

So did his aunt.

Chapter Three

Kathleen had propped the kitchen door back open. She announced that supper was ready, then told Devon she wanted to hear about what had happened today, too. She didn't seem to notice how quickly Devon turned from Sara, certainly not how grateful he was for the interruption.

He hung back for a moment, occupying himself with refreshing his drink while Sara, somewhat reluctantly it seemed to him, left the room. There had been disappointment in her eyes at his aunt's interruption, as if she'd felt cheated of what he'd been about to share. For a moment, he'd actually felt as if he could bare his soul to her.

He had no idea what had come over him during those few moments, but he wasn't at all comfortable with the way he'd felt: a little too vulnerable, a little less in control.

Kathleen was being her usual nosy self. He'd no sooner seated himself at her table than she wanted to know what he'd been about to tell Sara. He was surprised she hadn't heard already. The village grapevine operated just short of the speed of light. Figuring she must have been too busy entertaining Sara to gossip with the neighbors, he decided to tell her the same story Kevin had told him and to keep his reservations about its truth to himself.

First, though, plates were passed. Kathleen was always generous with her hospitality. But as she carefully filled Sara's glass with milk and set it precisely so by her plate, Devon couldn't help noticing that her attitude toward her guest was an odd cross between cautious and solicitous. That definitely wasn't Kathleen. He'd never known her to be that anxious to please anyone. Remembering her earlier remark about not wanting to take any chances and her cautious respect for the mystical lore that had undoubtedly prompted it, he could only conclude that this Sara had really rattled her—and obviously to the point of distraction. There were flowers in the salad.

Neither woman appeared to notice anything strange about the blossoms in the salad bowl, and his aunt's impatience to hear what he had to say precluded his mention of it. With a quick frown of puzzlement for the deceptively harmless-looking woman seated across from him, he turned his attention to this morning's incident.

As he related what Kevin had told him, Devon was careful to keep his doubts about Kevin's part in the incident to himself. There was no point in his aunt knowing he suspected his friend of such deception. She'd only chastise him for it. Or worse, mention it to someone else. What never occurred to him was that Sara could so easily hear what he wasn't saying.

The certainty in her gentle observation made her question a statement. "You don't believe him, do you?"

"What makes you think that?"

She hadn't touched her casserole, but her salad was almost gone. Poised on the tip of her fork now was a pale orange blossom. "You keep saying 'he'd said' or 'according to Kevin.' If you believed him, would you qualify everything you said that way?" The delicate line of her eyebrows arched with the inquiry and the flower disappeared.

Thinking she hadn't realized what she'd just eaten, certain she'd discard it when the taste registered, he deliberately moved his glance from her mouth. A frown centered on his brow when, from the corner of his eye, he saw her swallow and pick out another. "I wasn't there, so I can only repeat what he told me."

Kathleen reached for her tea. "It sounds to me as if you've finally ruffled the feathers of the wrong goose. Your Uncle Thomas and I keep telling you that people like things just the way they are here. Other folk have tried to tell you that, too, but you've stopped listening. Could be someone is trying to get your attention so you'll hear them."

"How will destroying what pays their wages prove anything?"

"It'll keep you from getting your new machines, won't it?"

"What happened today will only delay that." His knife clattered to his plate. "Nothing is going to put it off forever."

"It," Sara discovered as the meal progressed, was Devon's plan to bolster both the population and the economy of the village by expanding the three-hundred-year-old mill. For the most part, the flax mill was the only real source of employment in the area. The Brennan and Healy families raised sheep and supported themselves by selling wool and mutton. They delivered most of their milk to the Murphys, who earned a modest living with a small cheese-making operation. Just about every other family in Brigen Glen grew flax for the mill or had at least one member working there. That meant the majority of the families were directly dependent on Devon for a living. According to Kathleen, every one of them liked things just the way they were.

As Sara listened, in silence because that seemed the more prudent approach given Devon's inflexible expression, she had to admit that his progressive point of view made perfect sense to her. After all, there had to be some room for improvement after so many years and she could certainly see where modern safety features and improved methods of production would benefit the people who worked there. She didn't say as much, however, because her bias began to change when Kathleen, offering her more bread to keep her entertained while the debate continued, brought up her misgivings about the new road Devon wanted.

It was Devon's opinion that the road was a necessary part of the expansion. A wider, paved road would be the only way cars and delivery trucks could get to and from the mill. The road, though, would pass right through the quiet little village and Kathleen feared the vehicles would frighten the horses the villagers used for transportation.

And ruin the idyllic peace with their noise, Sara couldn't help but think. "Not to mention what the exhaust would do to the air."

She hadn't realized she'd spoken until the words were out of her mouth. Glancing up from the bread she was buttering, she found both of her dinner companions staring at her. The look Devon sent her over the jam server said clearly that he wished she'd kept her observation to herself. Kathleen looked more encouraging.

It quickly became apparent that, having lived her entire life in Brigen Glen, Kathleen regarded Sara as a woman of the world. At least in the sense that her travels had exposed her to so much more of the world than Kathleen herself had ever seen. She therefore wanted to know what Sara thought of a plan that would cause such drastic changes.

"You're always saying I don't see the whole picture," she told Devon when he started to protest Sara's input. "Perhaps an unbiased view will help."

"It would only help if she knew the village," he insisted, sounding reasonable despite the way his jaw tightened. "It's unfair to ask her to form an opinion with so little information. She's a stranger. What would an outsider know of the problems here?"

"Actually," Sara cut in, reasonably certain that "fairness" wasn't his reason for not wanting her to speak. "I've known of Brigen Glen all my life. I may not have spent any time here, but I've heard enough to care about it."

"Where have you heard about it?" Devon wanted to know while Kathleen sat there looking most pleased with Sara's defense.

"From my grandmother."

"Oh, yes." His expression grew faintly sardonic. "The grandmother with the faeries."

Kathleen's eyebrow shot up, her glance darting between the man and the woman frowning at each other. Sara didn't know if it was the mention of the faeries or the hint of some previous familiarity between her and Devon that had piqued the woman's interest, but Kathleen wasn't given a chance to do any prying. Sara's swift irritation with Devon wouldn't allow it.

Though her tone was calm, her eyes held an uncharacteristic challenge. "She thought this a very special place. A place of possibilities. She never said it in so many words, but one of the things she loved best about Brigen Glen was its character. Obviously one would have to have an open mind to appreciate that."

It sounded to Sara as if Kathleen choked on her tea. But when she turned from Devon's implacable glare, the older woman seemed to be perfectly fine.

"So tell me, dear," Kathleen encouraged, dabbing her mouth with her napkin, "what *do* you think of Devon's plan?"

The phrase "damned if you do, damned if you don't" sprang to mind. Suddenly appreciative of its meaning, Sara said only that she'd think it sad if such a lovely place were yanked too abruptly into the twentieth century. Industrialization and growth brought their own unique problems and there were so few truly pristine places left as it was. Certainly few so charming.

Sara thought her response quite diplomatic. If his expression was any indication, Devon definitely thought otherwise. Too bad, she thought and, eyes wide, she met his scowl and shrugged. He didn't have to like it. But it was her opinion and she was entitled to it.

"Charm doesn't feed people," he pointed out as reasonably as his irritation would allow. "Places like this have to either catch up or disappear. This mill is the only chance this village has." His eyes shone with the fierceness of his belief. But a weary resignation entered his tone, threatening to take the fight out of him. "Not that I'm in any position to do anything about it. With that lot ruined today, it'll be months before we can afford the new equipment we need."

Devon stared at his glass, mindless of the two women witnessing his frustration. It might be months yet, but he would do it. This town desperately needed the changes it fought.

Kathleen's voice gentled. "You know, Devon, it could be the way you went about cleaning up that flax had something to do with what happened today. It didn't help at all when you brought in those tinkers and paid them to clean up the bundles you found scattered along the stream last week."

Sara saw his grip tighten on the glass. "I didn't bring them in. They were passing through and needing work. It made more sense to me to have them rebundle it than to take the men off their jobs to do it. I'd only have been farther behind if I'd done that and it was bother enough that someone had broken in and made the mess in the first place."

"But *tinkers,* Devon," she stressed, clearly thinking that if he didn't feel guilty about giving away good work, he could at least feel guilty about who he'd given it to. She turned to Sara as if to enlist her aid. "He's always saying there isn't enough work here for the villagers. That we're needing more jobs. Yet he goes and hires the likes of them instead of paying his own for the work."

Having already earned Devon's displeasure, Sara thought it wiser to stick to questions rather than conclusions. For the moment anyway. "What's a tinker?"

The inquiry was directed to Kathleen. It was Devon who responded, preferring to put his own slant on the description. "They'd rather be called travelers. What they are is Gypsies. There aren't many of them left anymore, but those there are support themselves by traveling from village to village doing odd jobs."

"And by begging and thievery." Kathleen pursed her lips in disapproval. "But I don't suppose you could expect less from a lot that worships a goat."

Impatience shadowed Devon's tone. "They don't worship a goat, Aunt Kathleen."

"Then what do they do at that pilgrimage they make to Killorglin every year? I've been hearing of that since I was a babe."

"The Puck Fair? That's all done in fun. It's mock homage at best."

Kathleen wasn't to be dissuaded. "Mock homage or not, everyone's heard the tales of their magic. And don't be telling me it's all superstition," she warned her nephew. "Their powers may have been embellished over the years, but stories have a way of being rooted in fact.''

Suddenly Kathleen cut herself off. Sara missed the quick, wary glance the woman shot in her direction, though. She'd been watching Devon. Having already encountered his less than accepting opinion of lore and legend, she wouldn't have been surprised if he'd told his aunt exactly what he thought of her gullibility.

All he did was shake his head, no doubt having already expressed his position on more than one occasion, and re-iterate that hiring the tinkers had nothing to do with the load coming off the cart today.

Kathleen didn't look convinced, but she said nothing else, either, seeming quite relieved when Devon changed the subject.

He nodded to indicate Sara's fork. A petal was poised on its tip. ''Why are you eating those?''

The answer seemed obvious enough to Sara. ''Because I like them.''

''I'd never thought to put them in a salad before,'' Kathleen cut in, ''though I have used rose hips to scent tea. What do you think of them, Devon? A bit like bitter greens, aren't they?''

He didn't look at his aunt. He looked to Sara. After holding her glance for a couple of seconds, he reached for his bread. ''I prefer them in the border, not for supper.'' A moment later, sopping up the gravy from his plate, he dismissed that matter, too. ''Have you heard from Molly today?'' he asked Kathleen, and his aunt was off and running.

Sara sat back, trying to figure out what she'd done now. She decided not to waste any energy on it, listening instead to Kathleen go on about Molly's year-old son, Joey. When pictures of the child were brought out, she immediately recognized Mickey, whom she discovered was one of Joey's two brothers. Trying not to be wary of the way Devon's glance kept returning to her, she recounted for Kathleen how she'd met Mickey and his puppy this morning. The story brought a smile to Kathleen's eyes as well as a skeptical "Oh, really?" when Sara mentioned what a nice conversation they'd had.

All in all, the rest of the meal was fairly pleasant. It wasn't until after Sara had helped Kathleen with the dishes that the wariness returned. Devon, having come in from the bedroom where he'd unjammed a window his aunt had complained about earlier, announced that he was leaving.

"We'd best be going," he told Sara. "I'll take you back to the inn."

Before Sara could think to protest, he'd dropped a kiss on his aunt's forehead, thanked her for supper and disappeared out the back door.

Seeing Sara's confusion, Kathleen smiled. "He'll meet you out front. He went to get Skye."

"Skye?"

"Thomas's horse. Devon's been exercising him while Thomas is away. Being as the inn's a good mile down the road, I'm sure he's thinking the ride will do the pony some good."

Sara was perfectly capable of finding the way back herself. The moon was full and all she had to do was follow the road. She felt safe in this place time had forgotten, not the need to be guarded and watchful as she always did in cities. At least, she would have felt safe alone. What she felt about being alone with Devon was another matter entirely.

She couldn't very well decline the offer to Kathleen, though. She didn't quite know how the woman had done it, but she'd just made her feel as if she'd be depriving a pony of its exercise if she'd be so ungrateful as to refuse the escort.

A few moments later, having thanked Kathleen for her hospitality, Sara stepped out the front door and into the night.

Clouds scudded across the sky, their edges illuminated by the brightness of the moon. It could be a beautiful evening or an eerie one, depending on how she chose to think of it. Had she been alone, she might have entertained that thought. Devon's silhouette loomed ahead of her. With him waiting for her by the gate, his hand loosely holding the reins of a huge black stallion, she could think only of how formidible he appeared.

The magnificent animal gave an impatient snort as it shook its enormous head. Some pony, she mused, wondering at Kathleen's gift for understatement.

"He won't hurt you."

She hadn't realized how warily she'd approached. That caution had been unconscious. It also had nothing to do with the animal.

"I know," she said, absolutely certain that the great beast would do her no harm. The horse shied a little. Slowly she reached up her slender hand.

Instead of lifting its nose to avoid the unfamiliar touch, Skye went still. A moment later, after snuffling the tips of her fingers, he lowered his neck so she could rub his forehead.

Sara had an affinity for animals that tended toward the uncanny. An animal could sense the potential for harm. A threat was responded to with aggression or flight. Trust was shown by allowing closeness. She understood that about them. People were like that, too. But their reactions weren't usually so easy to define. With animals, she could almost feel their anxiety, or their acceptance, and she loved them all. Except for cats. Perhaps it was their stealth that bothered her about them. It was so like the sneakiness some people were capable of. Whatever the reason, she'd always been wary of cats.

She dropped her hand. The horse danced at the end of the rein Devon held, anxious now to be moving. She could appreciate the feeling, aware as she was of Devon's eyes on her.

"Why don't you go on and take him for his ride?" She added a smile with her not entirely selfless suggestion. "I can see myself to the inn. It's not that far."

"It's far enough," Devon returned, refusing to allow her a gracious out. "I said I'd take you back."

"It's not necessary. Really. But thanks for the offer."

For a moment, the only sound to interrupt the stillness was the crunch of gravel as she turned and walked away. Then came the heavier thud of Devon's boots and the rhythmic clop of the horse. Sara refused to turn around. She wasn't going to argue. He could follow her all the way back to the inn if he wanted. That didn't mean she had to talk to him.

The lights of Kathleen's cottage were a faint yellow glow in the darkness when the strain of waiting for him to say something got to her.

"I give up." She spun around and planted her hands on her hips. "What do you want?"

Man and beast continued their approach, halting a few feet in front of her. With the moon behind him, she couldn't see much of Devon's expression. He sounded mildly offended, though.

"Can't a gentleman see a lady safely home?"

She'd like to believe that was his only purpose. If it were true, that meant chivalry wasn't dead. Yet while there was much about Devon O'Donaugh to compare with the less flattering notions of medieval knighthood, Sara was sure he was no knight in shining armor. He was a man of too much purpose to do something with only altruism in mind.

"He could if I thought that was all he wanted."

"Are you usually so suspicious?"

"Only when I'm made to feel that way."

He took a step closer, the horse snorting his impatience with the delay. Stroking his hand along its massive neck, Devon absently soothed the huge animal. Skye wanted to run, to expend the energy stored in his powerful body. He could feel the muscles of its neck quivering beneath his hand, the raw, elemental power of them needing release.

Devon's glance moved to the enticing line of Sara's throat. All evening he'd been busily ignoring a very elemental need of his own. A good, hell-bent-for-fury ride was exactly what both he and the horse needed.

First he had to protect his own.

"The ring you came to give my uncle," he said. "Do you have it with you?"

The ring. So that's why he was following her. Relief dissolved some of the starch in her stance. Of course he would want to know about it. As adamant as he'd been about wanting to know her purpose here, she was surprised that he hadn't shown some curiosity about it before.

It wasn't curiosity prompting his interest. She had no sooner nodded to indicate that she did have it and reached into her pocket to show it to him when his next words stopped her cold.

"I want you to give it to me."

She left her hand in her pocket, securing the ring in her palm. She didn't trust his tone. His demand was entirely too incisive to be a request. It was more of an order. Sara didn't take orders very well. "Give it to you to look at? Or give it to you to keep. Which do you mean?"

"To keep. There's no reason for you to waste a week waiting for Thomas to come home. He's an old man and schedules don't mean much to him. It could even be longer than that before he shows up."

"I'll wait."

"I give you my word that he'll get it."

She didn't doubt his word. She felt sure Devon would do as he said. Saving her time wasn't his motive, though. She was just as sure of that. "I don't mind staying. I haven't seen that much of the village, and nothing at all of the area."

"You've seen as much of it as there is. Believe me, there's nothing for you to do here. You'll be bored to death in another day."

A certain bitterness clung to his last words, a bitterness that lay with what the village lacked. She didn't need to see his eyes to know the hardness that had slipped into them. She'd seen that chilling intensity when he'd first spoken of the accident today that had set his plans so far back. She'd seen it again when his aunt had reminded him of how the villagers didn't want to accept his changes.

Knowing better than to taunt a coiled snake, she jockeyed around the subject as best she could. "I think I'll enjoy the quiet for a while. I really don't mind staying," she repeated. "You see, I have to give your uncle the ring myself. I promised."

He was standing too close to her. He'd realized that as soon as he'd breathed in the scent she wore. Soft, like spring, and slightly wild, it teased his senses, delivering all the erotic havoc it promised. A knot had formed in his midsection the second he'd inhaled it. In the past couple of minutes, that knot had tightened into an ache.

As near as he was, all he'd have to do was lift his hand and he could draw her to him.

The moonlight touched her, making her skin appear impossibly translucent. Her hair, caught up in its loose coil, gleamed like pale threads of gold. But it was her eyes, warm even in the cool blue light, that he found so haunting. She wanted him to understand, to accept what she had to do. At that moment she was pleading for that understanding.

His voice sounded unnaturally rough to his ears. "This ring means a lot to you?"

"The promise I gave means more."

She was making what he had to do so much more difficult than it needed to be. He didn't want to appreciate what she must feel, let alone respect her for it. Having never understood sentimentality, he could have overlooked an emotional attachment to an object and thereby dismissed her concerns as inconsequential. But a person's word was a commitment and that was something he did understand.

He had a strong suspicion that, like himself, her sense of loyalty ran very deep. If that was the case, he definitely needed a different approach.

There didn't seem to be anything else to say just then. Sara must have realized that, too. She turned to continue down the road.

With a sigh for the woman's stubbornness, he reached out and snagged her arm. Beneath his fingers, he felt her muscles tense as he turned her around. "We might as well ride."

The moon had been playing hide-and-seek with the clouds. A moment ago, all had been in shadow. Now its light slowly illuminated the long, winding road. That light also made it easy for him to see the shock of awareness that had sprung into her eyes at his touch.

He let her go before he could pull her closer. The knowledge that she might feel some of the same perturbing tension he did didn't help at all. It changed nothing, though. He still had to figure out a way to get rid of her.

He watched in silence as she looked up at the horse, then back at him. He knew she wasn't afraid of the animal.

"I don't mind walking," she said, and that only confirmed that her hesitation was because of him.

"Skye does. Another few minutes at this pace, and he'll want to bolt. At least let's let him move a little."

Sara drew a deep breath. She really didn't want to ride with Devon, but she would do it for the horse. A few moments later, seated behind Devon with her arms locked around his waist as Skye cantered off, she fervently hoped the animal appreciated the effort she'd made for his physical well-being.

Devon didn't say a word to her as they rode. For that, she was grateful. Being stuck like flypaper to his disturbingly hard body only served to make her undeniably aware of what she'd been so busy ignoring. With her heart beating faster than normal, her blood running warmer and the feeling of him making her aware of nerve endings in the oddest places, she couldn't ignore it now.

He had demanded responses from her from the moment she'd first seen him emerge from the mist. Perhaps that ability had something to do with his underlying intensity. There were no half measures with a man like Devon. With him, it was all or nothing.

She found that thought remarkably compelling. It also scared the daylights out of her. Yet despite some very basic philosophical differences, Devon made her feel something she hadn't ever felt before. He made her feel truly...alive.

The inn sat to the north side of the crossroads, well back from the road itself. Protected by its stone fence, it looked quiet and still in the inky darkness. A light shown softly in a front window, another over the door welcomed weary travelers. According to Mrs. Carrigan, fewer than a half dozen people stayed there in any given month. At the moment, Sara was her only guest. Even the pub next door seemed deserted tonight. But then the hour was late.

"Thanks for the ride." Sara muttered the words to Devon's back the moment Skye halted by the gate. Peeling her arms from his waist, she slid off. The past ten minutes had felt like forever.

Devon's feet hit the ground like an echo. His hand shot out to keep her from moving away, falling back to his side the instant she turned around.

"Look, Sara. I appreciate the promise you made. But you really will be happier if you go on to Cork or to one of the cities on the coast. Just let me know where you'll be, and when Thomas returns I'll send for you. You can come back then and give him the ring."

The man was nothing if not persistent. When she'd first discovered that Thomas wasn't here, she might very well have done as Devon suggested. But she'd heard too much today to leave without learning more; too many questions had been raised that needed answers. At the top of the list was the place where her grandmother had once lived. She needed to know what there was about the woods that had kept her grandmother from mentioning that she'd lived there. She couldn't do that if she left. And though her presence wasn't wanted by the man who had unwittingly released a disconcerting restlessness within her, she had to find someone else who had known her grandmother.

The evening breeze carried the scent of the sea and the earth. Elemental smells that comforted in a way Sara couldn't describe. She breathed deeply of the damp night air, hoping for the calm she'd felt when she'd first arrived here. The peace eluded her.

Her voice was quiet, like the rustle of the wind through the grass. "This would be much easier if you'd be honest with me. Instead of pretending concern about how I spend my time, why don't you just say you don't want me to stay here? Then you can tell me why and I'll know what we're really talking about."

He tipped his head, considering her. "You surprise me."

"Because I'd prefer you to be honest?"

Among other things, he thought, unable to reconcile her steel with her softness. "For many reasons."

Matching the tilt of his head, she crossed her arms beneath the gentle swell of her breasts and repeated the question she'd posed a moment ago. She wanted to know what those reasons were. "Why don't you want me to stay here?"

"Let's just say that I've got all the problems I can handle right now."

"So I gathered," was her sympathetic reply. "But what's that got to do with me?"

"I don't want you causing more."

Genuine surprise flashed in her eyes. "Me? What am I going to do?"

"It's not what you're *going* to do. Though God knows, the possibilities there are a little frightening," he muttered to himself. "It's what you've done already."

"I haven't done anything."

Disbelief. He felt sure his expression betrayed it. Disbelief and a certain amazement at her guilelessness. "To begin with, that little speech you gave about industrialization bringing on its own problems. The points you raised would never have occurred to my aunt if you hadn't mentioned them. Thanks to you, she's got a whole new set of arguments to nag me with."

"Will they make any difference?" Sara ventured.

"The mill is mine to run as I see fit. She can nag all she wants."

Sara took that to mean no. "Then I don't see where my leaving now can really help anything. According to you, the damage has already been done."

He hesitated, looking very much as if he wished she'd be a little more cooperative. "That's not the case at all. But if you were anyone else, it might not matter so much."

He could see her confusion. He could appreciate that. He was a little uncertain about how to approach this part of it himself. He just hoped he wouldn't sound as if he'd lost his mind when he did bring it up.

Raking his fingers through his hair, he decided that needn't be a concern. After all, how crazy could she think him to be talking about nonexistent woods people when Sara herself had been waiting for faeries to show up this morning?

"What was your grandmother's name? Fiona?" he asked, going on when his own memory confirmed it. "Well, it seems that your being her granddaughter has my aunt all concerned about a bunch of superstitious nonsense that should have died out years ago. *I* certainly don't think you're anything other than what you appear to be. But Kathleen has always been susceptible to suggestion and she seems to think you might have inherited some kind of...

Oh, Lord, he thought when he'd almost said "magic." He sounded like a fool. No mature, intelligent adult would even consider such idiocy.

Nevertheless, his aunt believed the old myths. And though she'd tried to cover it, he knew Sara's presence bothered her. Kathleen's meddling might drive him around the bend at times, but he wasn't going to let an outsider upset her. He did a perfectly acceptable job of that himself.

"That I inherited some kind of what?" Sara prodded.

"Power," he muttered, irritated. "The woods people were supposed to have some power that could change people into animals. Or maybe it's the other way around. I don't know. All I do know is that she's acting like she thinks you might have it. It's as if she's afraid that if she's not nice to you, you'll put a hex on her house."

Sara didn't mean to. She really didn't. But she nearly choked on the giggle that sprang to her throat.

Devon did not look overly pleased with her response.

"I'm sorry," she said because she didn't mean to offend him. He was quite serious. "It's just that I didn't exactly expect what you said. I've never cast a spell over anything or anyone in my life." She crossed her heart with her index finger, hoping he couldn't see the amusement in her eyes. "Honest."

Devon could have argued that point. Her laughter was music, the allure of her scent a sweet seduction. She possessed intelligence and wit, and whether she acknowledged it or not she was perfectly capable of casting spells. At least as far as any breathing male was concerned.

Skye gave a great shake, the metal rings of his bridle catching the glint of the moon. Devon's hand splayed over the horse's shoulder, his stroke assuring the animal that it wouldn't have to be still much longer.

His expression when he turned his attention back to Sara was grim. "How can I get you to leave?"

Her smile faded. "You really think I'll cause you trouble, don't you?"

There was no doubt in his mind. "Yes."

"Then I'll do my best to stay out of your way."

"That's not good enough."

"It will have to be. And contrary to what you might think, there's plenty around here that I'd like to see. I'd like to start with the mill. Kathleen said she'd show it to me in the morning."

He wanted her gone. Her opinions would only cause more of the same kind of problem he'd worked so hard to overcome. More importantly, he didn't want her around inciting or upsetting his aunt. Right now he was simply too tired to argue anymore. Maybe after a decent night's sleep—something he'd found hard to come by lately—he could think of some other way to get rid of her.

Before Sara realized what he was doing, he swung up into the saddle. Reining back to curb Skye's eagerness, he kept the horse dancing a few feet from her. "I doubt Kathleen will have the time," she heard him say. A moment later after a curt, "Good night, Sara," he was gone.

Sara stared after him, wondering at his arrogance. Kathleen had said herself that she would show her around. And knowing what little she did of the woman, Sara doubted that she'd let her nephew decide what she did with her days.

She hadn't overestimated Kathleen. Not really. What Sara had done was greatly underestimate Devon.

Chapter Four

The horse-drawn jaunting car, a vehicle resembling a convertible version of Cinderella's coach, continued down the road, its occupants waving to Devon as he drew his big bay horse to a halt in front of Mrs. Carrigan's Inn and Pub.

Not particularly anxious to dismount, he watched the road until there was nothing to see but the morning mist. His cousin Molly and her mother were on their way to Durry for a few days. After stopping by Molly's to check the buggy's wheels and axles—something he always did for his female relatives to lessen their chances of a breakdown when they left the village—he'd ridden this far with them. On their way to the crossroads, they had dropped Molly's boys and her sister Beth, who'd be watching them, off at Kathleen's. The visit had been Devon's idea. He disliked the maneuvering, but he'd gotten Beth to keep Kathleen busy. Having his aunt angry with him for circumventing her plans was better than having her unduly distressed by the company of a woman she thought potentially capable of other-worldly feats.

Fortunately Beth was always looking for an excuse to avoid housework and the idea of having Kathleen help with the boys had added appeal. To be on the safe side, he'd told Beth just enough about Sara to ensure that she would stick around Kathleen's for the whole day. The O'Donaughs could fight among themselves, but they were fiercely protective of their own.

Having occupied Kathleen, he now had to tend to Sara. Until he figured out how to get her out of the village, he thought it best to keep an eye on her himself.

Two hitching posts guarded a wooden watering trough. He'd just reached the nearest one when the door of the inn swung open and the inn's owner stepped out. Wiping her hands on her white apron, she bent to pick up the bottles of milk sitting next to a potted rose.

She glanced up, her round, pleasant face beaming with her smile. "A good morning to you, Devon O'Donaugh. What brings you here?"

"Mrs. Carrigan," he returned with a nod. "You've a guest I need to see. Sara Madigan. Is she up yet?"

"Aye. She's up."

"Would you tell her I'm here."

"I'd be happy to, but she's out."

Patience, he warned himself, wondering what quirk of nature made his Aunt Kathleen so verbal and this woman so reticent. Mrs. Carrigan never volunteered anything. "Do you know where she is?"

"I'm right here."

His head jerked toward the sound of Sara's voice. She came from around the side of the building, following the path that led from the meadow behind the inn. In her arms she carried a bouquet of purple heather so huge she could barely see over the top of it. She had on a sweater that seemed to swallow her up and jeans that fit like a second skin. And when her face lit in a smile, he was reminded of sunshine.

The smile wasn't for him, though. It was for Mrs. Carrigan as she handed the woman the flowers. "I got a little carried away," he heard her say, then watched as Sara picked up the rest of the milk and they disappeared inside. Sara was back out before he could do much more than wonder if she was ignoring him, her arms crossed protectively as she approached his mount.

Despite her defensive stance, a hint of mischief danced in her eyes. "I don't suppose you've come to give me a ride to your aunt's."

"Why would I do that?"

"I told you she said she'd show me around the mill this morning."

"And I told you she'd be busy. If you want to see the mill, you'll have to come with me."

"You're going to show me around?"

There was as much disbelief as inquiry in the gentle lift of her eyebrows. But when she saw his tight nod, she seemed to find it unnecessary to press the subject. Devon appreciated her diplomacy. This morning would be easier to get through if they avoided challenges.

"Where's Skye?"

"At Thomas's." He watched as she stroked the bay's black, velvety nose, her hand looking amazingly delicate next to the horse's huge head. "This one's mine."

"He's beautiful." Looking up at Devon, she carried her touch along the animal's thick chestnut-colored neck. "What's his name?"

"Merlot."

"Like the magician?"

"That's Merlin." His brogue must have made the word difficult for her to understand. "Merlot," he repeated. "Like the wine."

She laughed. "You named your horse after a bottle of wine?"

"It was a very memorable night."

Her hand stilled as she regarded him. Feminine curiosity moved into her eyes, quick and intent.

Deciding he liked the idea of her wondering about him, but not interested in a stroll through memories of the year he'd lived in London, he shifted forward in the saddle. "I'm already running late this morning. If you want that tour, we leave now."

The Industrial Revolution certainly hadn't touched Brigen Glen.

That thought accompanied Sara as she followed Devon past the shallow ponds behind the mill. Retting pools, he'd called them. They were where the flax stalks were submerged in water so the fibers could rot away from the stalks.

"That process used to take over a year." He moved ahead of her, not quite rushing but not taking his time, either. "By adding natural enzymes to the water, that time can be reduced to about ten days. These two batches," he pointed out, indicating the pools nearest them, "are the first to use the new method. The water from here will be filtered and reused for the same purpose."

He spoke as if he were leading a group of tourists, something Sara knew he never did because she'd asked. Devon had told her that if anyone came to the mill wanting to look around, an occasion that only happened about once a year, he'd send for his Uncle Thomas.

It seemed that until Thomas's hands had become too gnarled to handle the fibers, he had been in charge of the mills hackling operation—the time-consuming process of combing through the fibers to separate the long ones from the shorter. For linen, the long fibers were combed repeatedly with finer and finer combs, then spun into threads and finally woven into cloth. The leftover short fibers were bundled off to the other end of the mill to be made into twine. According to Devon, his uncle liked explaining all that. Thomas lived to talk. Thomas also loved the mill, Devon said, so expounding on all that went on there could keep him and a hapless tourist occupied for hours.

Sara liked the picture that had begun to form of Thomas. She saw him as a man aging but not aged, generous like his sister, Kathleen, and not burdened by youth and ambition and drive. Schedules were impositions and he could give an entire day to a perfect stranger and enjoy it immensely. She couldn't begin to imagine Devon whiling away his time in such a manner.

It was true that Devon was showing her around, but she didn't lull herself into thinking he was enjoying it. She had the distinct feeling that what he was really doing was keeping an eye on her. Certainly he wasn't attempting to entertain her—or himself, as his uncle might have done. She didn't think that Devon was very much like his uncle at all. With Thomas, she suspected she might hear a certain affection or pride in his tone when he spoke of the place he'd worked all of his life. What she heard in Devon's voice was the subtle defensiveness she'd come to expect any time he talked about his mill. That and a certain protectiveness that surrounded everything he cared about. She had the feeling that, despite the gruff exterior, he was a man who cared a great deal.

The huge overhead door leading into a cavernous storage room gave with the groan of tired wood. She followed him into the damp interior, shivering a little at the chill. Another shiver chased that one when he pulled the door closed again. The light was poor, what little there was supplied by what could filter in through the high rain-stained windows nearly a full story above. It was dead silent, too. Three centuries' worth of stems and stalks had been worked into the dirt floor and the surface absorbed the sound of their footsteps like a sponge.

Following Devon a little more closely, Sara glanced around her. The room appeared to be storage for the shocks of flax destined for the retting pools. The yard-long bundles lay in piles against the dark stone walls. Farther ahead, other shapes replaced those forms. Boxes, horse carts, broken looms. Curiously, a child's cradle.

"That you, Devon?"

The deep male voice came from the shadows off to her left. Startled by the unexpected sound of it, Sara moved to the right and bumped into Devon. He had turned at the sound of his name. As a result, she collided with his chest. When her head snapped up, she found herself a breath away from his remarkably bland expression.

"It is," he said, never taking his eyes off her face—or his hands from where they'd caught her arms. "What do you want, Kevin?"

"I need to talk to you. Let me put these away first. Otherwise I'm likely to forget where I left them." A tool hit the ground, its sound dull and heavy. It came from up ahead, beside the cart.

Devon's glance lingered on Sara for a second longer, this time on the fullness of her mouth as she drew a deep, decidedly shaky breath. "Come to my office in half an hour." His grip tightened for a moment—whether in reaction to Kevin's statement or to her she couldn't tell. She only knew that she felt a vague sense of disappointment when his hands suddenly slid away. "We'll talk then."

"I think it best be now, Devon. While there's no one else around."

Occupied as he was, Kevin didn't seem to realize that Devon wasn't alone. Sara thought Devon would comment on that circumstance. But preoccupied herself with the strangely expectant way his behavior had made her feel, she hadn't noticed his impatience. Devon's mood hadn't been all that inviting to begin with. Kevin's presence didn't improve it.

Leaving her in the middle of the huge, shadowy room he muttered, "Wait here."

Sara's frown followed him into the shadows. The man had just said that he didn't want to talk to Devon with anyone else around. She was there. Obviously Devon didn't think her presence worth mentioning.

Her offense at that thought died a moment later. The man she assumed to be Kevin met Devon not far from the cart. He didn't appear quite as broad as Devon through the shoulders, but he was about the same height and bore himself with the same confident gait. She thought he might have a beard. The faded gray light was too unreliable to tell for sure and they were several yards away. Far enough away that Kevin hadn't noticed her, but certainly close enough for her to hear their every word.

"I'm surprised you're here today," she heard Devon say. "I told you to take the day off and tend your feet. It won't do you any good to get those blisters infected."

There was a definite edge in Devon's voice. Still, Sara couldn't help marveling at the concern he could show for someone he suspected of having betrayed him.

"It takes more than a few blisters to keep me from my work. You know that." Kevin squared his shoulders. "I noticed the containers when I had the boys burn the trash a while ago. You added that stuff to the pools, didn't you?"

"I did," Devon said, seeming to stand straighter himself. "Why?"

"You know why, man. No one's going to want to work the fiber that comes from that water. They'll think that if the stuff you put in there can eat away the stalks so fast, it's got to be too strong to be putting their hands in."

"They won't be thinking it if they're given the proper information. Did you read the material I gave you?"

The defensiveness in Kevin's stance now entered his tone. "I did. But it stands to reason that the people who make the stuff say it'll be safe."

"That stuff," Devon stressed in a tone just short of daunting, "is called an enzyme. It's protein. Natural. Properly used, it isn't going to hurt anybody or anything. You know me, Kevin, and you know I'm not going to put anyone at risk."

If there was one thing that couldn't be challenged it was Devon's sense of responsibility for the people under him. He took care of the people who worked for him. No one could argue that. And as Devon stood there waiting for Kevin to deny that, he couldn't help but question the reason for this latest challenge. Coming on the heels of yesterday's "accident," it felt very much as if Kevin was attempting to shore up an advantage. To capitalize on that loss somehow.

Kevin's posture lost its challenge. Challenging Devon on this subject was futile anyway. He sounded now as if he were trying to reach someone too close to a situation to see the whole picture.

"I know you wouldn't do anything that might hurt somebody. When we were kids you couldn't even drown the extra litters that old Yorkie of your ma's would have. But be reasonable about this. What's the sense of having people worked up about something that isn't even necessary? You wanted to ret the flax faster because you thought you'd need a quicker supply of fiber for those new power looms you wanted. Now that you won't be getting them, you don't need to change the way we do anything else."

"What makes you think I won't be getting the looms?"

Devon's voice was eerily calm. For a moment, as Kevin considered the question, an uneasy silence hung in the air.

Hesitation laced his answer. "Without the money from the load we lost, it just seemed that you wouldn't be able to afford them. Not soon anyway."

Silence returned. The two men stood motionless, facing each other over a widening gap. Devon wouldn't ask how Kevin had come to know that he'd earmarked that money for the looms. As his foreman, Kevin was close enough to the operations to know what was going on even though he never saw the books. But there was one thing Devon had to know.

"Did you untie the ropes on the cart yesterday?"

Kevin stiffened. "I'm going to pretend you didn't ask me that. A friend doesn't question another man's honor that way. Though God knows you've alienated most of us with your stubbornness, I still consider you a friend. I told you what happened. All I'm trying to do now is make you see that your beatin' a dead horse."

"Are you through?"

"Damn it, man. You won't listen to anyone anymore, will you?"

The question wasn't unfamiliar. His Uncle Thomas had asked it himself not too long ago. People accused him of not listening to them. But no one was hearing him, either. With both sides being deaf, Devon could see no point in talking.

Doing what he always did when he considered a subject closed, he moved directly to something else. "Since you're working today," he told Kevin, who was intimately familiar with the tactic, "I'd appreciate it if you'd see that a case of twine gets delivered to the O'Tulle farm. Casey's flax is about ready to harvest and he'll be needing it to tie the shocks."

He glanced at his watch, then back toward where he'd left Sara. Instead of seeing her, he saw nothing but empty space. "Damn it," he muttered into the yawning room. "Where'd she wander off to?"

"You don't need to swear." Her tone was faintly chiding. "I'm right here."

Sara slipped off the box she'd been sitting on, brushing the seat of her jeans as she did. Kevin did have a beard, she discovered. A neat, well-kept one that took the harshness from his blunt features. He also wore a tweed cap similar to the one little Mickey had worn. Grasping it by its bill, he pulled it off at her approach. His curly brown hair fell over his forehead as he nodded. "Ma'am," he said, glancing over her shoulder to see who else might have been there.

For a moment, Sara stood back, studying him. He had an open honest face and though he was a bit hesitant, he didn't look at all the type of man to deceive a friend. Still, the fact that he might have betrayed Devon colored her initial impression of him.

That she should feel even that much loyalty to a man she scarcely knew gave her considerable pause.

"Hi," she finally said, thinking it awkward to simply stand there staring. It didn't seem that Devon was going to introduce them, so she took it upon herself. "I'm Sara. You're Kevin Connor. Right?"

"I am. And you'd be the lady who's come looking for Thomas." He flipped the cap back onto his head. "Well, I've work to do," he said to Devon. Then to Sara, "You have a good visit." Another nod, and he turned back to the cart he'd been unloading.

Without a word, Devon started for the door they'd headed toward earlier.

"How did he know who I was?" she asked when she'd followed him into a much brighter storage area. This one was filled with row after row of foot-long spindles, all neatly wound with thread.

"I doubt there's anyone in the village who doesn't know about you by now. A stranger is news in a place like this."

"Devon."

He turned when he realized that she wasn't right behind him anymore. She'd stopped just inside the door.

"What?"

"Is Kevin right? Is there a chance that the additives you're using are harmful?"

A bear sticking its paw into a beehive had a lesser chance of getting stung than she did at that moment. Still raw from his encounter with Kevin, Devon steeled himself against the accusation he was sure he'd heard.

It wasn't accusation he'd heard at all. It was simply inquiry. Her eyes held his easily, her expression open and patient. She hadn't already made up her mind about anything, he realized. She wasn't prepared to attack. She'd simply asked a question and was waiting for an answer. *His* answer.

"No, Sara," he said, feeling some of the tension drain from him when he said her name. The sound of it was soft, soothing. And oddly, saying it seemed to soothe him. He didn't care to examine that phenomenon too closely. "There isn't. I looked into all different kinds of processes and this was the only one that was really safe. Kevin knows that, too."

Her brows puckered with her frown. "Then why was he going on about it?"

"Because it's something to pick on. The additives aren't the issue. The issue is the whole expansion." With his thumb and forefinger he pinched the bridge of his nose. A headache seemed to be forming there. "Losing that load yesterday may have slowed me down. But it isn't going to stop me.

Come on." He motioned her forward. "I'll show you the rest of this place."

The weariness in him was becoming difficult for him to ignore. That she could see it, if only for the brief moment before he turned away, made that very clear to Sara. But Devon wouldn't give in to it. And had she not just felt herself wanting to ease that weariness, she might have asked why he was so bent on doing something no one else wanted. One man against the world couldn't possibly be a comfortable position to be in. But now wasn't the time to pursue the matter. She was drawn by the strength of his determination. She admired it. Envied it. And being that attracted frightened her.

Sara had gone through most of her adult life with a decided lack of direction. Her only constant had been the restlessness that had caused her to move from one job to another until she'd found one that paid her to *keep* moving. No matter where she was, she always felt as if she were searching for something that hung just out of reach. Yet for a moment, when she'd seen the defensiveness slip from Devon's expression, she'd felt the tug of something that promised an end to that search. She couldn't identify it, though. Nor did it last long enough for her to do more than wonder if it had only been her imagination.

Left with only the all-too-familiar feeling of restlessness, she followed Devon inside.

With what were cursory explanations at best, Devon hustled her through the hackling room. There, curious eyes smiled at her over the paper masks that kept them from breathing the miniscule fibers their combs freed from the silvery yellow fibers. In the background, a lilting Strauss waltz set the pace of their work.

When she asked where the melody was coming from, he mumbled, "Portable compact disk," and pushed through the next door before she could say anything else. All she could hear then was the wheeze and clank of the steam-driven engine that supplied power for the spinning mechanisms—power once supplied by the human foot—that made the linen thread. The next series of doors led into the area where the fabric was made. These were the looms he wanted to replace, she guessed as they walked between the two cumbersome machines. Old and antiquated, they produced a fabric that was serviceable and, to her professional eye, of a standard grade. Two men battled the mechanisms to keep all the threads feeding into it properly, the task taking a kind of skill Sara could only call remarkable.

Devon would have passed right on through the next area with little more than the wave of his hand if Sara had let him. They had entered another section, much quieter than the last. This one contained the buzz of voices, which faded to little more than an occasional murmur as Devon led her down a long, narrow aisle. She hung back, taking her time where Devon would have hurried on. He saw this every day. So to him it must all seem very mundane. But Sara was fascinated.

Drawn by the rhythmic clack of shuttles being thrown, she stopped in the middle of the brightly lit space. A dozen looms lined the walls. Not the bulky behemoths she'd just seen, but wood-framed ones, each about five feet wide and each with its own weaver. With the exception of the spinning process, the linen here was all handmade.

One of the men she'd seen earlier in the spinning room was taking a bolt of finished cloth from a loom operated by a diminutive lady with wire-rimmed glasses. Sara moved closer.

Impatience flickered in Devon. He didn't have time for this as it was and now she was slowing him up even more by talking to Mary. He started to tell her that, but then he saw her smile at him and the impatience died. "This is wonderful," she said, skimming her fingers along a length of finished fabric. She glanced back to Mary, who was stretching the kinks from her back. "You do beautiful work."

Mary was beaming as Sara, absently flipping her long hair over her shoulder, moved on to the next loom. The weave there was a little nubbier, but just as exquisite. Her comment to that effect made the lady making it blush like a schoolgirl.

Instead of following her, Devon stayed by the door. The looms and the weavers all faced toward the other end of the room and he could watch her here without anyone noticing. Not that the dozen women waiting their turn to get a better look at the lovely stranger were paying any attention to him. The shuffle and clack of shuttles carrying woof threads across warp had slowed considerably. Conversation, usually animated and always filled with gossip, had come to a halt. Everyone was too busy trying to overhear whatever conversation Sara was having. At the moment, she was asking Kevin's sister-in-law, Leah, to show her how the threads were tightened to get such a close weave.

Crossing his arms over the cables in his knit sweater, Devon leaned against the doorjamb. He had to admit that he was pleased with Sara's enthusiasm for his product. But it was a guarded kind of satisfaction. Almost as guarded as the pleasure he found in simply watching her.

Her interest was visible in the way her fragile features pinched in concentration while Leah lowered and raised the loom's harness to show Sara what she wanted to know. That interest was real, not the polite curiosity he'd seen in some of the tourists Thomas had brought through. Devon felt his guard slip a little. Sara was completely absorbed with the process of making the linen and he, in turn, was unwillingly enchanted with her fascination.

Mary reset her loom now that the finished bolt had been carried off. Sara moved to watch her, stepping into a beam of sunlight coming through the windows. The walls in this room were painted white to make it as bright as possible for the weavers. When the sun shone, the room became as light as outdoors. As Sara hunched down to see what Mary was doing, the air in the sunlight around her seemed to shimmer.

Devon pressed his thumb and forefinger to his eyes, thinking his headache must be affecting his vision. Or maybe it was fatigue. The decent night's sleep he'd promised himself last night hadn't materialized. Leaning against the wall, doing nothing but waiting, he could feel his tiredness clear to his bones.

He glanced back up. There was still a surreal quality to the light. Only now a halo of gold dust followed Sara as she moved. It glittered around her gleaming hair, danced on the air currents when she lifted her hand to punctuate a thought. And when she stopped in a sunbeam, the sparkling dust made her look much as he imagined one of her fanciful, otherworldly creatures might appear—had he believed in such things.

Shaking his head didn't help his headache, but it did seem to clear it of the nonsensical thoughts. There was nothing unusual about the light. It had taken him only a moment to realize what caused the odd effect. Yet even though he knew that the "gold dust" was only miniscule fibers of flax floating in the air and lit by the sun, he couldn't quite shake the feeling that Sara might be something rather extraordinary. Not in any fantastic sense, of course. His head wasn't hurting that much. Just an extraordinary person. He didn't know many people who took the time to appreciate another person's effort the way she did. Her curiosity about what each person was doing was equaled only by her admiration for their particular skill. Everyone she spoke with sat just a little straighter when she left them. And every one of the ladies seemed a little more enthused about what they were doing. The shuttles had all picked up speed. She had a way of making a person feel special. Necessary.

Maybe that was why, when she approached him with her easy smile, he couldn't help but smile back. The movement felt rusty. And Sara, by the inquiring tilt of her head, seemed to realize it was something he hadn't done in a while.

The acknowledgment of the unfamiliar spontaneity jolted him. Calling back the rigid control he held over himself, feeling protected by it, he pushed himself from the door-jamb and swung the door open. A dozen pairs of eyes were watching as he motioned their visitor into the hall outside.

Whirling around as soon as she stepped into the narrow space, Sara pointed over Devon's shoulder. The rush of the women's conversation was shut out with his closing of the door. "What do you do with the fabric made in here?"

They were in a short hallway lined with sepia photographs of the mill. Had Sara not been so preoccupied, she would have taken a closer look. She loved old pictures. There was a romanticism about them that invited her imagination to wander—which was why she spent much of her free time in museums and galleries rather than the clubs and cafés many of her peers frequented. All that interested her at the moment was Devon's response.

"Most of it is sold locally," he told her, putting no particular import to her inquiry. "Some of the women use it for the embroidered handkerchiefs and tablecloths they sell to shops in Cork."

"Do you ever export it?"

With a droll, "Hardly," he crossed his arms. She'd seen him assume a similar stance back in the weaving room. Only in there, as he'd leaned against the wall, it had seemed surprisingly casual. Now it seemed to close him in. "I sell mainly to a small broker in Cork. He buys all the machined cloth I can make. I could get a better price from one of the bigger brokers, but my output isn't enough for them. Yet."

It was clear enough that Devon saw the fabric produced by the automated equipment as the backbone of the business. Sara wasn't interested in that, though. What she wanted was the handwoven fabric. The linen the women behind that door produced was of a quality and fineness she'd never seen before. It would sell for a fortune on the right market.

"Can I have a sample of what just came off Mary's loom?"

Her interest was far from idle. She could tell he realized that by the way his eyes narrowed when he asked her what she wanted it for.

Sara was always on the lookout for quality merchandise. The clients she bought for had widely varied needs and she'd long ago learned to appreciate unexpected discoveries. Two of her clients were top-notch designers. She felt certain that at least one of them would be interested in the rare and luxurious fabric.

Devon's shrug told her he thought little would come of her effort, but he said he'd get her a yard of it, then directed her to the room at the end of the hall when she asked if he had a telephone. She wanted to call the designers to let them know the fabric was on its way—and to make arrangements for its delivery. She had a hunch there wasn't any express mail out of Brigen Glen.

Devon's office was small and far from tidy. For a man who seemed very much in control of himself, he seemed to have little control over his immediate surroundings. It looked as if a bomb had exploded in the middle of the room.

Two coffee cups, both half-empty, sat on a dark wood desk. An old adding machine sat to one corner of it, half buried beneath files. Its tape curled to the floor. The wastebasket overflowed with matching crumpled papers, evidence of an idea that wasn't jelling. Magazines were everywhere: atop the gray metal file cabinets, on the ledge by the window, stacked next to a bolt of fabric propped against the wall. The publications were devoted to horses, the textile industry, computers, sports. One, which she took from the chair behind his desk just before she sat down on it, addressed the subject of woodworking.

With a smile, she lay it next to a sheet of neatly columned figures and leaned back in the deep, tufted chair. The leather was cracked and worn and it creaked a little with its age, but it was comfortable in the way of things that have grown accustomed to their owner. Her glance fell on a child's yellow plastic airplane. It was on the floor by a table leg. The table itself had nothing on it but rolled-up sheets of paper. They looked to be plans of some sort. One of the rolls was spread out, its edges held down by books.

This was the first real glimpse she'd had of the man behind the indomitable facade. And though chaos was hardly a good recommendation, she liked what she saw. All the clutter made him seem more approachable—which was more than she could say for his expression when he appeared in the doorway just as she picked up the phone.

He stood with his hands on his hips as his forbidding glance swept the room. It skipped right past her, indicating no satisfaction at all when it fell on the item he was looking for. Without a word, he pulled a wrench from the pocket of a jacket hanging on its peg. A moment later, he was gone.

It didn't take much for Sara to figure out that something must have broken. It took even less to realize that Devon wasn't too happy about it. Feeling pity for whatever the object was, she reached for the phone again.

Sara didn't think of herself as spoiled by technologies that shrank distances so efficiently, but she had grown accustomed to them. The telephone, a squat black instrument with a rotary dial, appeared to be Devon's only link with the present decade. His invoices were typed on a manual typewriter. Copies were made with carbon paper. And after getting the number for an international overnight delivery company with an office in Cork, she discovered that mail went by horseback rather than cart. At least as far as Durry, a town ten miles down the road. From there it went by truck. Her packages could be on their way out of Cork by tomorrow.

It could have been worse. Another buyer she knew had made a fabulous find of brass bells at a tiny foundry in Tibet. She'd had to bring them out herself, by yak.

It took her half an hour to make her calls. Devon returned just as she was concluding the last one. He had his hand clamped over the back of his neck and a preoccupied look on his face. It seemed he'd forgotten she was there. When he glanced up to see her at his desk, her presence didn't register for a moment. Then with an expression that seemed to say, "Oh. It's you," he started to leave.

"I'll just be a minute," Sara hurriedly said, and returned her attention to her call. He had a streak of grease on his cheek. For some reason, she found it terribly distracting. Her glance kept returning to it as she patiently repeated her pickup instructions. Her accent was apparently making it difficult for the woman on the other end of the line to understand her. Two more calls, quick ones to let the designers know when to expect their packages, and she was finished.

Devon was at the window, his back to her. He'd laid the sample she'd asked for on the desk, along with a couple of large manila envelopes. She left them where they were.

"Do I dare ask what happened?"

He seemed confused by the question. "With what?"

"With whatever it was you took after with that wrench."

The shrug of his shoulders was weary, designed more to relieve the tightness in them than as a commentary on her observation. "One of the looms jammed again. Both of them are so damned old it's a miracle they don't just quit completely. Hell," he muttered. "If I were their age, I would."

It was difficult being so close to him. Too easily, she could feel his frustration. It made her edgy, and she already felt restless enough. She rose from his chair, thinking he might want it, and walked over to the table. The plans unrolled on it appeared to be those for his expansion. But a quick glance at the meticulously drawn sheets weren't only of a building. It was a layout of an entire town.

"I can't see where anyone would object to your getting new ones if the old ones keep breaking down."

"It isn't that simple. The new looms are high-speed. Their output is triple what these old machines are capable of producing. Making that much more cloth means we need a more efficient method of transportation. That means trucks. But a truck is no good here because every time it rains, the thing would get bogged down in the mud on these dirt roads. Even if it didn't get stuck, the bridge over the stream couldn't hold a truck's weight."

"Why not just buy one loom, then? You'd only have one-third more product instead of six times as much."

He gave a shrewd, assessing look. "You playing devil's advocate?"

Maybe, she thought, wanting to understand what was going on in this village. She wanted, too, to understand him, though she wasn't sure why that felt so necessary. "It just seems that wouldn't put as much strain on your transportation. You'd come closer to maintaining the status quo."

"I suppose I could," he said with deceptive calm. "But that really solves nothing. As I've said before, expanding this mill is the only thing that's going to keep this village from disappearing as so many like it have done."

"Why is everyone so opposed to what you want to do, then?"

"Because it means change. And change scares the hell out of them."

"The people here aren't unique in that," she pointed out gently. "Change scares a lot of people."

She saw his glance jerk toward the plans, then back to her. It didn't appear that he was going to offer to explain them. As he had so graciously pointed out, she was an outsider and what went on here had nothing to do with her.

She supposed that, technically, he was justified in that rationale. But Sara wouldn't accept that limitation. "Just how much change do you have in mind?" she ventured.

He hesitated. For a moment, she thought he might do what she'd expected him to do soon anyway—tell her he really didn't have any more time to spare and send her on her way. After his insistence last night, she'd also anticipated a renewed attempt to get her to leave the village. Perhaps he still would. But for now, Devon apparently needed to talk about what no one else wanted to hear.

With a rustling of paper, he unrolled a larger view of the plan she'd first seen. There was a scope to his expansion that she'd never even suspected.

Devon wanted much more than to replace the looms with the faster ones. The increased production meant he'd need to hire more people. They would need housing, which meant craftsmen and their families would be drawn from the surrounding areas. The population of the village would increase and that would bring in merchants who, in turn, would bring their families. It was Devon's hope that Brigen Glen could grow from its present size into a small town, with all the conveniences a small town could offer. He envisioned stores, medical facilities, other manufacturing.

"I want it to be a place people will want to stay in, rather than move away from," Devon told her, and Sara couldn't help but wonder at his intensity when he expressed that desire. "I want everything they need to be right here."

Having people stay seemed very important to him. But she didn't interrupt to ask him why. She was too fascinated by what she could hear beneath his words as he spoke. He firmly believed that what he wanted to do was right. Essential. Unavoidable if the village was to survive. He also seemed to be one of those rare men with the discipline to follow his conviction. That trait was certainly commendable. But while she admired his dedication, she couldn't help feeling a certain ambivalence about what he wanted to do.

Evidently her mental struggle was visible. She hadn't meant for him to witness it.

"You don't approve."

She wished she could shade the truth, soften it. She didn't want to raise his defenses. "Not really."

His laconic "Why?" was expected.

Though outwardly Sara's life-style had a certain jet-set quality, beneath the trendy clothes and all the exotic travel lay a healthy respect for tradition. There was something solid and comforting about a way of life that had been around for so long. But three hundred years of tradition would go right down the tubes if Devon were to succeed with his plans. On the other hand, Brigen Glen could simply fade into oblivion if he didn't.

"Because a way of life will be lost. You want to save Brigen Glen, but what will save it will also destroy it. Once you start, the village will never be the same. I'm not saying that what you want to do is wrong," she hurried to tell him. A wistful longing entered her voice. "I just think it's rather sad."

He wasn't surprised that she should be sentimental. Rerolling the large set of plans, he muttered, "Nothing lasts forever."

She, in turn, wasn't surprised by his cynicism. "There are some things that do," she countered softly.

The rubber band snapped into place. The plans were tossed back on the table. He supposed she was talking about some romantic notion of love. The kind that was supposed to transcend time. He wasn't going to comment on her statement, though. It wasn't a subject he cared to discuss. His "forever" had lasted exactly three years and a month.

The door to his office had been left ajar. Kevin poked his head around it, excusing himself to Sara, before he glanced back to Devon. When he did, his brows lowered, but all he said was that one of the farmers had just arrived with a load of flax. The price the man wanted was high for the quality and Devon needed to take a look at it.

Devon told him he'd be there in a minute, then watched as Kevin's scowl bounced from him to Sara, then back again. More than a little guarded where Kevin was concerned, Devon didn't quite know what to make of the man's behavior.

Sara knew what Kevin had been frowning at. She also had the feeling that Kevin hadn't wanted to mention it in front of her—which was certainly polite but rather senseless since she could certainly see it. "I think he was looking at the streak on your face. You've got grease on your cheek."

Devon took a swipe at it, then frowned at the grease on his fingers.

"Do you have a mirror?" she asked, since he clearly couldn't see what he was doing. "All you did was smear it."

There was a mirror in the women's water closet, but he didn't go in there while the women were working. He took another pass at it, getting most of it except a faint streak high on his cheekbone.

"Here," she said and reached out her hand to help.

The pad of her thumb was already on his cheek when she realized what she was doing. Her glance jerked to his, her breath locking in her lungs when she found him staring straight into her eyes.

"Go on," she heard him say, his voice deliciously rough. "Take it off for me."

The breath she'd held released itself with a shudder. The next one she drew brought with it the subtle scents of soap and something unmistakably male. Its effect on her nervous system was insidious. She could feel her hand tremble as she drew the pad of her thumb over the streak. Pretending great concentration on the task, she rubbed the grease off on her index finger, then drew her thumb over his cheek again. The skin over his cheekbones was taut and smooth. Where the streak curved upward toward the corner of his eye, it was etched with a network of tiny wrinkles. Character lines, she supposed they were called. To her, they spoke of maturity—and worry.

His chest rose with the deep breath he drew. He blinked slowly, as if her touch felt good to him. She deliberately made it gentler, entertaining the thought of letting her fingers drift upward to his temple. She'd thought earlier that he might have a headache. If her touch could bring him ease...

Stunned at the track of her thoughts, she slowly withdrew her hand. "It's gone," she said and started to move away.

The feel of his fingers curling around her wrist stopped her. He picked up her hand, holding it palm out in his. For a moment, he did nothing but quietly scan her face, his eyes seeming to darken as they settled on her mouth. A sense of expectation hung in the air, taunting, teasing. But when he moved, it was only to slip the pad of his thumb over hers.

"Now you have it on you," he said, and held her eyes while he rubbed the grease away. The movement was slow, steady and undeniably sensual. The friction of their skin created heat. A kind of heat that seemed to transfer itself to inside Sara, softening her.

Its effect on Devon was quite the opposite. And when he realized how close he was to answering the invitation on Sara's lovely lips, he nearly groaned aloud. Had they been anywhere else, he'd have given in to the urge. But he could hear someone coming down the hall. Kevin probably. With the farmer.

It was just as well. Devon had the feeling that one taste of Sara's lips wouldn't be enough, that he'd want more. Much more.

Knowing how impossible that would be only strengthened his resolve to see that she left as soon as possible.

Chapter Five

The morning fog hadn't been as heavy as yesterday's. Still, patches of it lingered long past noon, hovering in the troughs between the hills where cotton-colored sheep grazed. Sara scarcely noticed the fog. Or the sheep. Or the tiny yellow flowers blooming in the grassy mound between the ruts in the road. With her hands deep in the pockets of her oversize sweater, her head bent to avoid the occasional hole, her thoughts were centered on Devon.

He was a puzzling man. He pushed her away, even as he pulled her closer. It was as if something within him responded to her, but he was determined to ignore it. To dam it up, the way she suspected he did with much of what motivated him.

Whatever his reason for doing that, she couldn't deny being drawn to him. She didn't doubt that to be a dubious development at best, given his attitude toward her. But she couldn't seem to help it any more than she could help drawing her next breath. She wasn't particularly pleased by the circumstance. Moths were drawn to flames, too, and what happened to them wasn't particularly appealing.

She couldn't deny, though, that for one incredible, heart-stopping moment, she'd thought he might pull her into his arms. The heat in his eyes had been so real, the need in him so visible, that she'd *felt* it, deep in a part of her that, until now, had lay untouched. Yet he'd done nothing. Just as he'd done nothing when she'd found herself a breath away from him in the storage room. When Kevin had returned with that crotchety old farmer, the cloak of control Devon wore so easily whipped back into place. Then he'd handed her a pen so she could address her packages and walked out.

The sound of horse's hooves joined the bounce and jolt of a wooden cart. Looking up, Sara saw it coming toward her and stepped from the middle of the road. The wagon carried two rows of large, galvanized-metal milk cans—empty, judging from the way they jostled and clanked together. The horse ambled past, the driver tipped his hat and Sara, with a wave, resumed her trek, very much as if she moved out of the way for horse-drawn milk carts every day.

Preoccupied as she was, she didn't stop to think of how foreign her surroundings were. Or how familiar. Dwelling on what Devon hadn't done also made her consider that he hadn't said anything more to her about leaving the village until Thomas returned. He'd seemed too adamant about it last night to simply let the matter drop. Yet he hadn't said a word about it today. That bothered her. Devon wasn't the type to give up when he was convinced of a necessity.

She took a deep breath of the cleansing air and let it out with a disgusted sigh. She was making too much of this. It was entirely possible that Devon felt it would be impolite to run her out given that she was trying to sell his fabric for him. Failing to see him as bending to that convention, she felt a more likely explanation would be that he'd simply re-

alized she was truly as harmless as she'd professed to be.
After all, except for displeasure at her having given his aunt
a few other things to think about regarding his expansion,
the principal reason he'd wanted her to leave was because of
his aunt's bizarre belief that Sara could have inherited some
kind of power from her grandmother. That was completely
ridiculous, of course. And though Sara would feel terrible
if her presence had truly distressed the woman, she didn't
think that Kathleen had appeared unduly affected by her
visit.

With that rationale in place, she felt her shoulders lift. She
wouldn't worry about what had taken place last night. What
she would do was act on it. Much of what Devon had said
had strengthened Sara's desire to learn more about her
grandmother's background—and thus her own. It was a
way to anchor her roots—something that, despite the con-
stancy of her grandmother's care, Sara had always felt she
lacked.

That need was what carried her toward the church at the
top of the hill. The priest might have some answers.

From a distance, the building had a serenity that such a
place was supposed to have. Gleaming white in the spo-
radic sunlight, its spire held a simple cross toward a cloudy
sky. The solace it promised was deceptive. The closer Sara
got, the easier it became to see that the building was as battered as the souls who'd come here seeking its peace. The
paint on the boards flaked and curled to reveal grayed
wood. Rust spots teared down from the iron nails that held
them together. The heavy, rough-hewn doors were the only
solid-looking thing about the place. And they were bolted
shut.

Sara's hand slipped from the pitted black metal handle
and she turned away. As with everything else she'd approached in her life, her sense of optimism hadn't allowed
her to think she'd have any difficulty finding out what she

wanted to know. She'd always had a knack for accomplishing by impulse what others planned for weeks. She simply did what she had to do when she had to do it and didn't spend much time on the details. The details could be handled once she got where she was going. That was why it hadn't occurred to her that she'd have any difficulty locating Thomas O'Donaugh. And why she didn't do much more than frown at the disadvantage of having found the church abandoned. She'd just have to look someplace else.

A small stone building sat at the back of the rise, not too far from the cemetery. It could have been a rectory or a caretaker's cottage. Whatever it was, like the church, it hadn't been occupied in a very long time. Cobwebs clung like little snowdrifts to the corners of the windows, an especially elaborate one adorning the knob and jamb of the front door. Sara cupped her hands around her eyes to peek through one of the hazy windows. A plain wooden table and a chair with a broken leg were all she could see.

It appeared that the church had neither a caretaker nor a priest.

"Sight-seeing?"

Whirling around, her hand flew to the base of her throat. Devon stood in the rocky grass a few feet back. His hands were on his hips, his expression remarkably bland for the start he'd given her.

The breath she'd sucked in was slowly released. "I was looking for the priest."

"You have sins to confess?"

"Undoubtedly," she returned, wondering if that was a smile in his eyes or merely a trick of the light. "But I just wanted to talk to him."

"I'm afraid that won't be possible. We haven't had a priest here since Father Flannigan died a few years ago."

That wasn't what she wanted to hear. She turned to the building, forgetting her disappointment for the moment.

Laying her hand on the peeling wood, she looked toward the church's steeple.

Is this part of what Devon had meant about the town dying? she wondered. "It's a shame to see it boarded up that way."

His silence implied agreement as to the building's condition—and a tacit refusal to discuss his position on the religion it represented. As cynical as he could be, she doubted that he subscribed to formalities. Even if he did, she was sure he would find fault with the local beliefs that blended lore and legend with religion to come up with a faith that was uniquely Irish. If she could rely on her grandmother's example, Sara was sure that many of the older folk here were as influenced by myth as they were a Sunday sermon.

She turned back to him. "Where do the people who live here go?"

"Those who do, go to the church in Durry."

So much for her finding anything in the local church records, she thought, making a mental note to see if the priest in Durry might have somehow acquired them. Then dismissing what she could do nothing about at the moment, she tipped her head in inquiry. "What are you doing here?"

He took a step closer. "You left before telling me what you wanted done with your packages."

She didn't think he'd sought her out for her company. But she didn't realize that she'd hoped he had until the disappointment set in. Not particularly pleased with her reaction, and finding no encouragement in his very businesslike tone, she told him that she'd left a note propped up by his telephone. It quickly became apparent that he hadn't seen it. The oversight wasn't surprising considering the clutter on the desk, though he didn't do much more than give her a wry glance when she mentioned its chaotic condition.

"Just tell me what it said," he muttered, and she quickly repeated what was on the note.

"Someone will be in from Durry this afternoon to pick the packages up. They'll deliver them to the airport in Cork tomorrow." She'd put her grandmother's ring on the chain she wore around her neck. It felt safer there, closer to her heart. Toying with it now, she added, "I hope to have a response a couple of days after that."

He accepted what she said with little more than a nod. His attention seemed centered on the motion of her fingers.

She'd slipped the tip of her index finger through the thick gold band and turned it in slow circles with her thumb. Her hand rested between the soft rise of her breasts and his eyes rested there, too, letting her feel their heat. A muscle in his jaw jerked and his focus shifted upward, stopping at the fullness of her mouth. His glance lingered.

"Where are you going now?" she heard him ask.

The hunger in his visual caress nearly stole her breath. She hadn't thought about where she would go from here. Even as she wondered why he wanted to know, if possibly he was keeping track of her, her glance fell on the cluster of gray tombstones rising in the distance. "Over there."

The heat dissipated, his eyes going hard. "It's one thing for you to kill time wandering around the mill. The cemetery isn't a place for tourists."

It was clear enough that he misunderstood her intention. Just as apparent was his regard of her as an outsider, someone prepared to trespass on the village's sacred ground. "I don't expect you to understand what I need to do," she told him simply. "You have family. I don't. But part of my family came from here. And there might be someone buried there who belonged to me."

Clutching the ring, seemingly guided by it, she moved toward the cemetery. The grass was lusher here, deeper, and the cuffs of her jeans grew damp with the clinging dew. She scarcely noticed. At first she didn't even notice that Devon had followed her. The only thought on her mind was that she had a right to be here, and that what she did was none of Devon's business.

She stopped beside a plain stone cross, her bottom lip between her teeth.

Grass rustled behind her. "Who would be buried here?" she heard him quietly ask.

The challenge was gone from his voice. The deep, beautifully accented tones washed over her, the question overriding the quick irritation she'd felt only moments ago.

She stayed with her back to him. She didn't know exactly who she was looking for. Perhaps the man her grandmother had married. "My grandfather. He passed away before my grandmother moved to the States." *When I left Ireland, it was just my little one and me,* was what Sara's grandmother had told her. "I really don't know anything about anyone else."

"You never asked?"

Her hair slipped forward, shimmering in the light as she shook her head. She'd said she didn't expect him to understand. And she didn't think he could. No one could who hadn't been raised as she had—alone with a wildly imaginative woman who trusted little of the outside world.

"It never occurred to me," she told him, because she really hadn't realized that there were questions she should have asked during the years she'd been growing up, answers she should have insisted upon. She'd been too easily satisfied by the fantastic stories with which her grandmother had teased her.

She could clearly remember how simple it had been to become caught up in the fantasy.

"What games did you play when you were little like me?" she would ask, and her grandmother's eyes would twinkle as she gathered Sara close.

"When I was little we liked to play hide-and-seek, just like you do. Only when we played, we had much better hiding places. My favorites were a knothole in a log, or under the leaf of a clover. The elves never thought to look there.''

''Oh, Grandma,'' Sara would say, sounding very grown-up. She did go to school after all, and she'd overheard the other children say how weird she was to believe such things. ''There's no such things as elves. And little girls are too big to hide in places like that.''

Her grandmother's expression would grow quite serious—except for that telling twinkle in her eyes. ''Oh, but there are. Remember, you don't always need to see something yourself to believe it exists. But you're right about little girls. They couldn't possibly hide in knotholes. When I was little, though, I wasn't a girl. I was a wood nymph. We could change ourselves into anything we wanted. Then we could hide anywhere.''

And so it would go. Fiona would describe herself playing with the faeries who were as light as the wind and whose gossamer gowns were spun of the most delicate webs. There were pixies and ogres and a great golden doe. The doe was special to Fiona, or so she would say, because with the doe rested the power to save Brigen Glen should the village ever be in danger.

The stories charmed the child. But as Sara grew older, entering those years when youth seeks its identity, the stories no longer satisfied. She began to wonder about her parents. The other children had them and not even knowing her own made Sara feel even more different. With a look of great sadness, her grandmother finally told her that her father, Fiona's son, had brought Sara to her after having been away for years. She'd never known the woman who bore her. Fiona had said nothing beyond that. But because the subject seemed to distress her so, Sara didn't push for more. She simply accepted the rootless feeling, along with the restlessness that followed.

Sara didn't mention that to Devon, though. Or how, once she'd left the protection of her grandmother's home and headed for college, she'd made herself believe it didn't matter where she'd come from because she had too many places now to go. She was a young woman tasting her first freedom, busy discovering; then, finally, a woman with a career, too caught up in the motions of daily living to need the details. As a child, she had accepted the incredible tales her grandmother had told her about her life because, like most children, Sara had seen her guardian as any child would see a parent figure. As a nurturer, teacher, warden. Not as a person in her own right. Certainly not as the eccentric others no doubt thought her. And when Sara had matured enough to realize how narrow her scope had been where her grandmother was concerned, and how sheltered and confined her own life had been, it had seemed that there would always be time later for the business of seeking answers.

But time had run out. Now she had to find the answers on her own.

She had been silent for a long time. Sara hadn't realized quite how long until she looked up from the leaf she'd shredded to see Devon quietly watching her. It was impossible to tell what he thought of anything she'd said.

Thinking he probably thought her foolish, and feeling too vulnerable with her memories to have her suspicion confirmed, she offered a dismissive smile.

Veiled sympathy touched his expression. "I hope you find what you're looking for," he told her, then added that he had to get back to the mill. "I'll see that your packages are taken care of."

She'd barely thanked him when, hands in his pockets, he turned to head back toward the church. She wasn't sure, but his manner seemed to indicate that he felt he was intruding. He wanted to give her her privacy.

Odd that someone who looked so hard could be so sensitive.

He hoped she found what she was looking for. Sara mulled the words over as she turned to find her grandfather's grave. She didn't know what she'd do once she found it. It didn't matter. It was just something that had to be done. So she searched every headstone, every marker. The dates went back for hundreds of years, time and the weather wearing away many of the inscriptions.

There were so many markers that for more than an hour, she walked between them, checking the name on each one. The name she was looking for was not to be found. Nowhere on any of the stones with their elaborate Celtic crosses or plain arched tops did she find the name Madigan.

Confused, Sara swept her hair back and stared at the stone she'd stopped beside. Her grandmother had said that her family had always lived in Brigen Glen. That she had been the first to leave it. So why weren't the deceased members of the family buried there? Why wasn't there a single Madigan to be found?

Confusion was joined by a sense of loss. It tugged at Sara, wanting to be felt. She pushed it away, refusing to mourn what she couldn't even identify. She always felt too much. And here in this silent, shadowy place, she'd begun to feel something she'd never experienced before. A sense of hopelessness. Her roots should have been here. But all she'd found was . . . nothing.

A small stand of oak guarded the back of the cemetery, many of the older headstones sheltered by the graceful limbs. The flash of movement from that direction caught her eye, her thoughts freezing as she glanced up. There was nothing to be seen but the gentle motion of the leaves. Their rustle was joined by the chatter of a bird answering another.

It hadn't been Devon. He'd gone the other way, back to the mill. Had it not been for the strange, prickling sensation crawling up her neck, she'd have thought the motion caused by an animal. She felt as if she were being watched.

Attributing the disconcerting sensation to the nature of the place, she slipped between two elaborate monuments and hurried toward the open field surrounding the abandoned cottage. She glanced behind her, again seeing nothing that shouldn't have been there. "Just your imagination," she muttered, then gave a disgusted sigh when she realized she was talking to herself.

The disturbing sensations that had encroached upon her seemed to ease with distance, allowing more productive thought. She hadn't found any Madigans, but she had found O'Donaughs. An O'Donaugh was just the person she needed to see right now. Kathleen hadn't known much about Fiona, but maybe she knew of someone who did.

She headed back past the church and down the hill, all the while ignoring the fact that while Devon hadn't exactly asked her to stay away from his aunt, the request had certainly been implied. Actually, with Devon, it was more of a directive than a request. But she was prepared to overlook that, too.

She wasn't, however, prepared for what she encountered at Kathleen's cottage.

A pretty young woman in her late teens with long, burnished curls and a smattering of freckles on her pert little nose answered Sara's knock. A toddler clung to her leg, his head of dark copper curls peeking around her yellow cotton skirt. She said simply that Kathleen was "not available."

The chill in the woman's voice would have frosted the equator. "Can you tell me when she will be?"

"I'm afraid not."

"Will you tell her I stopped by, then?" Sara asked, bewildered by the woman's attitude. It so opposed Kathleen's graciousness. "I'm..."

"I know who you are. Please. Don't come here again."

The woman bent down and picked up the baby. Hugging him to her as if Sara might snatch him away, she stayed in the doorway, looking very much as if she intended to remain there until Sara was off the property.

Not knowing what to make of the woman's unfriendliness, Sara stepped backward, instinctively distancing herself from the hostility in the woman's pale blue eyes. The little boy's stare was much easier to meet, though he did seem wary of her as he tucked his head beneath the woman's chin and popped his thumb into his mouth.

Sara had no choice but to leave. But there was one thing she had to know first. "Is Kathleen all right?"

"She fine. She's just not here. Please," she repeated. "Go away."

Her last words overlapped the high-pitched whinny of a horse. Another whinny preceded an ominous thud. The sound seemed to echo, bleeding into the more frantic noise of boards being battered.

The horse's cry was so desperate that a shudder swept Sara, replacing her bewilderment at the woman's open dislike. The commotion came from the small building behind the cottage, just beyond the yard.

The woman in the doorway whirled around. "Mickey?" Sara heard her call. "Are you in here? Mickey?"

Another crash sounded, this one of wood splintering. Sara was around the side of the house, heading for the back gate before she realized that the woman from the doorway had the same thought in mind. She'd come through the cottage and out the back door. Her yellow skirt lapped at her legs and her freckled arms were wound tightly around the little boy. Veering toward the garden, she quickly put the child in the playpen beside it, stuffed a toy into his chubby little hands and darted for the gate. Sara had already reached it. The woman didn't bother to stop her. Eyes frantic, she followed Sara into the corral.

The slat gate of the narrow hut was open. Skye was in the back of it, by the high open window. Nostrils flared, he looked positively frantic.

Both women skidded to a stop. Skye reared back on his hind legs, his front hoofs clawing air before striking the wall. His eyes were wild, his ears bent back flat against his massive head. He'd destroyed the wood slats that had formed the front of his stall. All that kept him in was whatever perception of restraint he imagined. There was nothing to prevent him from tearing right through them.

Sara started to back up. Skye was frightened, his terror a tangible thing. But what she saw next didn't allow any kind of protective retreat. In the back of the hay-filled stall, balled up tight in the corner, was Mickey. Huge tears rolled down his cheeks, but he said nothing. He simply sat there, clinging to his puppy and never taking his eyes off the horse.

"It's going to be all right," Sara said, forcing a conviction she didn't dare question. She kept her eyes glued on the great black stallion herself. A thousand pounds of frenzied horseflesh was nothing to turn one's back on. "We're going to get you out of here."

"No one can handle him if Devon or Thomas isn't around," the woman at Sara's shoulder said. The panic in her voice was controlled, much like Sara's. And like Sara she was nearly whispering. "We need Devon."

"Believe me, I'd feel better about this if he were here. But I don't think either one of us wants to wait while the other goes and gets him."

Skye reared back again, his knife-sharp hoofs coming precariously close to Mickey when he landed. The little boy flinched. The dog started a high-pitched yip that only seemed to increase the horse's agitation. Both women sucked in their breath.

The red-haired lady's panic broke through. "Skye is frightened of children. We're always telling them to stay away from him. Mickey's being in here is what has him so upset."

It was clear enough that Skye wasn't going to settle down until Mickey was out of his stall. But they couldn't get to the little boy with the horse blocking their way. Whatever they did, they'd have to do it soon—before those flailing hoofs connected with something other than a wall.

In the second she had to think about it, Sara saw only one solution. Her companion hadn't said as much but it was fairly clear that she wasn't crazy about the horse herself. Sara knew that Skye didn't mean to be upset. He was only obeying his instincts, reacting to a perceived threat. Her own instincts had her heart thudding so hard she could feel each pulse in her temples.

"The window," she said, mentally calculating its height from the floor. It looked to be a little more than four feet from the ground, high enough for a horse to stick his head out. And too high for Mickey to crawl out on his own. "If I can get Skye away from Mickey long enough for him to get to it, can you lift him from the outside?"

It was impossible for Sara to know what the woman's silence meant. A moment later, the woman had backed out the door and it didn't matter. As Sara took a tentative step forward and slowly raised her hand, she saw a head of coppery curls appear in the window.

"Easy, Skye," Sara coaxed, making her voice as soothing as her fear would allow. She tried to mask that fear, knowing Skye could pick up on it. "Easy," she repeated and, still keeping her attention on the rearing horse, began speaking to Mickey. Since she was trying to approach him, Skye had turned all of his attention to her.

Her heart bumped and her mouth went dry. She backed up a little, hoping the horse would follow her.

"Keep your back to the wall," she told the terrified child; "and move down to the window. The other lady is there," she went on, having no idea what the woman's name was. "She'll lift you out. Do you understand?"

She didn't dare take her eyes off the horse to see if Mickey nodded. Skye's upper lip was curled back, baring his teeth, and she didn't think it a wise move at the moment. Still, she kept talking, telling Mickey not to move too quickly. She told him to scoot along the wall real slow, and to hand the puppy out first. By her cajoling tone, she hoped to encourage the boy and soothe the horse. There was a selfish motive in there, too. As long as she kept talking, she didn't have to think of how frightened she was herself.

"I've got him!"

That was all Sara needed to hear to start backing out the door. She was no sooner out it, though, than the puppy raced past her on its way back in. Snatching it up, she saw the woman hurriedly carry Mickey toward the gate. Sara was nearly to the gate herself when Skye shot out of the hut like a great black cannonball, racing for the perimeter of the stone fence. Sara's heart slid to her throat. She'd thought he'd been about to leap it. Instead he slowed to a trot and, giving his head a vigorous shake, headed for the water trough. It seemed now that he was outside and he didn't feel threatened, he was fine.

That was more than Sara could say for herself. Now that she could think about it, her knees felt awfully weak.

The lady in yellow seemed just as shaken.

Safely on the closed side of the gate, the young woman put Mickey down and dropped to her knees in front of him. Her hands were trembling as she took his hands in hers. "Are you all right, lad? The horse didn't hurt you, did he?"

Wide-eyed and his bottom lip sucked between his teeth, he shook his head.

Immense relief swept the woman's pretty face. Gathering the child to her, she gave him a fierce hug, then set him back, her hands on his little shoulders. He truly did appear to be all right and the way his eyes shied from her now made him look more guilty than frightened.

Seeing his unease, the woman took a deep breath to calm herself. "Did the puppy go back in the pen like he did this morning, Mickey? Did you go after him to get him out?"

Again Mickey's nod was as solemn as his expression. The woman's was just as grave. "You should have come to get me. You know that," she told him, but it was apparent that her heart wasn't in the scolding. She obviously figured he'd learned his lesson well enough and was too grateful for his safety to be stern with him.

That gratitude was in her eyes as she glanced toward Sara. But the instant Sara started to smile her own relief, the woman turned her attention back to the boy. "I'm going inside to finish making your sandwich. You go stay with Joey," she told him and stood. "Do you want cheese?" she asked, inquiring as to his preference of filling.

Mickey shook his head.

"Jelly then?"

That earned her a smile.

It made Sara frown. But she said nothing as Mickey scooted off to watch the toddler who was entertaining himself by reaching through the bars to pile chunks of grass in his playpen. Sara was still holding the dog.

"Mickey," she called. "Don't you want your puppy?"

A quick wariness slipping into her expression, the woman moved to take the surprisingly subdued animal. Now that the crisis was over, she appeared to remember that Sara's presence wasn't welcome. Equally as apparent was her reluctance to appear unappreciative for what Sara had done.

"I'll give it to him. The boy doesn't take well to anyone outside the family."

Children will make liars out of saints. The woman had no sooner spoken than Mickey raced over to Sara to claim his troublesome companion. Instead of taking the puppy right away, though, he reached into the pocket of his corduroy pants and pulled out a granola bar. Judging from its wrapper, wrinkled and squashed as it was, the bar was the same one Sara had slipped into his lunch sack yesterday.

With a grin when Sara smiled, he put it back in his pocket, took the dog and was off.

The woman beside Sara blinked at the back of his curly head, then turned, puzzlement etched on her face. She studied Sara for a moment, not knowing quite what to make of her. "What was that about?"

"I suppose he just wanted me to know he still had it. I gave it to him yesterday," she explained, wondering what he'd thought when he opened his sack to find it instead of his cookies. "Are you his mother?"

Sara recognized reluctance when she saw it. It permeated the woman's manner and put a faint defensiveness in her tone. She said that she wasn't. She was his Aunt Beth. Molly, his mother, was her sister. Having explained that, she paused.

"I need to thank you for helping Mickey. That horse has the devil's own spirit, but you didn't more than bat an eye at him." The way she looked at Sara seemed to indicate she wasn't sure if bravery or stupidity had prompted such behavior. "I just thank the saints you were here. I don't know what I'd have done alone." A small nod accompanied the woman's gratitude. "You'll have to excuse me now. Devon said I shouldn't talk to you."

It took a moment for Sara to get past the initial jolt of Beth's statement. Having been left standing in the path, she hurried to catch up. Thick burnished curls bounced around the woman's face as she turned at Sara's touch.

To her credit, Sara sounded much less annoyed than she felt. "When did he tell you this?"

"This morning."

Sara felt her back stiffen. He hadn't been able to make her say she'd go, so he'd decided to cover his bases by making it difficult for her to stay. No wonder he hadn't said anything this morning about her leaving the village. "Is that why I can't talk to Kathleen, too? He told you to keep me away from her?"

"He said you upset her."

It was easy to see that given her own, though admittedly brief, experience with Sara, Beth didn't quite see how that was possible. More curious than guarded, she crossed her arms and tipped her head in inquiry. "Would you mind telling me just what it was you did? Devon wasn't terribly specific."

Taking the inquiry at face value, it appeared that Beth had accepted Devon's order without question. She was sure that had been the case when she relayed Devon's concerns.

"I know this is going to sound odd, but he thinks your aunt thinks I might have inherited some kind of power from my grandmother because my grandmother was born in the woods here."

Beth blinked slowly and backed up. "You're joking."

"I wish I were," Sara replied, wishing, too, that Beth wouldn't look at her as if she'd just grown another ear. "But that's what he said. The other reason he doesn't want me around is because I mentioned that his mill project might cause some problems that his aunt hadn't thought of. He's afraid I'll give her other ideas to nag him about."

A look of profound understanding replaced Beth's frown. "He's impossible to reason with when it comes to anything concerning the mill," she said, shaking her head at all the futile efforts that had been made on that score. "He's been that way ever since his wife left him."

Sara felt herself go still. "His wife?"

"She left him three years ago this spring. It was about a year later that she died. He practically started living at the mill then," she went on, skimming over the matter of his marriage since that wasn't what they were discussing. "That was about the time he got it in mind to start making it over. If you were inclined to get Aunt Kathleen thinking about his project, I can see why he wouldn't care to have you talking to her. We try to avoid discussing it when he's around. Everyone except Aunt Kathleen, that is."

A hint of exasperation laced Beth's tone. Sara wasn't sure if it was there for her cousin Devon's inflexibility or her Aunt Kathleen's persistence. What did seem clear was that Beth, being fairly young, didn't seem to find the matter of the mill as compelling as the older generations. Her concerns were more immediate.

A quick glance toward the two children assured her that they were still occupied. When she looked back to Sara, her eyes held apology. "I need to fix them something to eat," she said, sounding very much as if she was about to excuse herself and go inside.

Sara still needed to talk to Kathleen. To do that she needed to know where she was or when she'd be back. She couldn't do either if Beth left her standing out there. "I'd be happy to help," she told Beth, then added that she could keep an eye on the boys from the window for her so she wouldn't have to worry about them.

The incident with Skye fresh on her mind, Beth, somewhat reluctantly, accepted the offer. To keep her from reconsidering, Sara posed her question the moment they entered the cottage.

"Is Kathleen with the boys' mother?"

Beth missed the point. Pulling out sandwich makings, she said that Kathleen wasn't with Molly, but instead of saying where Kathleen was, she explained that her sister Molly had gone to Cork. "Since I'm the only one left at home," she went on, mentioning that her other sister and both brothers had moved to Waterford, "I get to watch the boys." Sean, the seven-year-old, was off with friends.

While Beth spread jelly on bread, Sara stood at the window watching the pair by the garden. Mickey lay on his stomach in the grass, intent on something crawling through it. Joey pulled at the eyes on his stuffed bear. Thus occupied, she listened while Beth told her that Molly's husband lived in Cork because it was the only place where he could find work. He wasn't making enough to move his family to the city, though, and Molly wanted to raise her children around family. It sounded very much as if the arrangement might be permanent.

"Devon looks after things for her," Beth went on, pouring milk from a ceramic pitcher. "So it's just like having a husband around anyway."

Sara doubted that, thinking such an existence must be incredibly difficult. She kept her thought to herself, though. Beth's dismissing comment had been most revealing—about her own attitude toward relationships, but about Devon, too. Devon took care of his cousin and her children, which explained his remark the morning Sara had met him about Mickey being his responsibility. He seemed to be responsible for so much: Molly's family, his Aunt Kathleen, the people at the mill.

And, in his mind, the welfare of the village.

As they spoke, Sara couldn't help but notice how Beth kept glancing out the window toward the road. But when Sara asked if she was expecting Kathleen, Beth was quick to say she wasn't. That made Sara suspect that the possibility of Devon's appearance might be making her anxious. Beth obviously wasn't comfortable neglecting his instructions by talking with her.

Not wanting to cause problems, Sara took her leave a few minutes later, stopping in the yard long enough to say goodbye to Mickey. When all he did was smile at her, she decided to make a point of meeting him on his way to school in the morning. Devon probably wouldn't like that, but he wasn't going to like what she was about to do, either.

His word might be law where some of his family was concerned, but she didn't have to obey his edicts. Having asked Beth which direction Kathleen would be coming from, she planted herself at the crossroads to wait. Beth had finally told her that Kathleen had gone to drop off the lace she'd made for the Connors' baby's christening gown, and to get eggs from a lady down the road who raised chickens. It didn't seem to Sara that either errand should take all that long.

Chapter Six

Sara waited at the crossroads for nearly two hours before Kathleen showed up. When she did, Kathleen was as pleasant as she could be—and most grateful to be relieved of her basket, which Sara carried a ways for her. She was, however, of absolutely no help in locating someone who might have known Fiona. According to her, the only person who might have known her grandmother was Father Flannigan. Sara already knew from Devon that he wasn't around anymore.

It was the mention of Devon's name that changed the quality of Kathleen's ever-watchful expression. Unashamedly inquisitive, she wanted to know everything that had happened during the time Sara and Devon had spent together. Devon had told his aunt this morning that he would show Sara around and Kathleen was especially interested in whether or not her nephew had shown her his plans.

When Sara said that he had, Kathleen's expression grew far too shrewd for comfort.

"I was wondering about this last night," she said as they ambled along. "Devon won't listen to any of us. Certainly he doesn't speak of his expansion with us anymore. Unless we bring it up. But if he showed you his plans, could be he'd listen to you. Would you consider talking to him?"

Sara's response was a very hesitant, "About what?"

"About leaving things as they are. Just think about it," she added before Sara could answer, then bent to pick a couple of flowers growing on the hump in the middle of the road—flowers that wouldn't be growing there if Devon laid cement over them.

Kathleen's question was what Sara pondered the next afternoon as she sat on a rock beside the rushing stream. The water wasn't nearly so calm here as up by the meadow. There it flowed at a placid pace, so lazy and clear that each ripple could be seen above the browns and ochres of the stony bed. Here among the trees, the water hurried over boulders and the fallen length of a lichen-covered tree, churning madly in its race around the obstacles.

The chaos suited the state of Sara's mind; the sound of the rushing water soothed it. The place was perfect for her and she felt grateful to have found it.

She drew her legs up. Wrapping her arms around them, she rested her chin on her knees. It was apparent enough that Kathleen knew how enchanting Sara had found Brigen Glen and was counting on her to join her cause. Sara had never been one for causes, though. She didn't believe that something was as cut and dried as most activists would have people believe. There was always more than one side to an issue and Sara always felt that the answer to a problem could only be found in compromise—something that wouldn't take place when both sides felt theirs had the only answer.

The issue facing Brigen Glen seemed to be suffering that fate. Only here Sara could feel herself being drawn into the problem no matter how she tried to convince herself that she should stay out of it. She didn't want to become involved in any disagreements between Devon and his aunt—much less between him and the rest of the village. In one respect he was absolutely right. She was an outsider. Without understanding the village, someone in that position couldn't possibly know the solution to its problems. It would be unconscionably arrogant to think otherwise. Yet she had fallen in love with the place nearly the moment she'd arrived and the feeling had grown enormously. Because of that feeling, she felt bound to protect it—even as she feared she might betray it. In the back of her mind was the nagging thought that she would somehow contribute to its demise if she were to buy Devon's goods.

The wind rattled the leaves, jarring the less tenacious from their limbs. They drifted downward. Some came to rest on the mossy rocks edging the stream; others settled on the water to be swiftly swept away. The gusts had grown stronger in the past half hour, and the air carried the damp smell of rain.

A sudden shift in the wind whipped her hair about her face and flattened her cotton shirt against her back. It was much cooler now than when she'd set out for her walk a couple of hours ago, but Sara didn't move. Clouds the color of old pewter shut out what little sun had managed to sneak through the heavy foliage, the dim light lending the setting the calming, worshipful feel of a sanctuary. This was a place where thoughts could roam free. A place where problems could be brought—and maybe even left behind. The feeling of peace she'd experienced when she'd first arrived could be found here, a feeling that promised to give order to her troubled thoughts.

Sara didn't feel as calm as she'd have liked, but she experienced the peace enough to realize that at least one of her concerns was completely illogical. The sale of a few bolts of cloth wouldn't have much of an impact on what happened to Brigen Glen. And while Sara wasn't always logical, she did have to admit that her worry on that point was undoubtedly exaggerated. She didn't feel settled enough, though, to cope with the question of whether or not she should say anything to Devon about his plans. Just the thought of him unnerved her—especially when she remembered what he'd done to keep her from Kathleen.

"How much longer are you going to sit there?"

Sara's hair flew as her head jerked around. It had barely settled about her shoulders when she realized that Devon must have been standing there for quite some time. He was leaning against a tree a dozen yards away. His arms were crossed and one knee was raised, his foot planted against the bark.

Apparently he was bent on giving her a heart attack. This was the third time he'd snuck up on her.

Willing her heart to return to a steadier beat, she swiveled on her rock. "That's one way to get rid of me. Scaring me to death."

"I don't believe I'd do anything quite so drastic. Though it does seem you aren't an easy one to discourage." With the thrust of his shoulders, he pushed himself from the tree. Twigs snapped as he moved closer. "What are you doing here?"

The curiosity in his tone didn't register. She only heard the impatience. He was still keeping track of her, and she was beginning to resent his surveillance. Maybe it *had* been him watching her in the cemetery yesterday.

She slid off the rock, her chin tilting up as her feet hit the mossy ground. "I could ask the same of you. This is an awfully isolated spot."

"This is the way I come home from the mill. And this particular place," he added as the wind gusted to flutter strands of his dark hair across his forehead, "is where I sometimes come to think."

She hadn't expected his explanation to be so reasonable. She certainly hadn't expected the insight he offered. The edge in his voice overrode both thoughts. He had accused her of trespassing before. He was doing it again. The man was as protective as a lion with his pride about what he regarded as belonging to him.

Her defensiveness, something she wasn't comfortable with anyway, eased as her glance was drawn to the tops of the trees. They swayed restively with the wind. "I can see why," she surprised him by saying. "It's a very restful place. I didn't mean to intrude."

"Didn't you? You seem to have such a knack for it. Everywhere I turn, you're there."

She met his glance. "Like a bad penny?"

The metaphor wasn't a familiar one to Devon, but he had no problem catching its drift. He didn't like having his space invaded. She'd obviously sensed that, which was why she'd more or less apologized. But her irritation at his failure to accept that apology didn't interest him at the moment. What did was the deep V of her shirt. It ended just above the swell of her breasts. The fabric's pale peach color made her smooth skin look golden and, with her head tipped as it was, the long line of her throat was exposed.

Despite her intended challenge, he could think only of how soft that inviting expanse of skin looked. His fingers itched to feel the pulse he could see beating in the hollow at its base, to slip up along her neck until he reached the delicate bones of her jaw.

She followed the path of his glance. Her hand slid up to protect her throat.

"I wasn't thinking of anything violent," he assured her. "It would be bad form to strangle a potential customer."

"It isn't bad form for you to make it impossible for me to talk to anyone?"

"I hardly made it impossible. You got past Beth, didn't you?"

Sara felt herself back down. She wanted him to know that she didn't appreciate what he had done, but she didn't want to score the point at someone else's expense. Her dilemma lay in that she didn't care to explain the circumstances that had caused Beth to ignore his instructions. Yet she didn't want Beth to be in trouble because of her. "It wasn't your cousin's fault. She told me you didn't want her talking to me."

"I know about Skye, Sara."

Devon's sense of protectiveness—for both his aunt and his project—had demanded his insistence that Sara be kept away from Kathleen. Though he didn't like that she'd gotten around Beth, his gut clenched when he thought of what might have happened to his nephew if Sara hadn't been there. "I thank you for what you did."

He didn't want to be obligated to her. Sara knew it, though she was gracious enough to keep that knowledge to herself. "No thanks are necessary. I'm just glad I could help."

"I still wish you'd leave."

"I still intend to stay."

They had reached an impasse. But instead of challenge, Sara felt a tacit acceptance hovering in the air between them. Each was aware of the other's position and neither was prepared to back down. Respecting one's adversary gave new meaning to the fight.

It wasn't until that moment, in thinking of Devon as her adversary, that Sara realized that she *was* prepared to fight. As she stood beneath the canopy of trees, a soft rain beginning to fall as she met the quiet intensity in his eyes, she just wasn't quite sure what it was she was fighting for.

Nature allowed her no time to consider the matter. The faint rumble of thunder sounded in the distance. Sara lifted her face toward the sky, squinting a little as a particularly fat drop landed on her cheek. A moment later, the churning gray clouds opened up and Sara released her breath with a delighted gasp. Within seconds the rain was falling so hard that it rebounded from the rocks, starting little rivers that ran toward the stream.

Over the noise of rain beating leaves, she heard Devon mutter something low and indistinct. An instant later, he curled his fingers around her wrist and took off, pulling her behind him.

She didn't bother to ask where they were going. She was too busy trying to maintain her footing on the slick ground. Wet moss was slippery enough. Wet leaves could be treacherous. The drenching rain beat through the trees, its steady din punctuated by the raucous chatter of birds scrambling for shelter.

Devon moved quickly, leading her through the thick and dripping foliage into a small clearing. Sara was quick, but his legs were longer than hers and it was difficult to keep up. Running was nearly impossible. The harder it rained, the muddier the path became. More mud meant less traction.

The ground was particularly slick where they reentered the trees on the other side of the small meadow. A puddle had already formed in the middle of what was little more than a deer path and Devon started to go around it. He cleared the patch of glistening leaves. Sara didn't. When her foot hit it, she grabbed for Devon's arm, bracing herself against him to keep from landing in the mud.

At the contact, he swung around, catching her to him so she wouldn't take him down with her. His arm flattened across her back, her chest smashing into his. He swore.

She laughed.

"This is wonderful!" She tipped her head back to let the rain caress her face. "I can't believe how warm the rain is."

He couldn't believe it, either. Not the rain. He'd been caught in plenty of summer cloudbursts. What he found difficult to comprehend was her lighthearted acceptance of what would thoroughly dampen most people's spirits. She was actually having fun.

Disarmed by her unbridled pleasure, Devon couldn't help but smile. A real, honest smile that did wonders to erase the tension from his face.

"I knew you could do it," he heard her say, the sound of her soft laughter inviting the chuckle that rumbled from deep within his chest.

"Do what?"

"That." She pointed to the curve of his mouth. "It looks good on you." With the abandon of a child, she gave her head a shake. Her hair was plastered to her head, so wet that it was several shades darker than its usual pale wheat. Beads of rain clung like tiny diamonds to her lashes. "Where are we going?"

"Not far. My cottage is just through the trees."

"Want to race?"

With the flat of her hand, she wiped water from her forehead, grinning at him while she waited for him to accept the challenge.

He would have accepted it, too. He'd been trying to ignore how good she felt pressed to his side and a good sprint sounded like a hell of an idea. But when she pulled back a little now that she had her balance, he could scarcely breathe.

Water sluiced down her face and throat, making her skin glisten with the luster of fine porcelain. The rain had soaked her cotton shirt. He nearly groaned when he saw how it clung to her. The wet fabric faithfully molded her breasts, clearly delineating what he'd lain awake last night trying not to imagine.

He felt his insides twist. Desire coiled through him, almost painful in its intensity.

Dragging his gaze back to her face, he saw her laughter die.

Slowly, reluctantly, he unlocked his arm from around her back. The breath he drew was deep and stabilizing. "I don't think racing is a very good idea. I can almost guarantee you'll end up in the mud."

He'd hoped his tone was teasing. He very much wanted to see her smile again. The awareness that had erased the laughter from her eyes made him uneasy. He was uneasy enough as it was. Having felt her against him, he now knew what he'd already suspected. Her slender body would fit him perfectly.

"Yeah," she muttered, turning away. "You'd probably trip me." She started ahead of him, hurrying along the side of the path. An inexplicable relief filled him when he saw her turn and smile. "Is that your place?" she asked, pointing through the small stand of oak.

It was. And after they had run to the door, he pushed it open to let her pass. Sara stopped just inside, hugging herself against the chill while Devon turned on a lamp as he crossed the room. Reaching the far side, he hunched down to start a fire.

She was grateful for that. It hadn't seemed so cold when they were moving, but she began to shiver as she silently scanned the room. What she saw there almost made her forget that she was soaking wet.

In many respects, Devon's cottage was much like the one Kathleen and Thomas shared. It was made of stone and thatch with paned windows and wooden doors. There the similarities ended. None of the little touches that add comfort to a home were visible here. Nor was there any of the clutter she'd seen in Devon's office. What she saw was a stark sort of order that made the room seem...deserted.

A brown plaid sofa sat in the middle of the room facing the squat black peat burning stove Devon stoked. To one side, bookshelves covered the wall. Filled with neat rows of books and magazines, the covers provided the only real color in the room. The single end table contained a lamp, and a small container of matches.

She ventured toward the sofa, her glance taking in the bare walls when she heard the metal thud of the stove door closing. Sara straightened.

"I'll get us some towels. Hang your clothes over there." Already tugging his own wet sweater over his head, he motioned with one arm to the rack behind the stove. Two pairs of dry socks hung over it. "I'll find you something to put on."

"That's all right. I don't need to..."

Change, she concluded to herself when he disappeared through the doorway to her right. She scowled at the empty space. Obviously he expected her to do as she was told.

She thought about ignoring his instructions. Being the independent sort, she didn't like him telling her what to do. She was also a little hesitant about the sudden intimacy of the situation. Another shiver slithered over her, raising gooseflesh on her arms and legs and everywhere in between. Trading wet clothes for dry did make a certain amount of sense.

Glancing out the window, she saw nothing but driving rain. Since it appeared that she wasn't going anywhere for a while, she accepted the shirt he brought her. It was one of his. A huge, cotton flannel that she changed into in the tiny bathroom. It felt deliciously soft against her skin and smelled of the outdoors. And of Devon.

She tried not to think about that.

By the time she'd stripped off her sodden clothes and hung them as Devon had his behind the stove, the rain had softened to a gentle patter. The sound was comforting, as were the noises coming from the kitchen. Devon was in there. Not wanting to intrude since she'd trespassed on enough of his territory already, she sat down on the braided rug in front of the stove to towel off her hair.

A pair of bare feet planted themselves on the floor in front of her.

Looking up, her hands pressing the towel to her head, she saw him hold out a steaming mug. "This might help," he told her.

He wore a pair of soft, worn jeans with a hole in the knee. A white sweatshirt sporting a logo for a well-known ale stretched across his imposing chest. He had its sleeves pushed back, revealing the silky dark hair on his corded forearms. He looked very male and, with his still-damp hair long enough to touch the crew neck of his shirt, very primitive. A twentieth-century Samson, living in a seventeenth-century world.

"Thank you," she said softly, and took the mug. She tasted the toddy, smiling as the flavors warmed her tongue.

Devon felt the corners of his mouth lift in response. There was an intimacy to their actions, to her smile, that felt unfamiliar to him. Unfamiliar, yet not at all unpleasant. It had been a long time since a woman had been in his home. In the three years since Maureen had gone, even his aunts and female cousins no longer dropped by. He spent so little time here that they were all accustomed to his coming to them.

Lowering himself to the couch, he rested his elbows on his knees, cupping his mug between them. Sara's back was to him, her legs bent and angled to one side. The green flannel shirt he'd given her covered her from neck to knees and, sitting as she was, only the feminine shape of her calves and her small bare feet were visible. Her head was tilted as she dried the ends of her hair. The comb she had asked for lay beside her mug.

She looked content.

Oddly at that moment, Devon almost felt that way himself. She softened the room somehow, made it more inviting. He didn't understand how that was possible. Energy seemed to radiate from her, enlivening the very air he breathed. Yet she had an amazing capacity to calm. The contradiction was only one of many. In some ways he'd found her to be as sophisticated as he'd expect a woman of her occupation and travels to be. Yet she was inexplicably innocent in others. This morning on his way to the mill, he had again seen her running along the stream, as fleet and agile as a gazelle. He'd followed her this time, but he hadn't intervened when she'd spotted Mickey and waylayed him long enough to catch a few salamanders from the stream before she'd walked him on to school. The child responded to her as he did to few others. Though Devon still had his reservations about letting her become involved with his family, he knew she wouldn't harm the boy.

He compared that behavior with what he'd witnessed the day before when she'd sat at his desk speaking with her clients. She had a no-nonsense approach to business, a sharp mind. She also possessed the enviable ability to take inconvenience in stride.

And she loved the rain.

The dichotomy intrigued him. Just as the woman herself intrigued him.

The admission seemed safe enough at the moment. With the summer storm closing them in, the fire warming her scent and surrounding him with its seductive allure, the problems that lay beyond the cottage walls didn't seem quite so immediate. Those problems would still be waiting for him when the clouds lifted. So for now, instead of feeling trapped by the storm, he would simply enjoy it.

He couldn't remember the last time he'd done something so indulgent.

"Did you find what you were looking for at the cemetery yesterday?"

She didn't turn. Only by the way her hands stilled did he know she had heard him. "No," she said after a moment. She started working the towel along the length of her hair again. "I think I'll go into Durry tomorrow. Maybe I can find out something there."

"What happens if you don't?"

"Then I'll find the answers someplace else."

He would have questioned her conviction, but the rain picked up just then, beating against the windows in a furious burst. The staccato sound drew Sara's glance toward the watery panes. A pensive smile curved her generous mouth.

"My grandmother used to tell me about these storms. How you would think that surely the earth would drown, but half an hour later the sun would be shining. It's no wonder the land is so green."

"You must find it very different here."

"Actually, where I grew up wasn't that different at all. We even had a schoolhouse not much bigger than what you have. And a creek that would overrun its banks every winter."

"What was it like?"

"Where I grew up?"

Devon nodded, not sure why he wanted to learn something more of her. It was unimportant. It was just something he wanted to know.

That was why he had her describe the small community where she had spent her first eighteen years. She told him that it straddled the border between New Hampshire and upstate New York and was a bucolic place of rolling hills where cows and horses roamed the greenest of pastures. Her grandmother had chosen to live there because it reminded her so much of her home in Ireland.

"I never realized how faithful she was to the way of life she must have had. Not until I got here anyway. Our little house was simple, and the curtains on the windows were all of lace she'd made herself. She kept doilies on every table, and pots of growing things in the kitchen windows. Just like your Aunt Kathleen," she added. "And she always wore a black dress and a black shawl, like the old women I saw picking heather this afternoon."

The shadow of less inviting memories crossed her face. Her grandmother had been so different from everyone else in town. Because of that, everyone had thought Sara different, too, and different wasn't an easy thing for a child to be. It set her apart, isolated her. Children needed playmates, but Sara's companions had been limited to fanciful imaginings and the dogs her grandmother kept to chase pests—both human and the four-legged variety—out of the chicken coop.

"I'd always thought that maybe she was just eccentric." Others had certainly thought her so. "Now I know she was just being who she was. She did the best she could with what she had. I never have understood why she always wore black, though."

Devon sat back as she spoke, slumping a little to rest his head on the back of the sofa. He balanced his mug over the snap of his jeans.

"Around here black becomes a woman's uniform when her husband dies. You said she'd lost her husband before she left. She was probably just wearing her widow's weeds."

The custom sounded inviolate. "Kathleen doesn't wear them."

"That's because she's not a widow. She's never been married."

"Is that why she seems to treat you as a recalcitrant son?"

Devon's glance narrowed. "I'm no more stubborn than she is."

"That's not the way she tells it. But that's not what I asked, either."

An animated light shone in her eyes. Half challenge, half teasing, it gave her a mischievous quality he found completely disarming. Instead of brushing off her curiosity, as he was first inclined to do, he found himself responding to it.

It wasn't often that Devon thought about the events in his life that had led him to where he was now. Certainly he'd never talked about them before. That was why he hesitated a little before the memories prodded him to recall how Kathleen had come to take him under her wing. He had to dig back nearly eighteen years. It had been that long since an accident at the mill had taken his father's life and left him on his own.

He had been nineteen and in school in London when he had found out what happened to his father. Kathleen knew how important it had been to Devon to graduate from college, but someone had to take over the mill. Thomas had retired the year before and there weren't any other male O'Donaughs left. It had been Kathleen who had encouraged him, made him stick it out when he was so sure he'd never be able to fill his father's shoes.

Sara shifted her position, turning to dry the back of her head. "It couldn't have been easy for you. Being so young. But you did it."

The empathy in her eyes was real. Having lost her grandmother, she knew what it felt like to be left alone. But it was more than that understanding that captivated Devon. It was her acceptance. Buried within this self-assured and otherwise mature woman was an almost childlike faith that everything in life eventually turned out all right. He found that quality impossibly idealistic. But he couldn't deny its appeal. Or the appeal she held for him as she sat running the comb through her hair.

His response to her was merely to shrug as he lifted his mug to his lips.

Sara wasn't fooled by his casual dismissal. Taking over the mill must have been an awesome, frightening responsibility. Human nature being what it was, she didn't doubt that many of the men who'd worked there had resented taking orders from someone so young. Devon had managed to earn their respect, though. That respect was still evident in his employees, even if it was tempered at present by their disagreement with his ideas.

The room had become silent except for the soft sounds of the rain and the hiss and sputter of burning peat. It stayed that way until a few seconds later when, more interested in what he was thinking as he sat there scowling at his mug than in what she was doing, Sara pulled the comb through her hair harder than she'd intended.

Her quick intake of breath was followed by a muttered, "Ow," as she started to pull the comb away. It was caught in a tangle. Closing her eyes against the faint sting, she tried again to free it. The comb wouldn't budge.

She was vaguely aware of Devon's movements. She heard the sofa groan in relief as he stood and the muffled thud of his mug on the end table. She didn't notice what he was doing, though. Not until she felt the touch of his hand on hers.

Her eyes flew open. He'd hunkered down in front of her. Her glance immediately settled on the double seam in the crotch of his jeans. Her eyes quickly shifted to the side, coming to rest on the worn denim stretched over his powerful thighs. The hole in the knee gapped from the strain of his position. Her pulse scrambling, she raised her eyes to his chest.

"Lower your head," he instructed, easing her hands aside to grasp the comb. "You've got your hair twisted around this."

She felt his fingers brush against her scalp. She'd noticed his hands before, how strong and capable they were. And she'd suspected his gentleness. Now she felt it.

"There," he said after what seemed an eternity, and held the comb between his knees for her to take.

She would have thanked him. Certainly that had been her intention when she raised her head again. But as he folded the comb into her palm, her eyes locked with his and she forgot to speak at all.

The gentleness she'd felt in his touch was nowhere in evidence. No emotion marred the hard angles of his face. What she saw in his cool blue eyes was stark and primitive. He didn't move and Sara couldn't seem to, either.

"I shouldn't have brought you here."

"Why not?" she asked on a whisper.

His eyes holding hers, he reached out to brush back a strand of hair from her cheek. His fingers lingered, moving to trace the shape of her jaw. His touch was exquisite. Light, sensual. And wholly capable of short-circuiting her entire nervous system.

"Because you tempt me." The pad of his thumb slipped to the corner of her mouth. It felt rough, deliciously so, against the smoothness of her skin. "I'm not sure I trust myself where you're concerned."

It wasn't wise. It wasn't prudent. But she didn't want him to trust himself with her. She wanted him to loosen the rigid control he held over himself, to let her learn more of the man she'd only begun to know. She wanted to discover the taste of him, to feel the hard line of his lips against her own. The restlessness he caused within her was more acute than any she'd felt before. More urgent. Far more unfamiliar.

"Would it be so bad to let yourself go a little?"

His nostrils flared at the impact of her quiet question, but he said nothing. Touching her bottom lip with his thumb, he pulled down on it ever so slightly. His eyes glittered, hard and hungry on her mouth.

An instant later, his jaw clenched.

"To be honest, I don't think it would do either of us any good." Withdrawing his hand, he clamped it over his knees and pushed himself up. "Your clothes should be dry enough to wear in a while. I'll see if I can find you a slicker."

Off balance from the heady heat flowing through her veins, Sara could do nothing but stare at his broad back as he left the room. The change in him had been so abrupt, his dismissal of her so total, that she felt as if he'd just slammed a door in her face.

Dragging a shaky hand through her hair, she tossed the comb aside. Its teeth had bitten into her palm. She had been horribly remiss in dropping her guard with him. But then she wasn't accustomed to having to protect herself. Not the way he did.

He was unlike anyone she'd ever known. In many respects. His sense of responsibility was enormous, the demands he made on himself as real as those placed on him by his family and most of the villagers. They all relied on him in one way or another. They all needed him. Yet it seemed that he wouldn't let himself need anyone. Not even for a while.

A cupboard closed somewhere in the back of the cottage. It was followed by scuffing sounds. No doubt he was searching for something she could wear so he could get rid of her without feeling guilty about sending her out in the rain.

The thought propelled her to her feet.

Grabbing her jeans, she yanked them off the rack. They were still quite damp and would feel awful against her skin, but she wasn't going to stick around while they dried. They'd just get wet again anyway.

The jeans felt worse than awful. She put them on despite their clamminess, struggling to get the cold fabric over her hips. She had Devon's shirt bunched up around her waist, her hands at the snap of her jeans to fasten them, when he stopped in the doorway.

He had a cape in one hand and a pair of dry socks in the other. He didn't look upset. Only distant.

Sara tried for indifference. "I'd appreciate it if you'd let me borrow this shirt." The thought of adding her cold, wet T-shirt to the uncomfortable pants wasn't at all appealing. "I'll get it back to you later."

"There's no hurry. Here. This should fit you."

He held out the cape. It was badly wrinkled from having been folded and would cover her to her ankles, but it would certainly keep the moisture off. The rain wasn't coming down that hard anymore as it was. It had softened to little more than a mist.

"Does this belong to one of your cousins?" Sara asked, noting the feminine touch of gathered fabric along the front plackets.

"My wife's. Kathleen made it for her, but she never wore it. I've meant to give it to Molly or Beth, but I never seem to think of it."

Beth had said that Devon hadn't been the same since his wife had left. Still suffering his rejection of a few minutes ago, she wondered if that might not well explain why he'd pulled away from her so abruptly. She knew she shouldn't ask, but she needed to know.

"Is she why you want me out of here so badly? Am I invading her territory?"

The question hung in the air. It was impossible to tell how far she'd overstepped herself. Nothing in Devon's expression betrayed his reaction. Nothing in his tone provided a clue. "There are no memories here, if that's what you mean. Maureen didn't like this place. It was too small for her. Just like the village was too small." He held out the dry socks. "She has nothing to do with why I want us out of here."

Just like the village was too small. There was an importance to those words that Sara felt she needed to remember. But that thought was overridden by his last sentence.

"Us?" He wasn't just kicking her out?

He was so close she could smell the clean, musky scent of him. He drew even closer, so close she could feel the heat radiating from his chest. A shiver shuddered through her, as much a reaction to him as her damp clothes. Standing in her bare feet, his large frame dwarfed her, making her feel very small and very vulnerable.

"I have to stop by Thomas's to check on Skye. I'll walk you that far."

She considered telling him that the escort wasn't necessary. But he was quite adept at derailing her train of thought. His glance skimmed her upturned face, caressing it as surely as if he'd touched her. The glittering intensity in his eyes might have been frightening had she not found the rawness of it so beautiful.

"Oh, hell," she heard him breathe. His hands framing her face, his mouth closed over hers.

Chapter Seven

Frustration. Sara tasted it on Devon's lips. That same frustration was echoed in his eyes when he pulled back just far enough to see her face. With a groan, his mouth came down again. Hard. He didn't tentatively test boundaries. He didn't seek acceptance or permission. She had already given him permission anyway. And what she felt when his tongue touched hers was heady. And hot. And wholly electrifying.

His hands fell to her waist, his fingers pressing into her back as he drew her closer. The hunger in his kiss when she opened to him was a raw, elemental thing. She felt as if he had just pulled her into quicksand. She was being consumed, absorbed. Rather than being frightened by the bewildering feeling, she seemed to come alive with it. It wasn't a threat so much as a promise of what could be.

The cape slipped from her fingers. Her hand flattened against his chest. Beneath her palm she felt the strong, rapid beat of his heart. A faint moan escaped her throat. The sound seemed to ignite him.

Locking one arm across her back, he drew her fully against him, trapping her hand between them. He angled her head to deepen the kiss. As he did, she felt his fingers drift up her side and over the swell of her breast. Her body tightened with the contact, then relaxed as his mouth moved over hers. His touch drifted beneath the roundness, testing its shape before trailing over its pebbled bud. She wanted him to close his hand over her, but he continued that tantalizing play upward, feathering the pads of his fingers along the bones at the base of her throat.

The pressure of his lips eased. Moving his fingers into her hair, he kissed the corners of her mouth. Spreading his hand over the back of her skull, he slowly drew her head back.

Several seconds passed. Long seconds that stretched the heavy silence. His breathing was ragged, like hers. And she could feel the chaotic beat of his heart.

With the pad of his thumb, he touched her kiss-swollen lips, liking the idea that he had made them look that way. "I shouldn't have done that."

"Why not?" she whispered.

"Because now I want more." His hand reluctantly fell away. "It's almost stopped raining. We'd better go."

Her cape lay on the floor. Picking it up, he offered it to her with a smile that was as much regret as anything else.

She answered with a smile so soft it nearly stole his breath.

Distance. That was what he needed before he did something utterly foolish.

"I need to get Skye's bridle," he said, loathe to let the silence become more intimate. He glanced toward her shoes, still drying by the stove. "I'll be in the workshop out back when you're ready."

The bit of Skye's bridle had come loose yesterday. Devon had brought it home to fix. He was at his workbench hammering the ring back into place—grateful for even that minimal physical activity—when a fluttering motion at the door caught his attention.

Sara stood in the doorway, the folds of the gray cape rustling around her. She had pulled the cape's hood over her head against the lingering mist. Cloaked as she was and with the pale light of a dreary day behind her, she gave the impression of something vaporous. Of something that was, but wasn't.

Devon shook his head, not at all certain where such a nonsensical thought had come from. He turned back to his task, the metal bit ringing with the contact of the hammer. "I'll just be a minute."

"No hurry," Sara assured him and pushed the hood back to get a better look around.

Devon's workshop had the lived-in warmth the interior of his cottage lacked. It was cluttered, like his office—a sort of efficient disorganization that felt far more inviting than precision and order. The frame of a bunk bed sat in the middle of the room. Half painted white, half raw wood, she could tell from the daisies carved into the headboards that it was intended for a girls' room.

"So this is where you spend your time when you're home." A soft smile touched her mouth. "It suits you."

"The mess, you mean?"

He didn't seem to mind her teasing him about the clutter. That pleased her. "That, too. But I was thinking that it seems rather like you. It's a room filled with purpose."

She could feel him watching her as she moved toward a very comfortable-looking chair in the corner. On the rough wood table beside it were hand tools and several small blocks of oak. Two of those blocks had been carved—one into a train engine, another into a coal car. A third hadn't yet completely revealed itself. But the beginnings of a caboose could be seen.

The planked floor was virtually covered with sawdust, and the smells of wood pitch and paint scented the air. Scattered over the floor in front of the chair were the curls of wood shavings. Sara could easily picture Devon sitting there, leaning forward to let the shavings fall while he methodically carved and listened to music from the tape player on the windowsill. She liked the thought of him taking time to relax in such a manner. She didn't like the thought that he probably spent much of that time more alone than he deserved to be.

She turned to see him holding the leather-and-metal bridle.

"It's for Mickey," he said, aware of her interest in the train. "For his birthday."

She was intruding again. She knew it and so did he. But he didn't seem to mind as much as he once would have. His interest in her reaction to his most private surroundings outweighed the threat of the invasion. Sara recognized the privilege he extended. Though nothing could be said to acknowledge it, she was touched by his wary willingness to let her enter further.

Her glance settled on a group of carvings jammed together with cans of paint and thinner on a shelf. She moved closer, a little awed by the scope of Devon's talent and by his curious disregard for his creations. It was one thing to build furniture and simple children's toys. The talent required to breathe life into a chunk of wood was something else entirely. The carvings were exquisite interpretations of the local wildlife: a doe with her fawn, a magnificent buck, a small fox. All were covered with a faint layer of dust, evidence that they had been neglected for some time.

She stopped by the shelf and glanced toward Devon. Her intention was apparent. When he did nothing to stop her, she took down one of the six-inch-high sculptures. The one she chose was unlike any of the rest.

Despite the coolness of the room, the dark wood was warm in her hand. Perhaps it was only her imagination. Perhaps he had just made the figure of a woman cradling a child that real. "A Madonna?" she asked, feeling the piece deserving of that kind of respect.

He shook his head. "Just a woman."

"No one in particular?"

Again the slow shake of his head. "Why?" he wanted to know.

She hesitated. Something other than imagination had to spark such sensitivity. Or so it seemed to her.

Three strides and he was in front of her. Taking the sculpture, he set it on the shelf between two carved hummingbirds. He glanced back at her. Reluctance warred with resignation. "Don't look at me that way, Sara. It's just a carving. That's all any of them are. It's not even something I do anymore."

"That's too bad. You obviously once found great pleasure in it."

In less than ten seconds she completely diluted his quick defensiveness. Genuine regret shown in her eyes. It was so pure, so real, that Devon couldn't help absorbing it himself. He didn't like the feeling at all, for with the regret came the acknowledgment that there were very few things he took real pleasure in any longer. What had once been enjoyable had now become obligation. He didn't mind the hours he spent in this room, but he certainly didn't look forward to the time as he once had.

There were other areas of his life where regret wanted to encroach, but Devon shoved the thoughts aside. He couldn't change the past, so there was no sense dwelling on it. The future was what mattered. He knew exactly what needed to be done there. He'd thought of little else in the past couple of years.

"I don't have time for it anymore," he told Sara, when what he really lacked was the patience. "Maybe I'll get back to it after the expansion is completed."

Her smile appeared, further easing his thoughts. "Your expansion," she repeated gamely. "I'm beginning to think that's all you think about."

He tipped her chin up with the tip of his finger. A moment later, he brushed his lips against hers. The touch was teasing, feather light. "That's not true, Sara. But it's what I must concentrate on. We'd best go while we can."

Kathleen was waiting for them. Actually, she was waiting for Devon and didn't bother to hide her curiosity when she saw Sara at his side. She motioned to them both from her post by the gate as they came down the hill.

"I've been watching for you," she called to her nephew, her glance bouncing between him and the woman at his side. Her glance swept over the dove-colored cape Sara wore. "They're needing you at the mill. Sean rode by not ten minutes ago. He said you were to be here. When I told him I hadn't seen you, he took off for your place. I take it you didn't come across him?"

They had come through the back pasture, which explained why they'd missed Sean. A man on a horse would have taken the road. The pasture was too rocky to run a horse in without risking a broken leg.

Since the answer to his aunt's question was obvious, Devon ignored it. "Did he say what was wrong?"

Kathleen shook her head. "Only that you'd best get to the mill."

The heavy drizzle had continued to fall, glazing the grassy fields and creating puddles in every dip and dent in the road. The clouds leaking the cold drops looked less ominous than the expression suddenly darkening Devon's face. He muttered something undoubtedly profane.

Kathleen pursed her lips at the oath. Sara stiffened. She knew from the way his eyes narrowed on her before skipping to his aunt that he still had serious doubts about leaving her alone with Kathleen. For a split second, Sara thought about assuring him that he needn't worry. The terseness of his order cancelled that idea.

"Go on to the inn," he told her. "I'll talk to you later."

He turned with a jerk toward the stable behind the cottage. The fastest way to get to the mill would be to ride, and he obviously intended to take Skye. The fact that he didn't give Sara so much as a backward glance seemed a fair indication that, having dismissed her, he intended for her to do as she'd been told.

The past couple of hours hadn't really changed a thing between them.

Kathleen immediately countered Devon's instructions. "You'll be going nowhere in this weather. Let's go inside and have us some tea. 'Tis miserable damp out here. No sense catching our death while we're waiting to hear what's happened." She gave Sara's arm a pat. "Devon will have to come back to put Skye in his stall, so we'll find out what the to-do is about then."

Sara started to say she didn't care what had happened, that Devon and his mill were no concern of hers. Denying, after all, gave the illusion of protection. The lie wouldn't come, though. She did care. Even if her caring didn't matter to Devon.

"I don't want to be any trouble," Sara said, willing to defy Devon's directive, but not wanting to impose on his aunt.

Kathleen had caught the hurt Sara tried to cover. Mercifully she said nothing about it. "Don't be talking such nonsense. You're not causing anyone any trouble. Except maybe for Devon and I'm not sure that's necessarily bad. Could be you're giving him something to think about besides the mill." She headed up the walk, leaving the door open after she'd stepped inside for Sara to follow. "Do you like currants?"

Sara hurried after her, grateful to be out of the rain—and for the incongruous change of subject.

"We've the red ones here," Kathleen continued, referring to the grapelike clusters of berries that grew above the banks of the stream. "But they're a bit difficult to come by. Deer usually get to them before humans can." She took off her shawl, her glance narrowing as Sara shrugged off the wet cape. "Deer love berries, you know. But the basketful I picked yesterday was enough for a batch of preserves. You do like them, don't you?"

"Very much," Sara replied, wondering why Kathleen was scowling so. Indeed, currant preserves were her favorite.

The puzzling woman gave a satisfied nod. "I thought you might. Those from the woods seemed particularly fond of them. I'm putting up preserves now. We'll have some with our tea while we're waiting to hear what all the fuss is about at the mill. I got another curiosity you can cure me of in the meantime." The woman's shrewd blue eyes once again skimmed the garment Sara hung on the coat tree. "If you're so inclined, you can tell me how you've come to acquire Maureen's cape."

Now understanding the reason for the odd way Kathleen had been watching her, Sara hurriedly assured her there wasn't that much to tell. At least there wasn't when Sara left out the parts too private to share. All she relayed to Kathleen—after the woman had raised her eyebrows at Devon's green flannel shirt and insisted that Sara sit next to the stove in the kitchen so her jeans would dry—was that she'd run into Devon by the stream and he'd let her borrow the cape, and his shirt, because she'd been caught in the rain.

A person was always left with the impression that Kathleen heard more than was being said. Sara had that impression as she sat in the homey kitchen and watched the spry old woman dip ladles full of bubbling, ruby-colored preserves into clean pint jars she'd lined up on the butcher-block table.

"Did he tell you much about Maureen?" Kathleen inquired blandly.

"Only enough to make me more curious."

Sara propped her chin on her fist. The steam rose from the neat line of jars, filling the room with the scent of memories. Next would come the paraffin. Sara remembered the process from her childhood. "He said she wasn't happy here." Sara looked up from the sparkling jars. "Was *he* happy?"

Kathleen wiped her brow with the back of her forearm. Frowning down at the big blue pot, she dipped the ladle into it again. "I don't know that Devon's ever been one to feel happiness the way some folk can. Oh, he had his pleasures, and many a night I've heard him singing over a pint with the boys. But even as a child he tended to have a more serious nature. His mother died bearing my brother Brian another child when Devon was only six. And that affected him, I know. When he married Maureen he seemed as content as I'd ever seen him. For a long while there, he'd felt very much alone."

"After his father died, you mean?"

The spare, red wing of Kathleen's eyebrow arched. If she was surprised that Devon had told Sara about his father, she didn't let on. She merely nodded.

"That was a difficult time for him. He'd wanted very badly to stay at the university and graduate. He'd worked hard to get there and coming back to run the mill wasn't at all what he wanted right then. I didn't think his going off to London was such a good idea to begin with. But you've never seen a man prouder than his father when Devon earned himself a scholarship.

"A man needed an education," Kathleen continued. "That's what Brian would tell Devon. My brother felt that times were changing and unless a man changed with them, he'd be left behind. Devon is very much his father's son in many ways. But Brian knew when he'd pushed too far. Devon once had that ability, too. Neither me nor Thomas nor anyone else can figure out what's become of it."

She made a faint clucking sound, shaking her head at the way she'd digressed. Kathleen loved to talk, no doubt about that. According to Devon, Thomas did, too. Devon, on the other hand, wasn't nearly as free with his thoughts. "You were wanting to hear about Maureen," Kathleen went on and willingly supplied the information Sara probably shouldn't have been so terribly interested in.

It turned out that Devon had known Maureen for most of his life. Her family had grown flax on their property outside of Durry. According to Kathleen, she had been a lovely girl who had seemed quite suited to Devon. She had been seven years younger than his thirty when they married. As far as Kathleen could tell—and she assured Sara that she hadn't pried any more than necessary—the problems between Maureen and Devon began after one of their yearly trips to a manufacturer's market in Dublin. Nothing seemed to satisfy her. She wanted Devon home more. She wanted him to take her on holidays over weekends.

Kathleen continued, careful not to place blame, though her prejudice still came through. As she spoke, Sara began to understand that Maureen had wanted excitement and variety in her life, not the same quiet routine she had known since the day she was born. She'd begged Devon to move to the city. But Devon wouldn't go. He couldn't. His responsibilities were here. Maureen knew that. Just as she ultimately knew she could never be happy in Brigen Glen. She moved to Dublin, then to London. She went to work in a cabaret and started saving money for flying lessons. They were too expensive, so she decided she'd rather jump out of planes than fly them. On her second jump, her chute hadn't opened.

Sara sat staring into her empty tea cup. She felt sorrow for Maureen. And for Devon. "It sounds as if the kind of excitement she was looking for would have been difficult for any man to provide."

The wind rattled the window over the sink, the breeze leaking through the sill, moving the lace curtain. Rain sluiced down the glass. "I don't know that what she wanted had anything to do with a man. I don't necessarily think it's a good thing to go looking for what lies beyond your own horizon. She had a good life here. She just became dissatisfied with it because she couldn't appreciate what was outside of Brigen Glen without wanting it all for herself."

Sara set her cup on the table. Devon had brushed off the demise of his marriage as a simple matter of fact. Sara hadn't been fooled, though. She'd seen the shuttered look in his eyes. He had been deeply affected by what had happened. But she sensed that his wife's leaving, and her death, were only part of the reason he held himself in check. He wasn't the kind of man to allow any one person such mastery over him. He was his own master, and being the kind of man who felt as intensely as he did, Sara would bet her grandmother's ring that he was determined to not make himself vulnerable again.

Still, she had felt the hunger in his kisses. She had seen the need in his eyes. He had even let her into his world for a while. Just long enough for her to sense that there was no room in it for anyone else.

The whinny of a horse brought her head up with a jerk. She felt cheated somehow, but now was not the time to dwell on it. Heaven only knew what had happened at the mill and Devon's mood could easily be less than amenable—especially when he discovered that she was still here.

She stood as Kathleen, wiping red streaks on her white apron, hurried into the living room to peek through the curtains. Hanging back, Sara quietly released her breath when the smiling woman announced who it was.

It wasn't Devon. It was Beth with Molly's boys.

Sara moved closer to see them pile out of an open buggy, red umbrellas blooming over their heads. Mickey and his older brother Patrick, a freckle-faced child with the same cinnamon-colored hair as his brother and a much more aggressive disposition, raced for the house. He headed straight through the murky puddle Mickey dutifully avoided. Balancing Joey on her hip, Beth called a quick thanks to the neighbor who'd given them the ride and hurried into the cottage herself.

Patrick headed straight for the pantry. Mickey walked in behind him, stopping just inside the doorway to pull off his rubber boots. His cherubic face lit with a smile when he saw Sara.

Unaccustomed to seeing him without the mischievous mongrel, she hunched down in front of him. "Where's your puppy?"

"We left him home" came the reply. Not from Mickey. From a weary-looking Beth who handed the toddler to Kathleen to unbundle while she slipped out of her raincoat. She opened her mouth to add something else when the sound of breaking glass cut her off. "Patrick! What are you into now?"

Beth was through the kitchen door, red curls flying, within a split second of the child's muttered, "Nothing."

Kathleen knowingly shook her head. "Must be she's had a day with them." Lowering herself into one of the "company" chairs by the window, she unbuttoned the squirming baby's sweater. "'Tis enough to deal with little ones when they're your own. Being as they're not, caring for them can be even more trying. Seems they're always especially difficult when their mother's taking her holiday." Her hands were gentle as they pried Joey's little fingers from the doily he'd snatched from the arm of the chair. He'd stuffed it into his mouth. "It's days like this that Beth swears she'll never marry. 'Children aren't for me,' she says."

Kathleen spoke the words lightly, a clear indication that she knew her pretty niece would someday fall for some eligible young man who would change her mind on that score. But her words had an impact on Mickey that Sara couldn't help but notice.

The boy's smile had died and his head hung as if he'd been scolded. Kathleen hadn't noticed. She was busy wrestling the fidgeting toddler, then chasing after him once she'd set him on the floor. When Beth appeared a moment later to set Patrick's boots by the stove, she didn't notice Mickey's dejected posture, either. She seemed to merely note that he wasn't getting into anything, while calling back to Patrick that supper would be ready as soon as Aunt Kathleen heated the soup.

With a quick smile to acknowledge Sara, Beth hurried back through the doorway. Kathleen had gone in ahead of her, leading the baby.

Alone with Mickey, Sara touched his soft auburn curls.

He wouldn't look at her.

She reached down to retie one of his shoelaces. It had no doubt come undone when he'd pulled off his boots. She couldn't help but note how he'd been so careful to take them off as soon as he'd come in.

He seemed like such a good child. Too good, almost. Was it possible that he tried to be good because being bad caused the exasperation that made adults not want children? That was what Kathleen's comments inferred, after all. If that were the case, had his desire to please those adults backfired? It seemed to Sara that by not causing problems, he didn't require the attention the other children demanded. As a result, he was ignored.

Thinking back to the other times she'd seen him with members of his family, it seemed they only paid attention to him when they were trying to figure out what he wanted. The longer it took them to guess, the longer he could hold their attention. Sara was no psychologist, but she was beginning to suspect the reason for his reticence. She knew Mickey could talk. She'd also seen how Devon and Beth answered for him. She suspected his other relatives did the same. Was it possible that they were reinforcing his uncommunicative behavior to the point where it simply wasn't necessary for him to speak?

Mickey stared down at the bow she'd just tied. She wanted very much to take his mind off Kathleen's unintentionally insensitive remarks. "Why didn't you bring your puppy?" she ventured, deliberately posing a question he couldn't answer with a simple nod or the shake of his head.

He shrugged.

"Mickey." A smile hid behind her gentle chiding. "You must know why you didn't bring him."

His solemn brown eyes peeked from under his long lashes. Though he hesitated, it was apparent to him that Sara wasn't going to suggest reasons for why he hadn't brought Tug. "Beth said I couldn't."

"Did she give you a reason?"

"She said he smells bad when he gets wet."

"Does he?"

He rubbed his nose as he thought about it. "Aye." A smile broke loose. "He smells like a skunk."

Sara laughed, tousling his hair as she'd seen Devon do with such affection the first morning she'd met them. She didn't blame Beth for wanting to leave the dog home under the circumstances and Mickey agreed that Tug would be more pleasant to sleep with tonight if he wasn't so pungent.

He was still smiling when Sara led him to join the others. She wanted to make sure he was occupied with his supper before she left.

As she'd told Devon during those quiet moments in his cottage, she wanted to go into Durry tomorrow. Therefore she'd needed to get back to the inn to make arrangements for transportation. It had become especially necessary in the past few minutes that she do something definite to assure herself that, tomorrow, she would discover some hint of who her family had been. Maybe that feeling was there because by being with these people—with Devon's family—she was reminded of what she no longer had. Of what she'd never had to begin with. The people in this house belonged to one another. Beth had had a hard day with her sister's children so she'd brought them to her aunt, who willingly shared the responsibility of their care. There was no question of an imposition or inconvenience. They were simply there for one another.

She quashed the feeling of emptiness that thought brought and quickly explained to Kathleen why she must say good-night.

"Oh, you'll not be going into Durry tomorrow." Kathleen handed her a cup of butter to set beside the bread, then pulled a chair from the table, indicating that Sara was to sit in it. "Certainly not if the rains keep up as they have. When the sky cries like this the stream becomes a river. There's no crossing it from here."

"Nor from anyplace for miles," added Beth as she ushered the boys to the table. "Sit and have some soup. And don't worry. It only takes a day or two for the stream to go down once the rain stops. Everyone is used to it."

Everyone might have been accustomed to it, but there was something Beth failed to mention. Devon had said that the bridge crossing the stream tended to wash out on occasion, which was one of the reasons he wanted to put in a better road and a properly engineered crossing. He had no patience for the delay a swelling stream could cause—a delay that Sara felt sure might last for days if a bridge had to be reconstructed.

From Beth's unconcerned attitude, Sara gathered that most of the villagers didn't much mind the inconvenience. They simply accepted it and adjusted their life accordingly. Normally Sara took matters in stride right along with the best of them. But the delay made her feel little less certain than she had been about finding the answers she was looking for. Though she couldn't begin to explain why she had the feeling, she also wondered if those answers might be something she'd be better off not knowing.

Beth didn't see Sara's consternation. What she saw was an advantage to the situation. She knew just what Sara could do with the time she'd now have available tomorrow.

"We take herbs and vegetables to market in Durry once a month so we can buy our flour and tea and such. Since Molly and my mother won't be back from Cork for a couple of days, and since next Wednesday is market, you could help us. I'd be pleased for the help gathering the hyssop and thyme. And for help dying the laces we make, if you'd be inclined. It's a deadly boring job to do alone and I'd be grateful for the company."

The invitation was as much an offer of friendship as a request for assistance. Sara, responding to her need to be included, was touched by it. That was why she told Beth she'd be happy to help, and tried not to think about how Devon would react when he got back to find her still here.

She had no choice but to consider his reaction when the back door swung open half an hour later.

Sara had just begun to help Kathleen clear the table while Beth cleaned up Joey when Devon walked in. His slicker dripped puddles on the floor and the ends of his coal-black hair were wet where his hat hadn't covered them. Slicker and hat were hung on the peg by the door.

Of the six people in the room, his eyes went straight to Sara when he turned. The room seemed to shrink as he moved into it. He filled the space with his presence, making her far more aware than she wanted to be of the tension radiating from him.

"I went by the inn. I thought you'd be there."

"To see me?" she asked quietly, her heart beating a little faster. "Or to check up on me?"

Sara didn't know what to make of his impassive expression. Kathleen, however, perceived only challenge and immediately rose to Sara's defense.

"I asked her to stay. No sense her eating alone at the pub."

He looked tired to Sara. As he turned from her, Beth must have seen his fatigue, too. Leaving Joey with a biscuit, she coaxed Devon toward the table.

"There's soup if you're hungry," she told him and took a bowl from the cupboard.

His aunt retrieved a clean napkin. "What had happened at the mill?"

"A water pipe broke in the storage room."

"They couldn't fix that without you?"

Wearily he drew his hand through his damp hair. The thick strands fell right back over his forehead. "They couldn't get in. The door was locked."

Kathleen seemed to find that odd. "Weren't Kevin or Mike there to open it?"

"They were there. But I have the only key now."

"So it's come to that, has it?" Kathleen's lips pinched. "You know, Devon, if your Uncle Thomas were here, he'd be telling you that it's a foolish thing to risk alienating your men by putting such little trust in them. Sure as the devil, your father'd be telling you the same."

"I know what I'm doing, Aunt Kathleen."

"Do you now?" she returned, making it clear she didn't think he had a clue as to what was going on.

Devon meant no disrespect. He just couldn't abide his aunt's harping tonight. His face was a study in stone when he looked up at the woman hovering at his elbow. His incisive glance was fleeting, but it was black enough to effectively silence whatever commentary she'd been prepared to offer.

Sara didn't need to hear anything else to understand the larger implications of the brief exchange anyway. Since he didn't know for certain who was sabotaging his plans, Devon wasn't trusting anyone. The chemicals in the storage room had already been destroyed once. By keeping the only key, he was minimizing the possibility of it happening again.

The brooding scowl etched in his forehead didn't ease at all as he sat down at the table. Propping his elbows on either side of the bowl of soup Beth set in front of him, he absently tore a chunk of bread from the loaf. Kathleen offered him milk, which he refused. Beth offered him ale, which he accepted. Sara, noting how the women skirted him, kept her back to him as she stood at the sink to wash the dishes. She knew exactly what he was doing, though. She could see his reflection in the window.

He ate in silence. The only sounds in the kitchen were those of dishes being washed and Beth's instructions to Patrick to stop teasing Joey. She'd taken the boys into the living room so their uncle could eat in peace. Mickey slipped back in. In his pudgy little hands he carried a pencil and pad of paper. He laid them on the table as he quietly slid into the chair beside Devon.

In the window's reflection, she saw the conscious effort Devon made to keep the affairs of the day from affecting his attitude toward the boy. His broad back expanded with the deep breath he inhaled, his red-and-black plaid shirt stretching over his strong shoulders with the motion. When he let out that calming breath, his shoulders visibly lowered. "You want to draw, eh, sport?"

Mickey grinned.

"Can I finish my supper first?"

Mickey's answer was a quick nod before he propped his chin on his fists to watch his uncle finish his meal. Sara kept an eye on the reflections, doing what she'd been doing since he'd arrived—wondering what Devon had wanted if he'd stopped by the inn. He was making no attempt to talk to her about it.

A couple of minutes later, she saw him push his chair back. Guiltily, because she'd been staring, she jerked her glance back to the suds in the sink. Behind her, she could hear his footsteps as he put the remaining bread in the larder.

He brought his bowl to her, saying nothing as he watched her grip the sturdy pottery so it wouldn't slip from her soapy fingers. It was impossible to tell what lay behind the cool blue of his eyes as he looked into hers. It could have been irritation. Or a question. Or a memory. Whatever it was, she found it so disturbing that she had to look away. When she did, she saw Kathleen staring at them over the plate she was drying.

"Do you want to draw your house?" she heard him ask Mickey, and Sara felt her breath slowly escape as he sat down again.

She turned back to the sink when the child nodded, too unsettled by her reaction to Devon to test her theory about the boy's silence. She wouldn't think about what was going on between her and Devon. For now she'd concentrate on simple things. Such as not putting cracks in Kathleen's dinnerware.

The house Mickey wanted to draw wasn't the one he lived in now. As Sara listened to Devon as he drew, the house turned out to be the one Mickey would live in when he grew up. Devon would help him build it and, in turn, Mickey was to help his nephews build houses of their own. It sounded like a familiar game, one they'd engaged in often because, though Mickey said nothing, he always knew when it was his turn to draw the next section.

It wasn't long before Patrick got bored with whatever it was he'd been doing in the other room. When he showed up, Mickey's house was set aside in favor of the rough and tumble play boys seemed to thrive on. Patrick had brought in several wooden soldiers and a battlefield was set up on the kitchen table. Mickey was put in charge of making barricades.

Kathleen threw her hands into air, invoking the protection of saints at the invasion of her space. She was secretly quite content being surrounded by family, but she had an image to maintain. Devon's image, however, was undergoing another change in Sara's mind.

She couldn't help but notice how Devon responded to his cousin's children. He was good with them. And they seemed good for him.

The observation was one shared by Kathleen.

"He needs his own," she confided, settling in the living room to keep Joey out of the war zone in the kitchen. "The good Lord no doubt knew what he was doing not blessing him and Maureen with children, but that's all behind him now. He's needing a wife and family. He needs sons." She made a faint tsking sound. "Even if he weren't naturally so good with children, you'd think he'd want to leave an heir. Someone to follow in his footsteps as he's done with his own father." She looked at Joey, comfortably ensconced in Sara's lap. "There's not a male child with the O'Donaugh name among the lot of us. Nor will there be unless Devon does something about it."

From the disapproving shake of her head, it was apparent that Kathleen found this lack of progeny disgraceful. She possessed a fierce pride in her family. Therefore, she also prided the O'Donaugh name. Molly's boys were all McMurtrys. All the other offspring were girls.

Knowing that Kathleen had tried on more than one occasion to find him a wife, Sara was certain that Devon's duty to continue the lineage had been pointed out to him. There was no doubt in Sara's mind how Devon felt about the subject, either. She had been playing with Joey as Kathleen spoke. When she glanced back at the woman, she saw Devon standing right behind her.

Chapter Eight

It hadn't been Devon's intention to interrupt the women's conversation. Beth had come in to tell the boys it was time to pick up their toys, and Devon had thought to help them by picking up the ones Mickey and Patrick missed. He'd just retrieved a wooden soldier that had slid all the way across the floor to the archway when he noticed Sara.

She sat in one of the wing chairs by the lace-draped table his aunt kept cut flowers on. Joey was in her lap. The child faced her and she held his pudgy little hands between hers, playing a clapping game with him while Kathleen, in the chair across from her, droned on.

At first, what Kathleen said didn't even register. Devon was aware only of Sara as he straightened. She looked almost like a child herself with her long, pale hair framed against the great back of the green wing chair he remembered his own mother once occupying.

His brow pinched. He had only the vaguest memories of his mother, but he remembered being held in her lap in that old chair. Just as Joey was held in Sara's now. He remembered, too, dimly, when he couldn't sit on her lap anymore because she'd grown so great with her second child that she no longer had a lap for him to sit on. He'd then sprawled on the rug at her feet entertaining himself with picture books while the rain beat against the windows and his mother and his aunts knitted tiny sweaters and caps.

He didn't know why he should recall such memories now. He'd been in this room hundreds of times over the years, had sat in that chair himself on many occasions. Yet he couldn't recall ever being so suddenly reminded of the woman he scarcely remembered. Certainly there was nothing about Sara that resembled her. His mother had been black Irish, a woman with alabaster skin, hair as dark as midnight and eyes the color of the sky. He'd inherited his own coloring from her. Sara's skin was golden tan, her eyes the warmest brown. There were no physical similarities between them at all. Yet seeing her holding little Joey had brought the memories sharply into focus.

As disconcerting as he found those sudden thoughts, more disturbing still was the image that encroached when she looked up to see him watching her.

Her lovely features were soft with a gentle smile, a warily offered sign that she was willing to forget his earlier behavior if he would let her. As had happened before when he'd met her eyes, he felt a certain ease come over him. It lasted only for a moment. Just long enough for him to regret its passing—and for him to realize how very right she would look holding *his* child.

That his aunt felt compelled to share her feelings along that line at that particular moment proved unfortunate. It wasn't that Kathleen had any ideas about him and Sara. To the meddlesome woman's credit, and to Devon's surprise,

Kathleen hadn't so much as hinted that the two of them should get together. What nailed Devon's defenses firmly in place was what he heard just as he started to turn away— Kathleen telling Sara that he needed a son and bemoaning the fact that there were no male children with the O'Donaugh name.

His nerves strained by the demands of the mill, agitated by the thoughts Sara provoked, Kathleen's reminder of yet another responsibility threatened to completely undo his patience. Muttering a terse expletive, which his aunt missed, and sending her an irritable glare, which she didn't, he decided it would be best to ignore what she was saying and continue his search for stray toys. He snatched a cannon wheel from near the china closet.

The prudent approach was lost to Kathleen. She'd realized what he'd heard and saw no point in wasting an opportunity to drive her point home.

"Now don't be looking that way, Devon O'Donaugh. You know that when a man is getting to be your age, he needs to be taking such considerations seriously. You can't say I've been interfering here of late. It's been since spring that I've tried to help you meet a girl." A healthy dose of self-defense joined her admonishing tone. She obviously prided herself on her self-restraint. "You can't fault me for wanting to give you a bit of a nudge now and then. Left to your own devices you might never have yourself a son. Anybody with the brains God gave them can see you ought to have one. Aside from the pride of it, it'd be nice to know our name won't be fading from the face of the earth."

Devon's fingers locked around the neck of the toy soldier. Strangling it, he faced the chair his aunt occupied. He didn't dare look at Sara. "I know you feel it's your duty to remind me of my obligations, Aunt Kathleen. But what you don't understand, what you've never understood," he added, his voice deadly calm, "is that I don't need anyone to tell me what my responsibilities are. You've never known me to walk away from them.''

"Well, it seems to me your being sadly remiss about this one.'' Her jaw set stubbornly. She'd missed Devon's hint of resentment. "It's like I was telling Sara, as good as you are with Molly's children, I think you'd . . .''

"I heard what you told Sara,'' he cut in, having heard the same argument long before now. "And it's none of her business. It's none of yours, for that matter. I've told you before I'm not in a position to take a wife. Even if I wanted one, which I *don't*,'' he added because his aunt was obviously unclear on that point, "I can't afford a family now. I certainly don't have time for one. All of my time and every pound of my money for the next few years will go to expanding the mill. The *family* mill.''

His jaw was tight with the reminder of whose property he was tending, his tone harsh, though he hadn't raised his voice at all. He didn't dare raise it. If he did, he feared the frustrations eating at him might make him say something he'd regret. As it was, Kathleen's pushing now had caused a few of those frustrations to surface.

"Just in case you've forgotten, the mill isn't just mine. It belongs to all of us. *I*,'' he emphasized, jamming his finger to his chest, "just happen to be the only one to run it. And since I'm running it, I'll do so the way I see fit. In one way or another, this family, this entire village, depends on its existence. Because of that, the mill is the only matter that concerns me. It will remain my only concern until it's producing enough to bring about the changes that will put some life into this place. Maybe once the expansion is complete, I can start to thinking about my other 'responsibilities.' ''

He pushed his fingers through his hair, angry with his aunt for wanting more and angry with himself for letting her get to him. "In the meantime,'' he muttered, letting his hand fall to a fist, "it'd be a damned sight easier to do what I have to do if I could just be left alone to do it."

The room went unnervingly silent. Beth and the boys had come from the kitchen to see what the commotion was about. They stood wide-eyed and watchful in the archway. Even Joey, who'd been playing with one of the buttons on the shirt Sara wore, had screwed up his face in puzzlement at his second cousin's forbidding tone.

"I'll hitch up Skye," he said to Beth as he strode past her. "Then I'll take you and the boys home."

A moment later the back door slammed.

"Is Devon mad?" a surprisingly subdued Patrick wanted to know.

Explaining that he wasn't mad so much as just upset, and that Devon's mood had nothing to do with either him or Mickey, Beth ushered the boys into the room. Handing them their boots, she suggested that it might not be wise to keep Devon waiting, and frowned at her aunt for upsetting Devon so.

Kathleen's eyes were worried. "That expansion has come to mean far too much to him, I'm afraid. Was a time it was just a dream. Now it's like an obsession."

An obsession. For Sara, the word added more weight to the troubled thoughts that accompanied her back to the inn that night. Devon came back to get her after he dropped off Beth and the boys, but he didn't say a word to her during the miserable ride to the inn. It was cold and wet and dark and she was sure Devon was most anxious to be rid of her. At least, she was until, through the drizzle, Mrs. Carrigan's Inn and Pub came into view.

"I'm sorry," he said when they pulled up alongside the buildings. No song came from the pub tonight, no raucous laughter. The weather had driven everyone into their homes.

Rain dripped in sheets from the top of the carriage. Wrapped in the gray cape, Sara shivered. "For what?"

"For losing my temper with my aunt tonight. I'm usually able to take her nagging better than that."

"You've had a long day."

"Don't make excuses for me, Sara. I meant everything I said. I'm just sorry I had to say it in front of you."

He was referring to how trapped he'd felt at that moment by the scope of his responsibilities, and how disappointed he was with himself for losing control as he had and admitting that failing aloud. He didn't know if his aunt had caught it. But he was sure Sara had. He was sure she understood when, by the pale yellow light of the porch lamp, he saw her hesitant smile.

That smile was one of the harder things Sara had ever managed. She'd recognized Devon's resentment, but his other admissions crowded in, making it more difficult than it should have been to accept his apology.

Even if I wanted a wife, which I don't...

It was foolish to let the words hurt as they did. After all, it wasn't as if she thought that they had any sort of future together. Certainly she'd never entertained such a possibility. They had little in common—except a love of Brigen Glen, and even there they didn't necessarily agree on what was best for the village. He was matter-of-fact, down to earth and unbelievably hardheaded. She believed that anything was possible. He was a dyed-in-the-wool realist. She wanted only impossible things.

She wanted the impossible now.

"You said you came by here earlier looking for me." In the darkness she could see little more than the shadow of his profile. Immobile, dark, unrevealing. "What did you want?"

"I'm not sure."

She waited because it seemed that he was struggling with something he might not reveal if she pushed. A few moments later, her silence was rewarded.

"I think I just wanted to talk to you. Not about anything in particular. I just wanted...to talk. It doesn't matter now."

How hard it must be for you, she thought, knowing he would hate her sympathy. How difficult to need someone to listen and to not find anyone there who cared about what was important to him. "I wish I'd been here," she said over the patter of the rain. Her voice grew quieter, encouraging. "I'm here now."

"It's late."

"Too late, you mean?" She hugged her arms more tightly around herself, shivering against the chill. She had no idea why she challenged him that way.

She should go in. She should say good-night and make the mad dash through the rain to the door. Twenty yards was all that stood between her leaving well enough alone and making a fool of herself.

"Good night, Devon. Thanks for the ride."

With a handful of cape in one hand so she wouldn't trip on it and her other hand on the side of the seat for balance, she started to step from the carriage. Devon's arm around her waist stopped her.

"Wait." The coach rocked with the movements. Balanced as she was, she had no leverage. His arm secure at her waist, he easily pulled her back to the bench seat.

She nearly landed in his lap. He didn't seem to care. Shifting his thigh out from under her, he moved his hands to her upper arms and turned her to face him.

He shouldn't have touched her. Beneath his hands he felt the tension he had caused, and the gradual shift of muscles as her shoulders lowered. Instead of pulling back now that she wasn't going to bolt, he left his hands where they were.

He needed to touch her. It bothered him to admit that need, but it didn't bother him enough to make him move.

The light from the inn couldn't compete with the veiling rain. What little penetrated the darkness did nothing more than create shadows.

"Talk to me," he heard her say. "Tell me why you're so angry."

The quiet sincerity in her voice begged for understanding. Fighting its lure just wasn't possible at the moment. "I'm not angry," he told her because he didn't really think he was. "I just get tired sometimes. Tonight it just seemed that no matter what I do, it's either not right or it's not enough. I shouldn't have let it get to me."

Some men might have sounded sorry for themselves under those circumstances. Not Devon. He made his inability to do it all sound like a personal flaw. Sara almost smiled at that because it was so like him. He'd missed the point of her question, though. Despite his denial, she could sense a deeper anger simmering inside him. It was what fueled his constant tension, what put the edge in his voice. Maybe, she thought, he didn't even realize it was there.

Just like he didn't realize how difficult it was for her to concentrate with him so close. His wrist was draped over her shoulder, his hand at the back of her neck. She had the cape's hood up so he wasn't touching her skin or her hair, but she could feel his fingers absently rubbing back and forth.

"What would you have done if you hadn't had to come back here to take over the mill?"

The question surprised him, even if he didn't need to think about the answer. "I'd still have come back." His fingers drifted along the seam of her hood. "But not for a long time. I'd have finished school and traveled more. Nothing that would make any real difference now, I suppose."

"Why wouldn't it have made a difference?"

"I taught myself what I could about the business, so not having a degree doesn't matter that much. Not here. And the cities I've never seen get along fine without me." She tipped her head to one side, seeming to unconsciously cradle his hand at her shoulder. "Why do you want to know?"

"You spend so much time taking care of everyone else that I guess I just wanted to know what you'd wanted for yourself."

"I wanted the usual things, Sara. But I didn't get them. Some of us just aren't meant to."

"That's awfully fatalistic isn't it?"

"Realistic," he told her.

The hood of her cape kept his hands from her hair. Grasping it by the sides, he slowly pushed it back. The breath he drew brought the freshness of her scent with it, the fragrance of damp wildflowers. He'd never smell rain again without thinking of her.

"Devon?"

He slipped his fingers under her hair, cupping his hand over the back of her neck. "No more questions, Sara." He lowered his head, touching his lips to hers. "Not now," he breathed and captured her faint sigh.

She shouldn't want his kiss so much. Sara knew that. Just as she knew that Devon didn't want to want her, either. Understanding didn't mean acceptance, though. She wouldn't accept limitations where Devon was concerned. A very vital part of herself responded to the strength in him and she couldn't let that go.

She felt his hand at her waist, seeking the opening of the voluminous cape. Wanting him to have that access, she slipped her hand past his and pulled the material apart. His hand slid inside, curving at her waist as he drew her closer. It wasn't enough. She ached to touch him, too, and a moan of frustration bubbled in her throat when the position of his

arms prevented her from lowering her own. Needing the
contact, she pushed her fingers through the damp curls
covering his collar. His tongue danced against hers, teasing, taunting. But the restraint she sensed in him was fading. His kiss became deeper, more urgent. He pulled her
against him, so sharply she could scarcely breathe. It didn't
matter. All that mattered to her was Devon.

God help him, he wanted her. Devon felt that need so
badly that he ached from the intensity of it. He could feel
her small, slender body tremble against him. When he
cupped his hand over her breast, he felt the nipple bloom in
his palm. Her response to him had been immediate, complete. She tasted warm and sweet and willing, and if he
didn't let go of her he would strip off the shirt that kept his
hands from her skin and pull her down on the floorboards.
He wanted her beneath him. He wanted her weak with the
same desire he felt for her.

He threaded his fingers through her hair, his mouth
moving over hers, seeking, tasting. He didn't want to let her
go, but he had to. If he didn't stop right now, he'd turn this
carriage around and take her home with him. He wanted
more than the physical release he could find in her body. He
wanted to lay with her, to experience the quiet comfort a
man can experience when he holds a woman. He couldn't
afford to feel what he did when he held her. Yet he couldn't
seem to feel any other way.

Slowly he lifted his head. His breathing was rapid and his
eyes glittered hard on Sara's face.

He didn't have to say a word as he pulled back for Sara to
know that he was closing himself off again. She could feel
it. Just as she could feel his reluctance when he finally
withdrew his hand from inside her cape and pulled her hood
back up. He wasn't nearly as unaffected by her as he wanted
to be. He just wasn't going to do anything about it—which
was why she had such an empty ache inside when he left her

at the front door of the inn. And why, after he'd gently kissed the rain from her lips and turned into the darkness, she spent the night wondering why he was shutting her out.

She wasn't the only one he was doing that to. He was shutting out friends and family, too. Knowing she wasn't the only one didn't help in the least. What it did do as she lay there tossing and turning that night was make her question what Kathleen had labeled his "obsession." Sara was sure Devon believed his idea of growth would be good for the village. But was it possible that he wanted those changes for the wrong reasons? Reasons that had nothing to do with boosting the local economy? Reasons that even went beyond wanting it because it had once been his father's dream?

Those questions still nagged the next day as she stood outside the mill. She wasn't waiting for Devon, though. Not exactly. She was waiting for his aunt.

After spending a companionable morning with Beth and several other women from the village gathering herbs and flowers from the fields, Sara had stopped here with Kathleen. The herbs they'd picked nearly overflowed the three large baskets sitting in the grass. Because of the dampness it was important that the herbs be sorted right away. That was why they'd stopped here. Indirectly anyway.

The necessary sorting was done on drying screens. Kathleen had loaned her big one to her friend Mary, though, and she had only a pair of small ones left. She'd meant to have Thomas build her another screen before he'd gone, but she'd forgotten to mention it. She was inside the mill mentioning it to Devon that very moment. Even though the mill didn't run on Saturdays, Kathleen had known that was where Devon would be.

Sara paced. Her restlessness was worse than usual. Wanting to see him, thinking that if he'd wanted to see her he'd have come out, she tried not to think of him at all. Instead, she scuffed at a rock and every once in a while glanced back at the building looming large and gleaming white in the sunshine. The mill seemed relieved, if that were possible, with the lack of activity within its walls. Even the water-wheel on the dammed-up stream beside the mill seemed to move a little slower than usual, and the geese who lived in the tall grass by the water seemed too lethargic to do much more than give a perfunctory honk at her intrusion. She wondered if Devon ever saw it like this. Or if he was so busy trying to change it all that the serenity it could offer was lost to him.

"He's working on the pipes," Kathleen announced when she emerged from the side door, the tail of her green scarf flapping in the breeze. Straightening her beige shawl, she picked up her basket. "He said he'd be by when he got to a good place to stop. He's keeping Mickey with him," she added, since Sara seemed to be watching the doorway.

Sara picked up her basket, along with Beth's since the younger woman had taken Sean and Joey home, and fell into step beside Kathleen. She was still talking.

"Used to be on a Saturday he'd have the likes of Sean or Kevin drop by to help with the kind of work he's doing now. It's for sure that at one time they'd have been here making less a task of it for him. It breaks my heart to see him fading away from his friends like he is. If he stays so bent on having his way, he's likely to not have a friend left."

"Can't one of them talk to him? Maybe make him see what he's doing?"

The look Kathleen gave her seemed to question Sara's basic intelligence. "You've been hearing enough to know that talking to Devon about something he doesn't want to hear is like talking to Stonehenge. I've never known Devon to raise a fist to a man, but I'm fearing it might come to that one day soon. I asked you the other day if you'd approach him about reconsidering his plans. If he'd do that, his other problems would take care of themselves."

A lock of hair, more silver now than red, fell over her forehead. As Sara had seen her do before, she blew it away rather than bother lifting her hand to brush it back. "It's not just for myself that I'm asking, you understand."

Sara balked at the request. "Why should anything I say make a difference?"

"It's just a feeling I have. There's something about you, Sara Madigan. I can't put my finger on it, but I learned long ago not to question the Fates. I've a feeling it was them that brought you here."

"The Fates had nothing to do with it. What brought me here was my grandmother's request that I give her ring to your brother."

"Maybe two things brought you here, then."

Sara smiled. She liked Kathleen, probably because in some ways she reminded her of her grandmother. She had the same good-natured bossiness Fiona had possessed. And the same smile. A devilish sort of grin that always made you wonder what it was you'd just agreed to.

Sara hadn't agreed to anything, though, despite Kathleen's conclusion.

"Now have you considered what you might say to him?"

Of course she had. But as they walked on to Kathleen's cottage, Sara told the woman that she suspected that her reasons for wanting Brigen Glen to remain as it was might be just as biased, in their own way, as were Devon's. Each morning when she ran along the stream, she breathed in air free of the smell of the city. The sound of cars and buses and machinery didn't hide the music of rustling leaves. Nor did those things interfere with the pace of life, speeding everything up and creating urgencies where none had existed before. Walking was a standard mode of transportation. An evening's entertainment was good conversation shared with friends. When the pantry was low, you shopped from your own garden. To be fair, she didn't see the changes Devon wanted as destroying all of that. What she saw was that a way of life would be lost. Once it was, a little more of what Ireland was all about—what she felt such an affinity for—wouldn't exist anymore.

"None of that will matter to him," Sara concluded as they reached the cottage. She went ahead of Kathleen, holding the gate for her, then heading into the yard by the garden. Setting her basket by the two small screens Kathleen had already set up, she tried to think of something to ask the woman to get her off the present subject. The diversion wasn't necessary. The sound of horse's hooves drew their attention back to the road.

The ground was far too damp for dust. But Merlot would have raised it had it been there. His black mane and black tail flying, his great chestnut body loped along with an easy, powerful grace. A powerful grace that reminded Sara very much of the man sitting astride him.

Devon had Mickey in the saddle in front of him. Mickey, grinning at the speed, was holding Tug. Devon didn't slow the horse as they approached the pasture beside the yard. Bending his head, he said something to Mickey, and in the next instant Sara sucked in her breath when all four of them went sailing over the stone fence.

Behind her, Skye came out of his stall, nickering a greeting for his company.

"I wish to the saints he wouldn't do that." Kathleen, holding her hand to her heart, glared at the back of Devon's head as he trotted the horse to a halt in the pasture. "Takes a year off my life every time he does."

Sara had thought the graceful leap quite beautiful. But then there was also a kind of beauty in Devon's sure movements as he lifted Mickey over the fence and jumped it himself a moment later.

Mickey came charging through the yard. Tug bounced along behind him.

"There's a biscuit in the jar for you," Kathleen called to the boy. Mickey immediately changed direction and headed inside. The puppy darted in after him. "Be careful pouring your milk! I just mopped the floor." Hands on her hips, she watched Devon stride toward her. "I didn't expect you so soon."

"Thought I might as well get it done."

His blue eyes swept toward the two small drying racks ready to hold neat rows of herbs. Three wicker baskets, filled with sprigs of hyssop and tiny-leafed thyme were near Sara's feet.

He didn't allow himself the luxury of scanning her slender frame. Without any reminders, he could too easily recall the tantalizing curves and swells hidden beneath her baggy sweater. His glance lifted quickly to meet hers. She seemed wary, uncertain of what to say.

He had too much on his mind to consider that he felt a little uncertain himself. Thinking only to finish here so he could get back to the mill, he acknowledged her with a stiff smile and reached for one of the screens. Tipping it, he glanced at the underside to see what his uncle had used to fasten the mesh to the wood frame. "How many more of these do you need?"

"A pair ought to do. I'll be putting on a chicken shortly," his aunt added, twirling a sprig of thyme she'd be adding to the pot. "As long as you're here you might as well stay to supper."

"I can't. I have to finish fixing that pipe and then I've papers to go through."

"I'll save the chicken for tomorrow, then."

"Don't save it on my account. I'll be leaving for Cork around noon tomorrow. Does Thomas have any more of this mesh around here?"

"You're going to Cork on a Sunday?"

"I've an appointment at a bank first thing Monday morning."

Kathleen's mouth pinched. "Now why would you be going to a bank?"

"For a loan," he replied, sounding quite reasonable despite the defensiveness settling over him. He regarded her levelly. "The mesh, Aunt Kathleen?"

"O'Donaughs don't borrow. They never have. If it's money you're short of, I've got a bit tucked away. There's no need to be getting it from anyone else."

"You don't have the kind of money I need. Even if you did, you wouldn't give it to me. Not to use for what I want."

Challenge shadowed his features. Kathleen recognized that much, but she didn't quite comprehend what he was talking about. It was apparent only that she wasn't going to approve of what she was about to hear.

Her eyes narrowed, she tipped her head in cautious inquiry. "What is it exactly that you'd be wanting, Devon?"

"The looms."

He wasn't going to argue. He wasn't going to defend. Plan A hadn't worked, so it was time to implement plan B. He'd have much preferred to have the mill pay its own way as it always had in the past. But that option wasn't available now. If he was going to modernize, he might as well do it the modern way. By going into debt.

"I'm going to borrow the down payment from a bank. While I'm there, I'm going to talk to them about financing the whole expansion."

Fortunately Kathleen knew nothing of finance. She therefore couldn't ask the kind of questions that Devon had been wrestling with the past few days. Questions such as whether the bank would even be interested in his collateral and how to substantiate the kind of growth he envisioned. That growth was essential to protect projected earnings.

He had the feeling Sara knew enough to verbalize the problems, though. From the corner of his eye, he saw her fiddling with a stem of hyssop. She appeared quite intent on what was being said.

Sara's considered silence wasn't lost on Kathleen, either. Though Devon's aunt was fairly ignorant of matters beyond her own borders, she was amazingly quick when it came to finding the right screw to turn.

"You know, Devon," she began in a tone as bland as the oatmeal he'd had for breakfast, "Sara and I were talking about your plans before you came. She's found a problem or two with them, though. Might be you'd want to talk to her about them before you go off to some fancy banker."

Appalled at the woman's audacity, Sara's glance flew from Devon to Kathleen. The older woman looked completely unconcerned at having so blatantly twisted what she'd said.

"Had you told me all your concerns?" she asked. "Or were there some we didn't get to?"

The woman was incorrigible. It was no wonder she gave Devon fits.

"I think we about covered it. But I don't think now is the time to discuss this, Kathleen." Anxious for an excuse to avoid Devon's glare, Sara glanced toward the baskets. "We shouldn't keep Devon. He has other things to do and you wanted to get the rest of this spread out before it molds. We can't do that until he makes another screen."

The woman was not to be dissuaded. "A few more minutes won't matter."

Devon seemed to agree. He moved closer, uneasiness falling over her like a shadow. He'd told her that one of the reasons he hadn't wanted her to stay was because of the ideas she might give his aunt. It didn't matter that she'd tried to keep her thoughts to herself. She'd done what he had said she'd do and his ominous silence now told her he wasn't overly pleased that she'd proved him right.

"I'd like to hear what you have to say."

"Devon, please."

"I'm going to hear it anyway. If not from you, from my aunt."

She didn't want to do this. She was afraid he would think her opinion another attack against him and she didn't want to be lumped together with all the other people he was no longer talking to. She needed to explain that what she felt he was doing was very different from what she felt for him. But how could she make him understand what she wasn't sure she understood herself. Especially with Kathleen watching so intently? Part of her wanted to protect him. Another part wanted to wring his neck for not just letting the matter drop.

A sense of self-preservation spurred her on. If he wouldn't drop it, she would. Glancing over her shoulder to the whitewashed cottage, she shielded her eyes against the brightness of the sun. "I wonder if Mickey's finished with his cookie. I promised I'd take him to the stream to see if it's gone down any. If it has, he said he wants to catch more salamanders." She smiled at Kathleen. "He wants them for your garden."

It took about three seconds for Kathleen's acknowledging smile to become an uncomprehending frown.

"He said you like them because they eat the bugs," Sara explained.

"He *said* that to you?"

"Aunt Kathleen," Devon cut in, impatient to have his own question answered. "Do you mind?"

"Yes, I mind. It's not possible that he'd have said as much to her. The boy scarcely utters a word."

"I'm sure that if Sara said he told her something, then he did. Now," he continued, dismissing the subject as well as his aunt by turning to Sara. The blue stripe on his gray polo shirt disappeared as he crossed his arms over it. "What is it you're not saying?"

"Please, Devon. Just let it go. Okay?"

As stubborn as he was, it was too much to hope that he would leave well enough alone. She already knew that he felt no one was on his side. What she didn't understand was why he was pushing her. Unless he was trying to push her farther away.

Fearing that was his purpose, she felt herself stiffen.

"Come on, Sara. What is it you have to say?"

"It's not that big a deal," she began, goaded by his insistence. "I just feel that Brigen Glen is special . . . and that it would be a mistake for you to try to change it."

He didn't like that. She hadn't thought he would. Just as she didn't think he'd let it go at that. His flat "Why?" compelled her to explain.

So she did. "Places like this are so scarce, Devon. There's a unity among the people here that can't exist if it gets bigger. A kind of peace. I've tried to, but I just don't understand how you can justify taking that away in return for all the problems your growth will cause. This village isn't prepared for the kind of issues it will have to face with your kind of progress.

"The women I met this morning," she offered as an example, "were talking about going to a market that to me sounds more like a country fair. It's a place people meet and gather and exchange what they have for what they haven't and they come away with a lot more than the sack of groceries I get when I go to the store. You put a store in here with the commercial goods your trucks will bring in from the city and those women will lose a lot of their sense of purpose. The cottage industries around here won't be able to compete. Then what happens to the people running them? It's their *job* to make or grow what they exchange or sell at the market. You'd be taking their jobs away.

"Not everyone can reeducate themselves to fit into what this place would grow into in ten years. They shouldn't have to. The people here are proud of what they do. If they don't have anything to do, if they can't do what they've done all their lives, you'll take that pride from them."

He'd asked for her opinion. Practically forced it from her. Devon reminded himself of that as he watched conviction play over her face. She believed in her position. But he believed in his just as fiercely. He'd just thought—hoped— that she might have appreciated his position, too.

"I'm not the tyrant everyone is making me out to be," he said, his voice far too calm. "I won't be taking anyone's pride, or their job, or their firstborn son," he added, since his temper was threatening. "I've thought about this a lot longer than you have and the advantages are stronger than the risks. I'd think you'd be all for this. You could stand to benefit, too, if your clients are wanting to buy my goods. As for the people in this village, they don't have the vaguest idea of what's in store for them ten years down the road if some changes aren't made now. That peace you talk about the people here feeling isn't peace at all. It's complacence. And if they don't stop settling for what they've always had, they're going to find they've got nothing at all."

"Now, Devon," Kathleen began, only to realize that he wasn't paying the least bit of attention to her. His narrowed eyes were fixed on Sara, who matched his glare beautifully.

Sara possessed a fair temper of her own. She just hadn't realized how quickly it could flair before she'd met Devon. "You're really incredible. You speak as if you're the only one around here with any sense. Don't you think the people who've lived here all of their lives know what it is they want? And what they don't want? That they should have some say in what happens to them and their children? You might be able to control your life and that of your family, but the power should end there. Serfdom went out in the past century," she reminded him. "Maybe if you'd stop trying to play feudal lord, you'd see that the only person truly served by your expansion is yourself. It's entirely possible that even if you reach your goal, you won't have what you want. Then all you've done is take away what this place once was."

For several seconds, all Sara could hear was the pounding of her heart. Devon said nothing. He didn't have to. The cool distance she saw in his eyes said it all.

She looked to Kathleen, who seemed inordinately pleased with the flying fur, and mumbled a quick, "Excuse me. I need to go for a walk."

Devon's fingers curled around Sara's arm, his grip insistent. "You're not going anywhere until you explain what you meant."

He could see confusion join Sara's agitation. Devon could appreciate the combination because he felt it himself. He also felt that a little privacy was in order.

Fortunately Kathleen was quick to catch that message.

"I'll be checking on Mickey," she said, looking as anxious to hear what they had to say to each other as she was to give them a chance to say it. A moment later, she was picking her way over the flagstones, casting a curious glance over her shoulder with every third step.

It wasn't until the slam of the screen door sliced through the heavy silence that Devon spoke. When he did, it was to voice the question Sara had been very much afraid he would ask.

Chapter Nine

Sara had spent most of her life as an observer. That was what one did when she grew up feeling like an outsider. Watching others' actions and reactions had been a way of entertaining herself. Seldom had she shared what she'd observed. Certainly she'd never spoken so boldly about her conclusions as she just had.

She enormously regretted her lapse.

"Tell me what you meant."

Devon's voice was low and insistent. Not angry as she'd feared it might be. Rather, impatient.

He'd yet to release her. Through the heavy knit of her sweater she could feel the heat of his hand. She kept her head turned away, her eyes trained on the herbs wilting in the basket. "About what?" she asked without challenge. "I said a lot of things. Far more than I should have."

"That may be." The pressure of his grip eased, his fingers sliding away with a certain reluctance. "But I want to know what you meant about my not having what I want when my plans are complete. All I *do* want is to see them finished. What else could there be?''

Pandora's box. Legend had it that all the world's evils had been contained in it and once the box was opened nothing was ever the same. The fate of the world hardly rested on what was happening on this tiny patch of it, but Sara felt very much as if she were about to take the lid off a potentially volatile issue now.

She met his eyes. The coolness there made her want to turn away. ''It's the reason you want all the changes that I'm talking about.''

''I've told you the reasons.''

''You've told me the surface ones,'' she countered, her voice soft. ''And I know you believe that growth is the answer. But it won't matter how much growth you can coax out of this glen, Devon. You can turn it into another Dublin with all of its jobs and excitement and hustle and whatever else it is that draws people to the city. But no matter what you do here, no matter how many changes you make, you can't force anyone to stay who doesn't want to stay. And none of your changes will bring your wife back.''

From behind them in the corral, Skye neighed. Merlot, as if in comment, whinnied from the pasture. The sounds were carried on the breeze, barely noticed by Sara as she fell silent. Her last words hung suspended between them, echoing with more import than she'd intended to give them.

Sara held her breath, waiting. No expression betrayed Devon's thoughts. All she could see in the rigid lines of his face was the fatigue etched in it and the stubborn determination that made him deny just how very tired he was. She didn't know if he would lash out or turn away. She wouldn't have blamed him for either. What she didn't expect was his weary admission.

"I stopped wanting my wife long before she'd left here, Sara. What I want has nothing to do with her, because once she realized I wasn't leaving here, nothing I did mattered to her. I'll go tell Mickey you're ready for him."

He turned before she could speak. Sara thought that just as well. There was nothing for her to say and she'd already overstepped herself as it was. But even as she watched him call through the open back door, she realized that he hadn't really denied what she'd said.

There was little time to consider that, however. Mickey, having been told that she was ready to catch salamanders, was ready to go. So with Tug in tow, the two of them left Devon to build a drying rack and Kathleen to wonder what Sara had said that left her nephew so subdued.

Sara was certain that four salamanders were enough for the average vegetable garden. That was how many Mickey had caught between the rocks within half an hour of their reaching the stream. By mutual agreement, they had come to the cathedral-like place where she'd run into Devon yesterday. Sara had chosen it because she badly needed the sanctuary the setting offered. Mickey had picked it because it was the best place to find the little brown lizards. Now, their catch prowling the sides of a jar with holes poked in its lid, Mickey set the container between his crossed legs and looked to Sara. She'd perched on a moss-covered stump after declaring the water too high to continue their search farther upstream. Though the water was already receding, the rains had swollen the stream beyond its normal banks.

Mickey didn't mind that their mission had met an early end. Sara was pretty sure he didn't care what he did so long as someone let him tag along. When he was with her, though, he liked to listen to her talk. He asked her now if she'd tell him a story. Willingly she gave him the attention he craved.

Being Fiona's granddaughter, she had heard a wealth of fantastic tales as a child. Therefore coming up with one wasn't a problem. From her repertoire, she ruled out those about wood nymphs and faerie princesses, since their appeal wouldn't have been so great to a little boy. And because Mickey was awfully young, she decided against those about the trolls who lived under bridges and routinely ate small children and gnomes for lunch. But the story that had always been her favorite seemed perfectly suited. It appealed to her especially here in this wooded setting. So on the very soil from which the myth had purportedly sprung, she wrapped her arms around her knees as if about to share some great secret and told him the legend of the golden doe.

The boy's eyes were wide as she explained how a druid priest, one of those practitioners of mysterious rites among the ancient Celts, had taken a young girl and changed her life forever. The girl, Sarina was her name, had displeased the priest by refusing to marry the man the priest had selected for her.

"She had never met the man she was to marry," Sara told a very attentive Mickey, "so he wasn't the problem. She just didn't want to marry anyone right then. Sarina had always been a strong-willed girl and had decided that she wanted to choose her own husband. Since she was still very young, she felt she had plenty of time to find the right man and to fall in love. But in those days marriages were often arranged, and young people did as they were told. Even if you objected, you didn't argue with a druid priest. Sarina did, though, because she was very outspoken, and she made the priest so angry with her willfulness that he cast a spell over her."

"What kind of a spell?" Mickey wanted to know.

"Well, the druids were very adept with their magic. And very creative. So the next midnight, when they met in the woods with the stream where they carried out their rituals..."

"Like this stream?"

"Probably," she agreed, wondering if his furtive glance toward the trees meant he expected a heavily bearded man in a hooded gown to appear. "They almost always held their ceremonies in oak groves and near rivers and lakes. This place would have worked quite well, I would think. Anyway," she continued, "that night he conjured up the spell that turned her into a doe. One minute she'd stood by the stream, a golden-haired child. The next she was a small deer, blinking at him with her big brown eyes. No one knows if she understood what he said, but he told her that since it was her wish to find her own mate, she could spend eternity doing just that."

Sara hugged her knees tighter. "The catch was that she would have only a short time every hundred years in which to conduct her search. She would come with the first light of day, when the fog was its thickest, and she had only until the full of the moon before she had to leave. Her search would never be easy. It wouldn't be enough that she just care for the man, she had to love him unconditionally, as he must love her. For without that kind of love, she had no hope of ever being human again, of ever being real. Each time she appeared, she would be given only one chance. And that was with the first eligible bachelor she encountered upon her transformation. If they didn't fall in love, she'd have to try again in the next century."

"She just went away?"

Sara nodded. "But she went away very unhappy. And because she would be forced again into that hundred-year isolation of living without love, if the man failed to win her heart she would take his happiness to sustain her. Without that she would die."

Mickey, possessing the literal practicality of a six-year-old, had only one other concern. "Where does she stay the rest of the time? Doesn't she have anyone to take care of her?"

"She lives in the mist with the wood nymphs and the elves. I don't think she's miserable or anything like that," she assured because she could see that Mickey didn't like the idea of the poor doe being all alone. "One of these days she'll probably find the love she's looking for and then the spell will be broken."

"I'll love her," Mickey said innocently.

The child's gentle offer touched Sara, making her smile. "And I'm sure she'd love you if you ever met. But no one knows when she's coming, or if she's ever been around."

Chewing his bottom lip, the boy mulled this over for a moment. Then having come to some conclusion he didn't care to share, he propped his chin on his fist. "Will you tell me another story, please?"

"She can tell you another some other time, lad. It's time you should be getting home."

Neither Mickey nor Sara had heard Devon's approach. Both looked surprised to see him, though Sara seemed more startled than pleased.

Mickey was on his feet in an instant, holding up his precious jar. "Sara was telling me about a doe. Not a real one," he clarified. "Not real most of the time, I mean. See what we caught?"

Giving the fabric at his knees a yank, Devon hunched down by the child. Mickey's features were animated, his eyes far less somber than they'd been for a long while. "I heard," Devon said. "And these salamanders are just the thing to keep the white flies off Aunt Kathleen's vegetables. Why don't you take them to her now? Patrick is waiting for you at my house with Tug. You'll be having supper at Kathleen's again tonight. Run along now and they'll walk back with you."

With a grin because he had a gift for his Great-aunt Kathleen, he started toward the path leading to Devon's cottage. Half a dozen steps and he turned around to walk back to Sara. He gave her a quick hug and, holding his jar like an offering, marched back to the path. She could hear Patrick yelling at him to hurry up even before Mickey's red shirt was no longer visible through the leaves.

Devon watched the faint smile fade from Sara's lips. She seemed more cautious now that Mickey was gone, a little more reluctant about meeting his eyes. She'd stood as soon as the child had run off. After absently brushing at a piece of moss clinging to her denims, she pushed her hands into the pockets of her pale pink sweater.

"You're good for the boy." He'd been watching her with Mickey. And listening. He hadn't meant to eavesdrop, but as he'd approached, the dulcet sounds of her voice had drawn him as they had so often before. It was soothing just to listen to her at times. A discovery his cousin's son had also apparently made. Between hearing those calming sounds and seeing the rapt attention in Mickey's face, he'd been loath to interrupt.

Seeing the way she hesitated now, as if she weren't comfortable in his presence, made him wish he hadn't.

Sara shrugged off the compliment. Alert to the tension in his powerful body, she felt her own nerves tighten in response. She didn't want to be that attuned to him. Nor did she want him to realize how he affected her. "He's a great little kid. He just seems to need attention."

"I've a feeling you're right." Keeping his distance, he shifted his weight to his other foot. He felt uneasy, though he was perfectly justified in being here. It was his property, after all. Yet she made him feel as if he were intruding on what belonged to her. "It's been difficult for him the past couple of years. His father's rarely around and his mother isn't very happy with her husband being gone so much. The arrangement seems necessary to them, but it's wearing on the boys.''

"It bothers you that you can't change that situation for them, doesn't it?"

"I care about them. I care about what influences them," he added, subtly veering the conversation from her observation. "I couldn't help overhearing what you were telling Mickey. I know you and I don't see eye to eye on this, but I don't think you should be telling him stories about imaginary does and elves and such. Believing in fairy tales does nothing for children but set them up for disappointment when they find out that the stories aren't true. At the very least you should have told him that the story was only a product of someone's imagination. Not something to be believed."

"You never had a make-believe friend when you were a child?" she asked. "Or believed in Santa Claus?"

He didn't remember, but he was sure he hadn't. At least the part about the imaginary friends. A belief in St. Nicholas had managed to survive until Devon was six, but that story had unraveled when his father had forgotten about Christmas the year Devon's mother died. Not that it mattered. Not to Devon. "Don't, Sara."

"Don't what?" She moved closer, drawn by the bleakness in his eyes. Already far too sensitive to him, she couldn't help aching for the little boy inside the man—the little boy who'd never been a child. "Don't ask questions? Don't disagree with you? Don't get too close?"

His jaw clenched. Her perceptions were too direct for comfort, too accurate to deny.

A gentle plea entered her voice. She didn't want him to close her out. Not again. "There's nothing wrong with letting a child use his imagination. Fantasy is a part of growing up. It's what is behind the battles Patrick wages with his toy soldiers. It's what will prompt the journeys for the train you're making for Mickey. I understand that you feel life is hard enough without adding more disappointments to it. But it's because it can be so difficult that a person needs an escape once in a while.'' She touched her fingers to where the muscles bunched on his jaw. His eyes jerked to hers. "Maybe it wouldn't hurt you to fantasize a little."

She hadn't meant to word her suggestion quite as she had. But there was no time to worry about its subtler implications. Devon slowly lifted his hand, taking hers to move it from his face. For one sinking moment, she thought he intended to push her away. Instead, he raised her hand to his lips and pressed a kiss to her palm. "I already do," he said and folded their hands together.

He drew her closer, holding her with the quiet intensity in his eyes. "You make me imagine totally impossible things."

Leaves rustled with the soft, sea-scented breeze. That same breeze lifted strands of her hair. Devon smoothed them from her face, leaving his fingers to caress the translucent skin of her cheek. His voice was deep and oddly pensive.

"I remember the first time I saw you. You were a little farther up the stream, drinking from it. Something about you reminded me of a gazelle, or a deer." He gave a quiet, disbelieving chuckle. "Actually, what you reminded me of was the doe in the legend you were telling Mickey about. I think I was about his age the first time I heard it."

"Did you believe it then?"

He shook his head, a faint disappointment entering his eyes. "No." He carried his touch along her jaw, seeming fascinated with the contrast of his callused fingers against her smooth skin. "You make me want to believe in that magic now, though."

Sara felt the bump of her heart against her ribs. His words, like his touch, wove a sensual magic of their own.

Her smile was soft, inviting. "Maybe if you'd stop being such a cynic, you would believe. Even if it's just for a little while."

"Maybe I'm afraid to believe."

They were speaking of more than fantasy. The words left unspoken had to do with love and trust and all things that made a person vulnerable. With his admission, Sara knew that he was just as vulnerable to her as she was to him. Sharing that risk made taking a chance a little easier.

"I'm afraid not to," she told him.

He regarded her warily, but the reason for his caution was difficult to discern. His eyes darkened, replacing wariness with heat. With the pad of his thumb he traced the fullness of her bottom lip. "I'm going to kiss you, Sara."

Longing trembled through her. "Please."

A faint groan sounded from deep within his chest. Anchoring one hand in her hair, the other around her small waist, he pulled her against him. A moment later, his mouth closed over hers.

She opened to him. With the touch of his tongue came the heat. She gasped with the quickness of it. She'd wanted his kiss, needed it desperately. But she hadn't expected the hunger, the raw urgency. Not his, though she felt his body harden as she moved against him. But her own hunger. She tasted need, and that need was coming from within.

Sliding her arms around his neck, she sought him as he sought her. Their tongues tangled, searching smooth and secret surfaces. Each breath she drew brought with it the essence of him. It filled her, breathing life into every cell and pore. It felt as if he were becoming necessary, an essential reason for her being.

She didn't know how it was possible, but he managed to deepen the kiss. Angling her head to his shoulder, his mouth creating sensual havoc with every nerve in her body, he worked his way under the hem of her loose sweater. His hand was cool on her heated skin, but she scarcely noticed. She noticed only his slight hesitation when he realized that she wasn't wearing a bra.

The moan issuing at the contact could have been hers or his. She couldn't tell. There was no barrier between his palm and her breast and when his fingers flexed over her fullness, she was aware of little other than the jolt of sensation his touch elicited.

Devon felt her delicate shudder. She was all warmth and sweet eagerness in his arms. He had known, somehow, that he had to have her, that he would have her. A vague sense of the inevitable had seemed to predict it. That sense of inevitability led him now to soften his kisses. The demands of his body threatened to override his sensibilities, and if he didn't slow down he'd take her right where they stood. He wanted her in his bed.

He pulled back, wondering how it was possible to want so badly. "Come with me, Sara?"

She didn't hesitate before she nodded. Nor did she ask where he wanted to take her. She simply slipped her hand in his. Something about that acceptance touched him deeply.

The sound of water rushing over rocks followed them as he led her by the hand, taking her deeper into the woods that would lead to his cottage. Rays of sunlight filtered through the trees, dappling the forest floor with shadow and light. Mosses and ferns boasted every shade of green, the moisture remaining on some plants making them shimmer like emeralds.

A moss-covered log lay back in the thickest ferns, the trees overhead enclosing the space like a protective canopy. Devon started to help her over the barrier, too impatient to take the long way around. But Sara had stopped.

"No, Devon. Here."

He turned at her soft command and felt a jolt of pure longing.

A shaft of light illuminated her hair, backlighting it with a golden glow. She reminded him of an angel, and when she smiled at him he could have sworn he heard the heavens sigh.

The hard line of his jaw was shadowed with the late-afternoon stubble of beard and felt abrasive to the touch. Laying her palm to his cheek, Sara leaned forward to touch her lips to his. There was no need for words. She wanted none. Promises could be broken. And she'd rather have never known a promise from Devon than to have him offer words he might regret.

He didn't seem interested in words anyway. Taking her by the shoulders, he pulled her back just far enough to be certain he understood her message. Raw need tightened his features as he searched her eyes. He must have found the answer he sought. As she whispered his name, he took the invitation she offered.

The touch of his mouth was teasing. He nipped tiny kisses to her temple, the soft skin behind her ear, the arched line of her neck. Sliding his hand beneath her sweater, he pushed the fabric up and over her head. Her hair fell back over her shoulders, cloaking them in a gossamer veil. Gooseflesh covered her skin and puckered her nipples.

Her shy smile was a combination of innocence and seduction. Already inflamed by the sight of her slender body, Devon quickly pulled off his own sweater. He drew her back to him, warming her against his muscled chest as he eased her onto the soft clover. The cushion of tiny yellow flowers was crushed beneath them. He didn't notice. Nor did he notice the wind that caressed them or the birds that filled the air with their sweet song. Easing his weight over her, his seeking tongue pushed past her lips. With the kiss came the fire.

Devon's touch was light, thrilling. He didn't demand. Not at first. For a while it seemed to Sara that he meant to drive her quietly out of her mind with the touch of his lips to her breast, the caress of his hand over her stomach. Strange, exciting sensations coursed through her. Tantalizing feelings that made her restive. He caused an ache to build inside her, an unfamiliar hollowness that demanded to be filled. She wriggled beneath him, seeking him through the restraining fabric of their jeans.

What she lacked in experience, she made up in instinct. Mimicking his touch, she followed his lead—where he would let her. Tension coiled his body—a tension far different from that which she usually sensed in him—and he insisted that if she wasn't careful this would be over before it started. She wanted to feel him. All of him. When she told him that, his low murmur told her he wanted it, too. But not until he had grown impatient with the barriers himself did he strip away the rest of their clothes.

Skin finally met heated skin. Smooth to rough, hard to soft. Devon ached with the pleasure found in those contrasts. Nearly ready to explode with need, he slid his hand beneath Sara's hips to align himself more intimately. His control threatened to snap when he felt the heat of her against him. But some shred of sanity held him back, making him realize that if he obeyed his body's demand to forget everything else and bury himself in her, he might hurt her badly.

Every muscle in his body stiffened. He hadn't expected the barrier he felt, though he truly hadn't given the matter of her experience any thought. He wasn't allowed to think of it now, either. The enormity of what she was offering barely registered when Sara arched instinctively toward him, urging him on when he would have taken it slower. A moment later, sheathed in her warmth, he drank in her shuddered gasp and gave in to the urgency. Moving beneath him, whispering his name, she wouldn't let him do otherwise.

Reality became a misty glen suffused with the fading light of day. Time had suspended itself, then led to the long minutes Devon held Sara close as their breathing quieted. A languid peace had seeped into him. The feeling was unfamiliar. Almost as unfamiliar as the tenderness he felt for the small woman nestled beneath him.

He lifted himself to his elbows so she could breathe. "You should have told me," he whispered, brushing the damp hair from her forehead. "I didn't mean to hurt you."

A soft smile touched her mouth. The matter of her virginity was a moot point. "You didn't hurt me. What we did was beautiful." A piece of moss clung to the smooth skin of his shoulder. She brushed it off, leaving her hand to lovingly caress the muscles there. "You're beautiful."

His light chuckle made his stomach flex against her abdomen. "I'm not sure if a man should be called that or not."

"Why not? It's the truth."

"Oh, Sara," he breathed, and leaned down to capture her smile with his own.

Devon was still smiling when he pulled back to draw her up with him. Clover was caught in her hair. He ignored that in favor of her sweater. Evening was rapidly descending and the cool air caused her to shiver. "Here. Put this on before you freeze."

He gathered his own clothes while she pulled on her sweater and jeans and shook out her hair. He'd thought to take her to his cottage to make love with her. Even now the thought of having her beneath him in his bed had him hardening again. But laying with her here in the woods had seemed very right somehow. This first time.

Tugging on his zipper, he watched her turn to him. She was oddly silent.

His belt buckle made a dull clink as he fastened it. "Is something wrong?"

"You're going to the mill now?"

He didn't know what to make of the hesitation that marked her expression. He hadn't even thought of the mill. Why, he wondered, the dark slash of his eyebrows arching in incomprehension, was she concerned about it now?

"You told Kathleen you had paperwork to do there," she clarified. Now that he wasn't touching her, she felt suddenly unsure. "For your trip to Cork."

"No, Sara," he assured, understanding her sudden insecurity. He folded her in his arms, his touch tender, almost protective. "I can stop by the mill in the morning. I'll have plenty of time before I have to leave for Cork. I know you've been wanting to go into Durry, so I thought you might want to come with me that far. Right now, I thought we'd go see what we can find to eat in my pantry. Then," he added as his head lowered, "I've another appetite I've a need to satisfy."

It wasn't long after the moon had risen that Sara fell asleep. Long after she did, Devon remained awake, holding her, listening to the sounds he hadn't noticed in a long time. An owl hooted nearby, so suspiciously close that Devon thought its nest might be under one of the eaves. In the distance, the bark of a nocturnal fox was joined by the yelping of its pack. The commotion died down within moments, leaving only the silence again. The silence sounded like peace. The peace Sara had said she'd felt here.

A sliver of moonlight filtered between the woven curtains. It fell across her arm where it lay on his chest. He scarcely felt the weight. He was more aware of her closeness, of how her head nestled on his shoulder, and of her deep, even breaths fanning the hair on his chest. He'd known all along that he'd wanted to make love with her. He'd known all along that he'd wanted to hold her. What he hadn't realized was how profoundly he'd be moved by what they'd shared. He could love this woman.

That knowledge would have shaken him had he not understood what had happened tonight. What he and Sara shared was special. That much he readily admitted. But it was also temporary. For now, because of her, he could let himself believe a little in the fantasy. He could enjoy the time he had with her. But soon reality would return. She didn't approve of what he needed to do and he couldn't offer her anything else. For now, he wouldn't think of tomorrow.

She stirred against him, rubbing her nose where his chest hair tickled it. He could tell the very moment she realized there was something different about where she slept. Her body tensed, then relaxed an instant later.

Moving her head, she blinked up at him in the pale light. The sheet fell back as she shifted to her elbow, and with the tips of her fingers she traced the furrows in his brow. "Can't you sleep?"

He didn't want to sleep, though for the first time in weeks he felt as though untroubled slumber were possible. He kissed the concern from her forehead. "I just want to enjoy holding you."

"You need your rest."

"What I need is for you to go back to sleep." The palm of his hand skimmed along her hip. "Or neither one of us will get any rest."

A soft, seductive smile played over her features. She moved like a spirit, weightless, effortless. The brush of her breasts to his chest was the merest tease of skin, the touch of her lips to his, a whisper of promise. "I'm not tired anymore."

"Witch," he murmured, grinning.

Sara's laugh was light, little more than a strangled giggle really when he flipped her over. It wasn't long before the laughter died. The love growing in her heart found its expression and she was lost again in the sheer beauty of what she and Devon shared.

She loved him. The knowledge didn't surprise her. It just felt right. Along with that feeling came another—a sense of coming home. In Devon's arms, she'd felt as if she'd finally found where she'd always belonged.

Unfortunately it wasn't long before that feeling was threatened.

Chapter Ten

"Whoever was here knew what they were looking for."

Paper rustled, the sound seeming magnified in the Sunday silence of the mill. Devon had searched the file cabinets next to his desk three times. His response this time to not finding what he was looking for was to slam his fist against the wall.

Sara jumped and hugged her arms to herself. They had come to the mill five minutes ago and she'd yet to step past the doorway of Devon's office. Still there, she watched helplessly as he began going through desk drawers he'd already been through twice.

Papers were everywhere. The mess wasn't just Devon's usual clutter. Papers, magazines, files had all been deliberately scattered. It would take hours to sort it all out.

The mug on Devon's desk nearly shook off the edge when he slammed the drawer. A curse, low and distinct, matched the fury in his face. Never had Sara seen anyone look as dangerous as Devon did at that moment.

An empty file folder lay at her feet. She bent to pick it up.

"Leave it."

She straightened. If he didn't want her help, she wouldn't force it on him.

Sara's sudden timidity made Devon wince. He drew a deep breath and let it out slowly, stabilizing himself. "The ledgers are gone. So is the file with all my projections in it."

"Those are what you needed for your meeting at the bank?"

"Those and my plans for the mill and the village. They took them, too. I'll have to use the drafts of the plans I have at home."

The desk chair had been overturned. Sidestepping it, he took Sara by the arm and started out the door.

"What about this?" Her glance swept the room. "Shouldn't we clean it up?"

"I'll do it when I get back. It'd take all day to straighten this out and I don't have that kind of time right now. I intend to keep my appointment in the morning. That's what this is all about anyway. Whoever did this knew I was going to a bank and they know what I'm going for. I'm getting the money to make my improvements, Sara. They're not going to stop me."

From the determination etched in his hard features, Sara didn't doubt his claim. She also didn't doubt that whoever was responsible for ransacking his office would be well advised to remain anonymous. But it wasn't until they'd locked up the mill and were headed back to Devon's cottage in his horse-drawn jaunting car that she considered asking who that person, or persons, might be.

Merlot's hooves beat a rhythmic cadence on the dirt road. Sara sat next to Devon on the padded leather seat, wishing she could absorb the tranquillity of the morning rather than his tension. Ever since she'd awakened this morning to find him drinking coffee at his kitchen table, her insecurities had threatened to take hold. Devon had staved them off that time by giving her a smile that turned her knees to butter. He had kept them at bay again an hour ago when he'd reminded her that he'd take her to Durry. She'd been afraid he'd either forgotten or regretted the offer. It wasn't like her to be so tractable.

Now that Devon was so silent, she again felt unsure of what she should do. Though he held the reins loosely, his elbows resting on the knees of his faded jeans, his jaw was locked so tightly she thought his teeth might shatter. Two days ago, if she'd had a question, she'd simply have asked.

Disgusted with herself, she started to do what she should have done five minutes ago. When she looked over at him, though, her question turned into a frown.

The frown wasn't for Devon. It was for what she glimpsed when she'd turned her head. From the corner of her eye she caught a movement in the distance behind them. She turned to get a better look. There was nothing there except lovely green hills dotted with stacks of golden hay. She looked back to Devon. He hadn't noticed a thing.

"I wonder who did it," she finally mumbled, thinking her anxieties were getting the better of her.

His tone was low, his voice tight. "I've just been wondering that myself. The only person I mentioned this meeting to was Kathleen." He paused, considering again what he'd considered before. "I can't very well picture her creeping around in the dead of night to do such a thing. She doesn't agree with me, but I doubt she's turned into a vandal."

They'd come to the road leading through the woods to his cottage. With a flick of the reins, he turned the carriage onto it. "I hadn't even told Kevin. All I said to him was that I had business in Cork. I had to tell him that much because, being my foreman, he had to know that I'd be gone for a couple of days.''

Would Kathleen have mentioned it to someone in passing? Sara wondered. Kevin's wife, perhaps? Kathleen had said that the young woman would be stopping by to show her how the lace Kathleen had made looked on their baby's christening gown. Or maybe one of the women from the mill? His aunt knew everyone, after all.

Sara was about to mention that when a vague prickling sensation skittered across the back of her neck. Touching her fingers to her nape, she turned again, her glance skimming the thick of the woods. Nothing looked at all unusual.

She looked back to Devon. He was too preoccupied to notice her perplexity. His cottage had come into view. "Hold these," he absently mumbled when he drew the carriage to a stop and handed her the reins. A moment later, he jumped down and disappeared inside to get his plans.

After another glance behind her, Sara forced her attention away from what was obviously her imagination. Toying with the thin strips of leather, she breathed in the pungent scent of the earth, hoping to relieve the odd skittishness she felt. She wished that Devon could feel the quiet as she sometimes could. She was fairly certain, though, that he relied only on himself for his solutions and didn't much allow anyone or anything to help. She took another breath, only to have its potential effect canceled by the sharp sound of his front door closing.

The progress she'd made toward her own inner calm was dubious at best. Her glance flew to him, searching the rugged lines of his face when he swung easily onto the platform and sat down beside her. Carefully he placed a cardboard tube under the seat.

He seemed a little less agitated now that he had something concrete to take to his meeting. Sara saw no point in undoing that small gain. Therefore she didn't mention that it felt as if they'd been followed. The feeling wasn't there anymore anyway. She concentrated on making herself smile. Her reward for that easy effort was the unexpected brush of his lips over hers.

"I'm glad you're with me, Sara," he told her and grazed his knuckles over the smooth skin of her cheek.

The admission came far easier than Devon would have expected. Some truths, it seemed, couldn't be denied. If it hadn't been for her presence this morning, he might very well have let his anger at this latest affront get the best of him. She had accepted his anger calmly, allowing him to feel it rather than chastising him as Kathleen would have done. His aunt would have told him that he was only getting what he'd asked for by not listening to her and everyone else. Sara might not agree with his plans, but she didn't agree with the methods chosen to oppose them, either.

There was something else about her, too. When he looked into her eyes, he could almost feel the weight being lifted. If there was one thing Sara could do, it was make him forget what troubled him. Or if not forget, to relieve the matter of its immediate import.

She did so now quite effortlessly.

On Sunday, those so inclined went to church in Durry. Since word had passed yesterday that the bridge had held and the stream could be crossed, they passed several families on their way back from that town. Sara returned the greetings and the stares, and being the curious sort proceeded to question Devon about who everyone was and who they were related to. They passed from the rolling mountains into the lowlands along the coast, the whole of Bantry Bay gleaming like a sapphire, and she spotted Dunboy Castle. He therefore had to tell her how the last garrison to defend it refused to surrender until the walls had been reduced to rubble. With a teasing smile, she told him she could see a little of him in that story, and instead of being defensive about the comparison he decided he rather liked it.

She managed to keep him talking for the better part of the fifteen-mile ride. But it wasn't until he noticed her toying with the ring she'd pulled from under the collar of her sweater that he realized there was more to her interest than simple curiosity. She was trying to keep her own mind occupied. Grateful for the escape she had offered him, he'd forgotten that the reason she wanted to go into Durry in the first place was because she harbored a few anxieties of her own.

Not knowing what to say to ease them, he took her hand, folding it in his so she couldn't worry the ring so much.

Durry was a place caught between centuries. Its population was five times that of Brigen Glen, but even with more than a thousand citizens, its streets were as quiet today. All the businesses along the flower-lined main street were closed, though a few horses stood dutifully guarding the posts they'd been hitched to and a couple of cars were parked along the curbs.

The old met the new everywhere one looked. A modern cinema boasted a fairly recent release from America, but farther down the street loomed the remains of a sixteenth-century battlement. Marketing was the district's livelihood, and though English signs marked the storefronts, on market days Gaelic was the vernacular.

Sara had only been here once before, on her way to Brigen Glen. Since then, she'd been told much about the town. Besides everything that Beth and Kathleen had mentioned, she knew that the messenger service she'd used to send the samples of Devon's fabric a few days ago was around the corner from the bakery they passed—and that the church was at the end of Ballingeary Hill Road.

It was to the church that they went now, and she couldn't help feeling a strange ambivalence about what she might find there.

St. Sebastian's looked as Sara suspected the church in Brigen Glen once had. Small and sturdy and with the same heavy doors, it sat on a nicely kept lawn surrounded by bushes of holly and yew. The cornerstone bore a date obscured by a particularly healthy shrub, but the sign near the sidewalk clearly indicated times of masses and confessions. Since it was nearing midafternoon, services were long over.

Devon cautiously watched her as they pulled to a halt in front of the rectory next door. She'd yet to let go of his hand.

"Would you like me to come with you?"

Her eyes swung to his, vulnerable and uncertain. "Would you?"

She hadn't dared ask him that herself, though the thought had been with her for miles. She didn't want him to leave her yet, and it was his intention to go on to Cork from here. Before he did, she needed to know if she would see him again. It hadn't seemed necessary to ask that until she realized he hadn't said exactly how long he'd be in Cork. Kathleen had received a card saying Thomas would be home on Tuesday. Once Sara gave Thomas the ring, she really had no reason to stay.

Devon's question, however, gave her a reprieve. If he went with her, he wouldn't leave right now. That meant she could concentrate on the other matter she'd also dwelled on. Days ago, the thought had planted itself in her head that she might not be meant to discover her family. She wasn't sure where the thought had come from exactly, but Kathleen's comment yesterday about the Fates had only compounded the feeling.

"Ready?" Devon asked.

Not really, she thought, but jumped off the seat anyway.

The priest who answered the rectory door was a kindly man in his middle years who possessed a manner as expansive as his middle. His hair was as black as his suit, except for his sideburns, which matched his white collar, and wire-rimmed glasses perched on the end of his ruddy nose. He listened to Sara's explanation about what she wanted and, telling her she was more than welcome to peruse the available records, he introduced himself as Father Walsh and invited her and Devon into his impeccably tidy office. The room was remarkably austere, its only decoration a cross on the wall and a small potted violet in the window.

The first question the priest asked when they sat down in the two ladderback chairs facing his well-oiled desk was if she had her birth certificate. Tracing one's roots usually began with the parents, he explained.

When she said she'd never seen it, the man's wiry eyebrows jerked in curiosity.

Devon apparently found her response interesting, too, though Sara found nothing unusual about it herself. She'd never needed her birth certificate. When she'd started school, usually the first place evidence of age or citizenship would be required, her grandmother had registered her. Sara had never learned to drive so she hadn't needed the certificate to obtain a driver's license. And when she'd needed a passport, her grandmother had already taken care of that, too. "My grandmother had hoped to bring me here herself one day. She'd obtained a passport for me when I was nine. You renew them by mailing in the old one," she added, just in case the priest didn't know that.

"I see," the reverend muttered in the manner of one who clearly doesn't. "What about your other relatives?"

She twisted the ring on its chain. "There are none that I know of," she quietly admitted.

There was something about saying that aloud that made her voice lose a little of its energy. It wasn't quite so easy to smile as it had been before, either. Brushing aside the tiny ache the words had brought, she told him that all she knew was that her grandmother's name had been Fiona, and her father's was John. They'd both been Madigans. She knew nothing of her mother.

"Your parents were born in America?" the priest wanted to know.

"My father was born here." *When I left, it was just my little one and me,* she remembered Fiona saying. "My grandmother left here with him when he was a baby."

It wasn't much to go on, but Father Walsh looked like a man who enjoyed a mystery, and Devon, though silent, was interested, too. With the three of them looking, it took less than two hours for them to go through the cumbersome volumes he brought from a panel behind the wall. Halfway into the project, the priest brought in tea. Shortly after that, he called the parishioner who'd invited him to supper to request half an hour's delay. The man was kindly and as helpful as he knew how to be. But having only been in the area for fifteen years and not having known anyone from Brigen Glen except the people who came to his church from there now, he was hard pressed to help further when their search turned up nothing.

He had only one suggestion. Taking off his glasses to pinch the bridge of his nose, he offered it. "You might try the presbytery across from St. Mary's Cathedral in Cork. They've records there of baptisms and marriages going back to 1748."

Devon stood, rotating his shoulders to loosen the kinks after two hours of bending over books. "Would they have records from someplace as far away as Brigen Glen?"

"They might, seeing as how not all those that were at the church in your village were brought here when Father Flannigan passed on. But mind you, they'll only have records concerning the faithful. Civil marriages and records of death would be matters for the county.''

"Would those records be at city hall or the court house?" Devon wanted to know, and the men, faced with a puzzle they hadn't been able to solve, pondered other possibilities.

Sara didn't really hear them. As they debated which place might be the best for her to go from here, she was aware only of the deep drone of their voices. Their words didn't register. She sat staring at the volume in her lap, the neatly penned names of people she didn't know blurring into dates that meant nothing to her. The anticipation she'd felt when she'd opened the first heavy book had slowly given way to disappointment. Now an odd sort of emptiness filled her. It was the same feeling she'd fought the other day at the cemetery when she'd searched the markers and monuments and discovered nothing but a vague sense of loss.

That feeling wasn't so vague right now. And she wasn't able to fight it as she had then.

Carefully she closed the book and placed it on the corner of the priest's desk. She hadn't moved abruptly, yet the men's conversation halted, as if they expected her to comment.

Her voice was little more than a whisper. "Thank you for your time, Father. I'm sorry I kept you from your supper." She backed toward the door. It was rude of her to leave so quickly, she knew, but the room suddenly seemed too small, the walls too confining. "Thank you," she added again and kept backing up.

She didn't realize how alarmed Father Walsh was by her lack of color. Nor was she aware of how closely Devon had been watching her—or how he stopped the priest from following her when she headed outside. She wasn't at all sure where she was going. She just knew she needed to walk, to move.

She started past the church, hurrying by the gate in the fence that led to its cemetery. She would find no one there who belonged to her. A dozen steps later, she stood at a curb. The road stretched empty ahead, leading out into the country. On the opposite side of the street, past a building that looked like a museum, was a little park.

It was there that Devon found her sitting on a bench beneath the wide arms of an elm.

The bench was made of wooden slats and it creaked when Devon sat down next to her. For nearly a minute, he said nothing. He simply studied her delicate profile as she stared across the park's wide lawn, her attention seemingly on the children playing in a wading pool beyond a splashing fountain. Devon doubted she really saw the children. Though her features were relaxed, her glance was unfocused, her thoughts turned inward. Her hand, where it held the ring on its chain, was clenched so fiercely to her chest that her knuckles were white.

Except for the slow blink of her lashes, she didn't move. Not even so much as to glance at him. "Are you leaving now?"

"Soon," he said. "But I'd like you to tell me what happened back there first."

She gave a dismissing shrug. "I just needed some air, I guess. It was awfully stuffy in there."

"No, Sara." He touched his fingers to her chin, coaxing her to look at him. When she did, he found her eyes suspiciously bright. "It was more than that. I want to know what's wrong."

"Don't be nice to me, Devon. It'll just make it worse."

"Make what worse?"

She turned away, refusing to indulge his curiosity. She supposed she owed him some sort of explanation. But she couldn't bare her soul to him and then watch him walk away. It was therefore necessary to reduce what troubled her to the simplest possible terms. Maybe by minimizing it to him it wouldn't seem that important to her, either.

"I suppose I just realized that I don't have anyone," she said as lightly as she could and immediately knew it had been a mistake to speak at all.

It was too late to take back the words, so she tried to cover the hurt that had come with them. "I've known that consciously, of course. I mean, I knew it when my grandmother died, and that was weeks ago. It always had been just the two of us, and then, when that happened, there was just me. So it's not as if I hadn't thought about it before."

Oh, Lord, she thought, as a knot formed in her throat. The more she explained, the more of an explanation her rationale seemed to require. And the more she needed the catharsis of having someone listen. By his patient silence Devon told her he understood, that having someone listen was a need with which he was intimately familiar.

"I'd always felt connected to something because of her. At least I knew there was someone I was linked to. When I got here, it seemed that if I found out more about her or my parents, I could keep that connection." She swallowed. Hard.

She still clutched her grandmother's ring. Prying her fingers from around it, Devon drew her hand away. Little half-moons marked her palm where her nails had pressed into it.

Holding her hand in his, Devon smoothed those marks with his thumb.

"It's too soon to be giving up." His deep voice was gentle, his brogue soothing somehow. "You exist, so it's apparent enough that you had some family somewhere. You didn't just pop up out of the mist. If you've a relative anywhere in County Cork, you're bound to come across some clue in time. There are still places you can look. Father Walsh mentioned a couple just before you left."

He was being practical, which she would expect him to be because he always was. Some of that practicality must have rubbed off on her. Being realistic wasn't easy for Sara, but it made more sense than holding on to a hope that led nowhere.

"I'm not giving up," she told him. "I'm just facing facts. Even if I did discover something more about my background, I'd still be just as I am. It wouldn't change anything." Her voice became even more subdued. "I wouldn't belong anywhere, or to anyone. And no one would belong to me."

Tipping her head back, she blinked to ease the burning in her eyes. Last night, for a little while when she'd lain in Devon's arms, she'd felt as if she belonged. She'd felt needed. Part of something. Someone. It hadn't been until then that she'd realized just how necessary that feeling was, and how isolated a person felt without it. Oh, she'd suspected its necessity. Intellectually she'd known its worth. But you couldn't miss what you'd never really known. And now that she knew, the loss was all the greater.

She wanted desperately to feel that sense of belonging again. But she couldn't look to Devon for it. He had commitments that held no room for her.

Still, because she loved him, she smiled.

That smile, made poignant by unshed tears, was like a crashing blow to his heart. "I have more relatives than I know what to do with," he said to keep from saying other words, dangerous words that held promises he wasn't free to make. "You can have Aunt Kathleen."

She laughed, shaking her head at his questionably generous offer, and brushed at her eyes. "You have a wonderful family, Devon. I know they must drive you crazy, but they care about you. They depend on you, too."

Devon knew the rewards and frustrations of an extended family. What he didn't have was the closeness of a woman, his own children. He seldom thought of such things. He didn't want to think of them now.

"We get by," he told her, and stopped rubbing the marks on her palm. "We're not talking about them, though. What are you going to do?"

The smile faded from her lips and she pulled back her hand. "There's nothing I can do."

"Not about what you were looking for back there," he clarified, nodding his head in the general direction of the rectory. "I mean what are you going to do right now?"

Closing her eyes, Sara drew a quick breath. He was getting ready to say goodbye. She knew it. "I guess I'll go back to the inn and wait for your uncle. He's coming back on Tuesday. You're sure you don't mind my using your carriage?" She felt very brave when she looked at him. Her head was held high and she was sure he couldn't tell that she was falling apart inside. As empty as she felt now, she had the awful feeling she'd feel even worse when he left. "I can hire a ride back if you'd prefer."

"I told you could use it. I'm taking a cousin's car from here, so there's no need for you to hire what you've already got. How do you know when Thomas is arriving?"

"Kathleen told me. She got a card from him."

Devon's ambivalence about his uncle's return etched a faint scowl in his forehead. It would be nice not to have to spend so much time looking after his aunt. But he and his Uncle Thomas argued about the expansion, too. A lot. Thomas would be furious when he learned that Devon had borrowed from a bank. He wasn't going to be too crazy about what had been going on at the mill in his absence, either.

Over the shouts of the children, he heard Sara quietly ask, "She didn't tell you?"

He shouldn't have met her eyes. The sadness she valiantly tried to hide tore at him, making him feel petty for indulging such a trivial concern. His uncle's attitude was bothersome, for certain. But it wasn't anything Devon couldn't handle. On the other hand, Sara was feeling very alone and being very courageous about it and he couldn't stand it when she looked so lost.

He couldn't leave her like this.

"She probably would have," he said to dismiss the matter. "But she was too busy reminding me of other things to remember."

Not caring to examine his motives too closely, he stood and reached for her hand. He pulled her up in front of him. Before she could ask what he was doing, he pushed his fingers through the silk of her hair and drew her face up to meet his lips. Her hands flattened against his chest.

She tasted soft and sweet, and he could have sworn he heard a sob catch in her throat. That tiny sound was his undoing. Gathering her to him, he deepened the kiss until her breath altered and his memories of last night threatened his sense of propriety. They were in a public park, only a block off a main street and with a dozen screaming children a hundred yards away.

"How I want you," he whispered into her hair. Rubbing his hand over her back, he could feel the smooth movement of her muscles as she lowered her head to rest it against his chest. "Come with me, Sara." Though he very much liked the feel of her in his arms, he drew back. "There's no sense in you sitting around for two days waiting for my uncle. Have you ever been to Cork?"

She looked as if she were holding her breath when she shook her head.

"Then you might as well see it now," he decided. "I'm taking you with me."

Sara didn't know how it was possible, but in the space of seconds Devon had carried her from melancholy thought to what felt suspiciously like happiness. Incredible, considering that less than ten minutes ago, she couldn't have imagined ever wanting to smile again. But that was what she did now because being with Devon made everything seem all right. And for now, she didn't have to wonder what would happen when she no longer had a reason to stay in his land. Being realistic, she decided, wasn't all that necessary at the moment.

That attitude held for more than twenty-four idyllic hours. Devon was wonderful, charming her with a side of himself she'd never seen. A side that delighted in teasing her, making her laugh. They arrived in Cork well before sunset and he took her everywhere in the little black sport coupe he'd borrowed from his cousin Anna who'd stabled the horse and stored the carriage. Only once was there an uncomfortable moment. That was when he asked if she wanted to go to St. Mary's as the priest had suggested. She told him she didn't, that she only wanted them to enjoy the day. Then she made him smile by insisting that he buy her a helium balloon with a four-leaf clover on it.

"For luck," she explained, "even though I know you don't believe in it."

That balloon accompanied them to an alfresco dinner along the River Shannon and into a lovely old hotel Devon chose for them to spend the night in. It even hung over the bed where his tender kisses led them. But in the morning the balloon didn't dance along the ceiling anymore. It was as deflated as Devon's mood when he returned from the bank.

"He said the west is dying and no reputable banker would sink money into an operation so far out. Hell," Devon muttered, tossing the purchases Sara had made while waiting for him into the trunk. He'd arrived seconds ago, meeting her as they'd agreed by the open-air market known as Coal-Quay. "He wouldn't even listen to me. I'm trying to do what I can to see the piece of the west *I* care about doesn't die off and all he could say was, 'It's an economic fact.' How does he expect it to save itself if no one's willing to take a chance on it?''

The honk of a bus prompted Sara to hurry since the car was double-parked. Devon's muttered curse was muffled by the sharp sound of their doors slamming. He cursed again as he shot out into the traffic, but she was pretty sure the last expletive was again for the banker since Devon had started in on the man's obvious lack of foresight.

"First thing he did was put the ax to financing the down payment on the new looms, ignoring completely that without them I couldn't produce enough to pay for even the basic safety measures. We need fire sprinklers built in instead of just extinguishers. And rubberize flooring would be a damned sight safer than the wood in there now. You bring the flax in from the retting pools and the floor gets so slick you could skate on it. Do you know what he said to that?''

Sara shook her head. That was all the response he wanted anyway.

"He said if the place is that old and that outdated, it'd probably cost as much to build a new mill. So I asked him if he'd be willing to finance that kind of construction.''

Needless to say, though he told her anyway, the banker had found that idea as unadvantageous as the rest of Devon's proposal. After all, the location of the mill was still in the same village he wasn't interested in risking capital on. And while the man had said that what Devon wanted to do was commendable, he thought the expansion too ambitious to work.

"Commendable,'' Devon seethed, regarding the man's assessment as a placating insult. "I'm not doing this to be 'commended' for it.''

Why are you doing it? she couldn't help but wonder. But she said nothing. She simply let him rant, suspecting as she did that another approach would occur to him. A man like Devon didn't give up. Like the sturdy Celtic stock he came from, he defended his ideals to the bitter end. His passion wouldn't allow him to do otherwise. And like other men who dedicated themselves to a cause, everything else in their life came second—if they thought of anything else at all.

It took an hour and a half to reach Durry. Sara spent most of that time watching the lovely scenery roll by the window and wondering if Devon realized she was still there. He'd fallen silent, absorbed in thought as she'd often seen him before. At least he was no longer angry. Having worked out his frustrations, he was once again his withdrawn, preoccupied self.

It was only after they had exchanged car for carriage and were on their way out of Durry that her presence seemed to make a difference to him. Then he still didn't say much, but his silence became comfortable, as if her being there eased him somehow. They stopped to picnic in a glen, and for a long time after they'd eaten the bread and cheese they'd picked up in town, he seemed content to talk of little things. No mention was made of the bank or the mill or of family. It was a quiet time that made Sara feel content just to be.

The time came to move on, though, and the closer they got to Brigen Glen the more withdrawn Devon became. From the intense concentration marking his brow, Sara was sure his thoughts had gone back to the mill and to some other way to raise the money he needed.

She didn't doubt that he would find one. What she didn't begin to suspect was that she held his solution.

Chapter Eleven

Two telegrams sat on the windowsill in Devon's office. One had been delivered yesterday. The other, a short while ago. Both were addressed to Sara.

Because he was up to his eyebrows in paper, Devon had set the wires aside to give to her later. He'd been sorting through the mess in his office since he'd arrived right after sunup, talking to no one. Not even Kevin. Most especially Kevin. His foreman seemed to be avoiding him anyway. It was now almost noon and the man had done little more than mumble a defensive "hello" as he'd passed the office door. He hadn't asked why Devon's office looked as if a bomb had been dropped in it, or if he could help put the files back together. Not that Devon expected him to do the latter.

There was no doubt in Devon's mind that Kevin was responsible for what had happened here. With all the other incidents, Devon had harbored just enough uncertainty to make the conclusion impossible. Now he'd have to be blind not to see Kevin's guilt. The man who'd once been his best friend had completely betrayed him. But because Kevin *had* been his best friend, because he had a family to support, Devon would find little pleasure in firing him.

Not looking forward to that unpleasant task, he decided to put it off until he'd straightened out his office. When he went looking for him later that afternoon, though, Kevin wasn't around. According to the men working the hackles, he was helping one of the farmers with an overturned load of flax.

The task, Devon decided, would wait until after supper.

His agitation lessened with his next thought. Sara was cooking supper for him tonight.

Fixing a simple meal turned out to be more of an adventure for Sara than she'd first anticipated. Devon didn't keep much in his pantry that wasn't canned, and his garden was overgrown with weeds. That explained why he never refused a meal at Kathleen's, but it didn't much help Sara plan what to prepare. She mentioned this to Kathleen when she stopped by to give her the scarf she'd bought for her in Cork.

Kathleen was delighted with the gift, but she seemed to take Sara's decidedly domestic project in stride. She didn't question that Sara had been gone for two days and a night with her nephew. Nor did she question that she was cooking for him at his cottage. Sara didn't know what to make of her lack of interest, though she was grateful for it. She didn't want to explain what was going on between herself and Devon, because she wasn't really sure herself. What Kathleen *did* do about Sara's quandary over food confounded her even more.

After giving her some vegetables from her own garden, Devon's aunt told Sara that she could get good mutton from the Brennans, eggs and chicken from either the Connors or

Margaret O'Day and butter and cheese from the Murphys. She made a point of making sure Sara wouldn't forget where each cottage and farm was located by seeing that Sara wrote all of it down.

"Now flour and oats and leavening and such you have to get at market in Durry, but I can give you what you need of those until you can get there. Oh, and milk you can get from Sean's wife. She's got goat or cow, whatever you prefer."

Sara's thanks were genuine, though she was sure she sounded a bit puzzled when she explained that she only meant to fix dinner. She hadn't planned on stocking his pantry.

"This gives you a choice of what you might be wanting to cook," Kathleen said as if she couldn't possibly be implying anything else. "Aside from that, it never hurts to know where to find things in case you're in need of something later."

So it was that Sara set out with a basket and at the end of two hours had collected the ingredients for chicken stew. She remembered Kathleen's comment the other day about it being Devon's favorite.

On her way, she also acquired Beth who, once she found out what Sara was doing, accompanied her back to Devon's. Sara was grateful for the company. But it was too much to hope that Beth wouldn't find her project of interest, and with the enthusiasm of the polite but nosy voiced the questions Kathleen hadn't asked.

Sara was as honest as she could be. She told Beth simply that she and Devon were friends, that they might do business together and she'd offered to cook for him because he'd been nice enough to take her into Durry and Cork. Aside from that it would give her something to do to keep her mind occupied. Thomas was due to arrive tonight and Kathleen had told Sara she should come by in the morning.

If Sara stayed at the inn, she'd do nothing but pace. This way, she had something productive to do.

A smile hovered behind Beth's bland acceptance of that lengthy and logical explanation. "The only reason you forgot to mention was that you like him. There's nothing wrong with being here because you want to be. Devon deserves someone to care about him." She leaned across the freshly scrubbed table. Sara had put a small glass of flowers on it and Beth now adjusted the angle of one of the bright yellow blooms. "Kathleen has her own theory about you and Devon, you know. She thinks you've put a spell on him."

Sara stood at the sink peeling potatoes. It was one thing to be as transparent as cellophane. Quite another to be suspected of some sort of sorcery. She turned to Beth. The young woman appeared far too sober to be joking. "You're not serious."

"Kathleen is. Molly and my mother got back Sunday evening and Kathleen spent all of Monday over there. She wanted to hear all about the trip, of course, but a good part of the time she was telling them about what's been going on here. She thinks because of some of it you've a special power."

Devon had been afraid his aunt would think that. Wondering if there were any chance Kathleen would spare him her conclusion, she turned her attention to the potato. "Because of what kind of thing?" she wanted to know.

Beth, being helpful, started slicing the carrots destined for the stew pot. "She said you could make Mickey talk. Now she admitted she hadn't heard him talking to you herself, but Devon apparently has."

"There isn't anything remarkable about that," Sara replied, inexplicably relieved that the woman's speculation could be easily answered. Digging an eye out of the last potato, she explained how she'd met Mickey and how intrigued he'd been with her accent. Then, adding the vegetables to the simmering chicken, she went on to offer her theory for Mickey's silence: how it was his way of getting the attention he craved, and how the adults reinforced his behavior by anticipating his needs.

"Try not guessing what he wants next time," Sara suggested. "I'm willing to bet that he'll eventually get so frustrated that he'll have to talk."

A budding skeptic, a trait no doubt inherited from her oldest cousin, though open-minded enough to entertain her aunt's position, she said she would do just that—and offered another of her aunt's observations. "Aunt Kathleen says you've a power over animals, too. Tug always quiets when you pick him up and when I told her about the way you handled Skye when Mickey was in his stall, she didn't seem at all surprised that you weren't scared to death of the beast."

Sara wasn't allowed time to address that erroneous conclusion. From their position by the window, both women saw that Devon had ridden Merlot into his small corral. Man and horse stopped in the middle and, with a quick and easy grace, Devon swung from the bay's back. Years of familiarity with the task made quick work of removing bridle and saddle.

Giving the sleek animal a pat on the rump, he carried the tack into the stable.

"I'd best be on my way," Beth said, her speculative glance bouncing between the quiet woman beside her and the window. "It'll only take him a minute to pour her a bucket of oats. I don't imagine he's in much of a mood to want me here. Everyone's heard about his office being broken into while he was away."

For the first time since Sara had run into her this afternoon, the youthful light left Beth's eyes. She looked worried, and uneasy. "Mary McMurtry found it all torn apart yesterday morning. I wish whoever is doing these things would stop. It's hurting all of us, not just Devon. We've never had this kind of trouble here before."

Beneath the freckles, Beth's beautiful ivory skin was paler than usual. She was in no way responsible for her cousin's actions, but there were those who could decide her guilty simply because she was related to the man who wanted to change their village. Any grudge they carried against Devon could be carried on to her—and other members of the O'Donaugh family—if he should actually start to implement his plans. Change was a threat and, when threatened, people defended themselves.

Trepidation settled over Sara. It was entirely possible that the real trouble was only beginning. What had happened so far was petty compared to the uglier actions that could be taken. In the future the mill might not be the only target. Homes and the people in them might become involved. And when a member of a family was threatened, that family drew together to defend itself. Lines would be drawn, the real fight begun.

The village could destroy itself with animosity before it had a chance to realize Devon's vision—or work out a compromise.

As Beth had spoken, Devon emerged from the stable, his long-legged strides carrying him purposefully toward the cottage. Sara had no time to decide whether or not he might find his cousin's presence awkward. With a rush of cool air, the door swung open and his imposing frame filled the threshold.

His glance skimmed past Sara and settled on Beth. He seemed first surprised, then a little disconcerted, to find his young cousin there. Turning to the rack of pegs by the door, he focused his attention on hanging up his jacket.

"You haven't been here for a while," he said to her, hoping she wouldn't comment on how different the cottage seemed since the last time she'd been in his home. Beth noticed that sort of thing.

The place had become cold and uninviting, as if no one really *lived* here. It hadn't been that way when it had been his father's home, or during the years Maureen had occupied it with him. He hadn't really noticed the difference himself until the first time Sara had been here. She'd been such a bright contrast to the lifeless surroundings.

"I hadn't thought you wanted any of us here."

At Beth's quiet reply, Devon swiveled on his boot heel and faced the room. Within an instant, the defensive set of his mouth softened. The smell of something delicious cooking had registered as he'd opened the door. Now, seeing the flowers on the table and Sara's hesitant smile, he noticed that the room didn't feel cold at all.

"I'm sorry if I gave you that impression," he told his cousin. It was entirely possible, he realized, that the contrasts were visible only to him. "You're always welcome here. You're staying to supper?"

There wasn't as much enthusiasm in the question as there should have been. He didn't mean to be inhospitable. Even with nearly a twenty-year age difference, he got along fine with Beth. He just wanted to be with Sara right now. This business with Kevin had him wanting to break something and he needed very much to talk to her. Alone.

Beth showed a sudden and remarkable astuteness. Rattling off a list of excuses why she couldn't possibly stay and grinning oddly at Sara as she spoke, the younger woman backed toward the door. On her way, she collected her cardigan from a chair back, gave Sara a surreptitious wink and waggled her fingers at Devon before she said goodbye.

He had neither the energy nor the inclination to figure out what that was all about.

Sara cautiously turned from the door when Beth had gone. Something wasn't right with Devon. She'd sensed it from the moment he'd set foot in the room. Though he'd been pleasant with his cousin, beneath the calm facade she could feel his agitation.

When she turned, she could see it in his eyes.

"What's wrong?" she asked and he reached for her.

"Not now." His fingers bit into her waist. Skimming his other hand down her side to her hip, he smiled and he pulled her against him. "I need to kiss you."

His ability to empty her head of any rational thought should have been frightening. The touch of his lips to hers was potent, powerful. What she felt when his mouth moved against hers was relief and gladness and need. That combination didn't leave room for much else. Beyond that was only feeling.

She was a little weak in the knees when he set her back, but she was immediately conscious of the tension she'd first noticed in him. When he turned from her, he was kneading the muscles in his neck.

"Before I forget," he began, heading for his jacket to pull the telegrams from its pocket, "these came for you." Four long strides and he was back across the kitchen. After he handed her the envelopes, he reached for the ladle on the white countertop. "I hope this is ready. I'm starving."

Tearing open the first envelope, she watched him sniff appreciatively at the contents in the pot. Devon was a man of healthy appetites. No matter what troubled him, he could always put away a good meal. When she was disturbed, she couldn't stomach so much as the thought of food. "You can dish it up if you want. There's bread and cheese, too. Just a minute and I'll get them."

The sound of rustling paper was joined by the dull clank of pot lid to counter. Staring absently at the ladle in his hand, Devon paused. He wanted to talk about what concerned him, but he wasn't in the habit of asking for someone else's opinion. He worked his problems out alone. This problem with Kevin troubled him more than most, though, and he thought Sara might be able to help. After all, she seemed to understand Mickey.

Two empty bowls sat on the counter. He picked up the nearest and filled it with succulent chunks of meat and vegetables. "How do you go about understanding how a man can change so much?"

A few seconds passed before he heard her quiet, "Who?"

"Kevin." One bowl filled, he started on the other, too preoccupied with his own thoughts to notice that Sara had sounded vaguely distracted herself. "I've known him forever. My father was like a father to him. Hell, he didn't even realize that Uncle Thomas wasn't really his uncle until we were twelve years old. He's always been close to my family." His voice grew a little quieter as he remembered. "He'd always been like a brother to me."

The second bowl was carried along with the first to the table. He sat them beside the utensils and napkins Sara had already placed there, then stood studying the nicks the years had worn into the tabletop he'd helped his father make.

"I'd have done anything for him, Sara. Until a few months ago, I'd have sworn he'd have done the same for me. Now he's changed so much I don't even recognize him anymore."

"Do you think it's possible that he doesn't recognize you, either?"

Devon's head shot up, his eyes narrow as he tried to comprehend. "What do you mean?"

She'd folded the telegrams in half and stood with them dangling, seemingly forgotten, in her hand. There was no accusation in her tone and her eyes were as guileless as he'd ever seen. "Maybe it's you who's changed."

"I'm just as I've always been."

The overhead light made her hair glint with shades of silver as she moved closer. "No one stays the same forever,

Devon. We grow, we learn, we struggle. We get older, and with any luck gain some maturity out of that. Sometimes we experience things that make us build defenses. Or have experiences that fill us with joy. No matter what part of any of that happens to us, we change a little because of it. For better or worse."

In Kevin's case it was definitely worse. But all Devon said was, "I suppose," and let the matter go. He'd intended to talk about his friend, but Sara had somehow turned the conversation around on him. Devon didn't want to talk about himself. Sara tended to get too close when they did that, and even though part of him craved that closeness, a more protective part of him insisted on denying it.

Feeling vaguely disappointed that she hadn't been able to help him find his answer, he changed the subject.

"What was in your telegrams? Since they were delivered to the mill, I assume they're responses to the fabric samples you sent. Are either of your clients interested in a few yards of linen?"

Sara cleared her throat and stuffed the papers into the pocket of her oversize white shirt. It wasn't like her to evade. Having had little practice at it, her attempt to do so now was laughably transparent. "We can talk about that later. Let me get the bread. Do you want butter? I bought butter and you have eggs now," she added. "Two dozen. You can give some of them to Kathleen. I wouldn't have bought so much except that I felt a little guilty for taking up so much of Mrs. O'Day's time. I'd noticed the buttons on her blouse," she explained, looking through a drawer for a knife. "When she told me she'd made them herself from shells she collected at the shore, I asked if she had any extras and she brought out all these boxes."

The buttons really were beautiful. They'd all been cut and filed by hand and as soon as Sara had seen them, she'd wondered if the clients she'd sent Devon's linen to would be interested. She didn't mention that to Devon, though. She didn't want to bring up either of those clients right now.

It was, however, as good a time as any to bring up something else she'd been thinking about.

She found a knife and reached for the bread. "You know, Devon," she boldly began. "It occurred to me while I was at Mrs. O'Day's that you might not need to expand as much as you think. There are jobs already here that aren't being filled. Mrs. O'Day said her son makes buttons, too. And the laces Beth and your aunts and the other women make are really quite beautiful. Instead of them selling their goods at market, you could buy from them and handle the distribution. They'd have to produce more to make it worthwhile, of course. But that's the whole idea."

To Sara, the thought didn't seem so farfetched. He already dealt with textile brokers. Notions such as buttons and trims logically went with that territory.

"There are bound to be other items you could stock and broker, too." she told him. "All it would take to find them is someone willing to scout around the peninsula. Once a month or so that same person could make the rounds to pick up finished goods." She turned, bread in hand, thinking such a job most appealing. "You might even inspire a few more cottage industries."

"It doesn't matter, Sara."

Puzzled, she set the bread on the table. "Which part?"

"It doesn't matter that neither of them want my fabric. I wasn't planning on anything coming of your inquiry anyway."

She didn't deserve the smile he gave her. It seemed to say that he appreciated her trying to spare him, but that her effort wasn't necessary.

Feeling like a louse, knowing she was only going to feel worse, she reached into her pocket. After a moment's hesitation, she drew out the telegrams and handed them to him.

The ticking of the clock on the living room wall seemed inordinately loud as he read first one, then the other, then read them both again.

Her client in California wanted a thousand yards as soon as she could get the manufacturer to ship the order. The client in Paris wanted to build an entire line with the fabric. He also wanted an exclusive for one season which meant he'd be willing to bid higher to get it. The price Sara had put on it was already more than Devon would have dared ask.

She knew the instant he'd finished making his mental calculations. He stood, still looking at the telegrams. His hands weren't quite steady. It was also as clear as crystal that he hadn't given so much as a passing thought to her suggestion.

"I can do it with this, Sara." His voice was hushed, as if by speaking too loud the bubble might burst. "This is my down payment. This is my start." He took two steps, then turned and paced the other way. "It's more than a start. I can hire a contractor with this. I can bring in men to widen the road. I'll need a truck and electricians," he said, unable to focus on any one area now that his dream could be reality.

As he paced, his expression more animated than she'd ever seen it, Sara shrank back toward the counter. Never in her life had she felt so torn. She wanted to be happy for him, to be as pleased for him as he was with his fortune.

Devon was elated.

Sara wished she'd never even seen his blasted linen.

Suddenly he scooped her up to his chest, laughing as he turned her in the middle of the room. "I don't believe this." He kissed her. He kissed her again. "I don't believe this," he repeated, still laughing.

It took a moment before Devon realized that Sara wasn't sharing his enthusiasm. Every time before when he'd reached for her, she'd come to him willingly, as she had just a few minutes ago. She'd invited his touch. Been eager for it. Now, though she'd settled her arms around his waist, he noticed a certain stiffness in her body. It was in her smile, too.

Her reaction baffled him. He searched her face, as if trying to understand the sadness in her eyes. "Don't you realize what this means?"

His arms felt so good around her, so strong. If she could simply curl up against him and stay there for the rest of her life, she would die a happy woman. But she wasn't being given options right now and once she said what was on her mind—and she knew Devon wouldn't let her rest until she did—holding her would be the last thing he'd want to do.

"I know exactly what it means," she said and waited to feel him withdraw from her. "It means that if I take those orders, I'll be as responsible as you for what might happen here."

It didn't help that she'd anticipated it. When his arms fell away, she crossed her own about her and stared down at the pink laces of her tennis shoes.

The elation had long since vanished from his eyes when she finally looked up. He stood three feet from her, waiting.

"I'm not sure what you're talking about, Sara, but I get the feeling you're thinking about not doing business with me. Tell me I'm wrong."

She couldn't do that. "I'm sorry" was all she could say.

"Why?" The word exploded between them. "It was your idea to send that fabric off in the first place. Do you realize how unfair you're being? This is my chance and you're thinking of taking it away from me?"

"I'm not taking anything from you. If you want those orders, all you have to do is pick up the phone and tell those people their fabric's on the way. I'm not going to do it, though, and I don't care if I lose the commission. You know who the designers are. You've got their names right there. I can't stop you from contacting them yourself.

"As for being unfair," she continued, goaded by his glare, "you've never for a moment stopped to consider how unfair you're being to the people who live here. If you go through with your plans, you'll cut the heart out of this place. And don't tell me the villagers will appreciate the growth once they see the benefits. People have tried to tell you how they feel about what you want to do, but you won't listen to them."

She hugged her arms tighter. "I hate the way you refuse to see anyone else's side of this."

Devon wasn't exactly overjoyed with her attitude, either.

"I have listened," he bit out. "Everything I've heard boils down to one argument. They want to keep things the way they are because it's the way it's always been. The way it's always been just isn't good enough anymore."

"It isn't good enough for whom, Devon? You're the only one wanting such extensive changes. Doesn't that tell you something?"

"It tells me that no one else is willing to take a chance. Don't you think I can do it?"

He was thinking about the banker who'd turned him down just yesterday. Sara was almost sure of it. "I don't doubt that you're capable, Devon. If anyone could tackle such a task and make it work I truly believe it would be you. I just can't help thinking that you're using this expansion to fight your own personal demons."

Her hand shot up, warding off his quick denial. She remembered the house he had drawn with Mickey, and how Devon had said his marriage had died. "Maureen left you for the city. You couldn't keep her here. Just as you can't keep Mickey or any of the other children here when they grow up if they don't want to stay. You can't hold on so tight, Devon. The village has always lost some of its young people to Durry and Cork and Dublin. That's one of the reasons it's remained nearly the same size for all these centuries. The people who do stay here like the village for what it has to offer as it is. Look at Molly. She stays here even with her husband working in another town so she can raise her children as she was raised. Don't you see any of this?''

He drew closer, his voice menacing. ''What I see is that we need a more modern plant for the people to work in. We need new automated looms. The kind of modern equipment that doesn't require its operator to risk a limb when he runs it. We need to increase production so we can afford to build roads and inns and stores that will draw people here. We need a clinic or a hospital so that a sick child doesn't have to be taken for a ten-mile ride in the rain to see a doctor.''

He thrust his hand through his hair, burning with frustration that no one could see what was so obvious to him. Abruptly he turned away, tired to death of trying to explain it. Just as abruptly, he faced her again.

''We need this, Sara. My mother might not have died if they'd been able to get her to a hospital instead of that old midwife letting her bleed to death. My father's accident could have been prevented if the loom he'd been operating had been updated with a few basic safety features. But people around here accept that kind of event as just being the way things are. A woman dies and leaves a young child and it's a pity, they say, but life goes on. A man electrocutes himself trying to jury-rig an ancient generator and they say it was a shame he had to go like that, then drink themselves silly at his wake before going back to those same unsafe conditions themselves.

''I've never been able to accept that, Sara,'' he insisted vehemently. ''It can be changed. It should be, and I should have found a way to change it long before now. Maybe if I had... Maybe if I had,'' he repeated, his voice suddenly losing its fervor, "I wouldn't have failed my wife. Maybe she wouldn't have found it so necessary to leave."

In the silence that followed, Devon moved to the window. Hands spread and flat on the counter, he lowered his head and took a deep breath. Beside him the pot still simmered on the stove. Ahead of him, his horse nosed at the grass in his corral. Crickets sang the approach of dusk. And behind him, he could feel Sara's bewildered eyes on his back.

His words had left Sara stunned. Abandonment. Failure. Blame. As she watched his broad shoulders rise with the stabilizing breath he drew, she began to realize the scope of emotions he'd tried to deal with for so many years. He'd said he'd failed his wife, as if her boredom had been his fault. She knew he'd felt the loss of his father because he'd spoken of him before, but he'd never mentioned his mother. Certainly he'd said nothing about how abandoned he'd obviously felt by her death. Kathleen had said only that his mother had died in childbirth years ago.

Once again she felt like an intruder. But caring for him as she did, she needed to let him know that finally she understood why he'd taken on such enormous responsibility. "You can't change any of what's already happened," she said quietly.

"I'm not trying to change what's happened." He let out a weary sigh. "I'm just trying to keep those kinds of things from happening again."

She started toward him, aching at his desolation. "I don't know of anyone who has that kind of power, Devon." Slowly, so her touch wouldn't startle him, she reached over and lay her hand on his. He didn't react to the contact. He didn't even look at her. "Maybe you're taking on too much responsibility. Some of those decisions aren't yours to make."

"Spare me the euphemisms," he muttered, and jerked his hand out from under hers. "What you mean is that I'm interfering in other people's lives."

A knot formed in the pit of Sara's stomach. Folding her arms over it, she watched him move away.

A moment later, he wasn't the only one she was hurting for. She was hurting for herself, too.

"I think you'd better go," he told her, then opened the door to counter any further discussion.

Clearly stricken by his dismissal, she couldn't seem to move.

"Please," he asked, more quietly.

She quickly averted her eyes from his. Not liking what he heard, he wasn't going to listen to any more. Sara understood. Far better than he realized. Shaken and silent, she fled past him, leaving so quickly that she didn't even close the door.

Devon closed it for her, not turning from its window until he'd seen her disappear, hair flying, into the woods.

He turned back to the room. The two bowls sat lukewarm and untouched on the table. Methodically he dumped one back into the pot. With the scrape of a chair, he sat down in front of the other. After staring at it for a full minute, he shoved it aside and drew his hands down his face.

When had it all gotten so out of hand? he wondered. When had the need to simply do what was required of him become a need to do it all? No. Not all, he corrected. Just the parts that mattered to him.

His fist hit the table. Sara had made it sound as if he were manipulating the village—as if it lacked the things he'd needed to keep his relationships intact, so he was trying to change it into what he thought it should be. If he were to take her little analysis a step further, he supposed she'd implied that his inability to accept the events of his past was making him try to control everyone else's future.

He didn't care at all for the way that conclusion made him feel.

Letting out a long deep breath, he glanced toward the window. Sara was wrong. And he'd been wrong about her.

A bottle of the local rye sat on the shelf next to a bowl of berries that hadn't been there the last time he'd looked. Ignoring them, he took the bottle and glass and sat back down at the table.

Chapter Twelve

A silvery fog wound its way through the glen, laying like a gossamer ribbon between the rolling hills. From the top of a rise beyond the crossroads, Sara could see that protective mist veiling most of Brigen Glen. It was eerie to see the village hidden that way, with only the emerald hilltops peeking above the mist.

She walked along the ridge, hugging to her the heather she'd gathered to give Mrs. Carrigan for her parlor. The view below her brought back old, familiar feelings. Feelings she'd managed to suppress or escape by being constantly on the move. She felt isolated. Separate. As if being a part of something lay forever beyond her reach.

Devon had called her an outsider. He'd had no idea that she'd been one all her life.

With the quick shake of her head to dispel the unwanted thoughts, she tried to focus on the beauty of the scenery rather than its less appealing reminders. The attempt was commendable, but she couldn't clear her mind enough to find calm in aesthetics. Adding another stalk of purple-pink heather to the huge bouquet she'd already collected, she wondered how much time had passed since she'd last checked her watch.

Kathleen had told her to come by her cottage midmorning. Thomas might want to sleep in after a long day of traveling, Kathleen had said, but he'd surely be up and about by then. Sara assumed midmorning to be around ten o'clock, which, checking the Roman numerals on her watch again, was still two hours away. Time, it seemed, wasn't moving any faster this morning than it had last night. She'd spent nearly every one of those interminable hours watching the moonlight shift across her ceiling, replaying the disaster last evening had turned into.

A dull ache centered in her chest when she thought of that. She had no one to blame but herself for the pain she felt now. Devon had made it abundantly clear when she'd first arrived that he didn't want her around. When he'd sent her away last night, she wished she'd listened. Because of him she now knew what she'd been searching for all of her life. Because of him, she now knew she couldn't have it.

A week wasn't much time, but it was all the time it had taken for Sara to realize that Brigen Glen was where she'd always needed to be. She hadn't even let herself think of how she would feel when it came time to leave, because just the thought made her unbearably sad. Even more important, more compelling, was that she knew she needed Devon. But Devon, she was certain, now thought of her as he did all the others who stood in the way of his plans—and those plans were all that mattered. Being with him, sharing, discovering, had made her forget that. It wasn't as if she hadn't been warned.

Still, she had to see him one more time. She wouldn't place the order for his fabric herself, but she couldn't stop him from doing it. It would be petty to make him search for those clients' phone numbers and addresses. They weren't on the telegrams, so she'd write them down for him.

Not giving herself time to reconsider, she headed down the hill. Sara never made it to the mill, though. She dropped off the heather with Mrs. Carrigan and was on the road not twenty yards from Kathleen and Thomas's cottage when she noticed two men standing near the gate. Had it not been for the fog, she would have noticed them sooner. Her glance was immediately drawn to the taller one. Big and brooding and wearing a dark turtleneck sweater, he was accepting the hug of an elderly white-haired gentleman.

Sara felt a rising lump catch in her throat.

She'd thought she'd have more time before she faced him. Time to don a mask of professionalism and figure out how to pretend she wasn't aching inside. She was still too raw from his curt dismissal to risk hurting herself even more. She loved Devon, but she needed to protect herself, too.

It was too late to turn around. In her anxiety, she thought about it, though, staring at the two men as she did. Anxious as she was, it took a moment for what she was seeing to fully register. When it did, her breath escaped in a rush. The man with his hand on the old man's shoulder wasn't Devon. He was about the same height and of the same brawny build, but his dark hair had more curl. When he turned, she could see that he had a beard.

She'd only met him once. But now that he faced her, she had no difficulty in recognizing Kevin. He looked angry and worried.

Immediately Sara stiffened. Had something happened between him and Devon? she wondered. Had Kevin then come to Thomas complaining about whatever had happened? It was possible, after all. Devon had told her himself that Kevin was close to his uncle. And now that Thomas was back . . .

Amazed at how quickly she'd been prepared to suspect the worst, she cut off her speculation. Now that Thomas was back, it was entirely possible that all Kevin was doing was welcoming him home.

She took a few steps closer, edging toward the stone fence with its border of lavender-headed clover. It hadn't occurred to her to doubt that the elderly gentleman was Devon's Uncle Thomas. Even from the road, she could see the familial resemblance. The man had the same squared and stubborn jaw as Devon, the same proud bearing he hadn't allowed his age to bend.

Both men hesitated when they noticed her. In the foggy morning light, she saw Kevin nod.

"Morning, ma'am," he said, and Sara nodded back as he slapped his tweed cap on his head. His glance was clearly speculative as he passed through the gate, his smile reserved.

Or was it guilt, Sara wondered as she watched him jog away.

She turned her attention back to the man squinting at her. It was early yet. She wasn't expected for nearly an hour and she didn't want to impose. Still, she was here. And so was the man her grandmother had sent her to find.

The ring felt cold as her fingers closed over where it hung at the base of her throat. "Are you Thomas O'Donaugh?"

"Aye. And you'll be Sara."

"I am," she returned, smiling because he did. At least, she thought it was a smile. It might have been a grimace.

In his hand he held a curved and unlit pipe. He stuck it in the corner of his mouth, jammed his hands into his pockets and dipped his head toward the cottage. The breeze ruffled his thick white hair as he muttered, "Come inside."

Hoping Kathleen was home, she followed him up the walk. Kathleen might have some strange ideas, but at least she was friendly. Sara very much needed to see a friendly face. Thomas obviously expected her, and just as obviously had little enthusiasm for the visit. There was no welcome in his manner, no real curiosity, either.

His sister was apparently there. At least, Sara assumed it was Kathleen he spoke to when he closed the door behind them. Calling out, "She's here," he began to check his pockets. After patting at all of them, his eyes narrowed on his guest. "Do you have a match?"

Since she hadn't been asked to sit, Sara remained in the middle of the cozy little room. "I'm sorry, I don't," she said and watched him shrug, seeming to forget about wanting a light.

Kathleen's voice cut around the corner. "Didn't Kevin want to come in?"

"We spoke outside."

"For all that time?" she wanted to know, but her brother wasn't paying any attention to her.

Thomas wore a gray cardigan over a blue shirt buttoned to his neck. His pants were heavy twill, serviceable looking and held up by suspenders. Bright red suspenders. Sara noticed them when he put his hands on his hips, their position drawing the sides of his sweater back, and he walked a slow circle around her.

"You've grown into a fine-looking lass," he told her, completely unapologetic about his studied assessment. "The last time I saw you, you were little more than a few pounds of mewling babe. Sickly, you were, but with lungs a banshee would envy. It was your carrying on that led me to find you, you know?"

The question was nothing more than a pattern of speech. But because Sara hadn't known—had, in fact, no idea what he was talking about—she shook her head. "You found me?"

"Thomas O'Donaugh," came Kathleen's chastising voice, along with Kathleen herself carrying a tea tray. "I told you you'll be needing to go slow with what you have to say. You can't just go babbling on without giving her a chance to wean into it all. As amazing as I found it, it's sure to knock the breath out of her."

The admonishment fell from her tone as she settled her tray and glanced up. "A good morning to you, Sara. Do sit down. Here. In this chair," she said, setting a cup of tea on the table near the arm of one of the green wingbacks.

As quickly as it had vanished, her scolding tone returned. She pointed to the chair on the opposite side of the lace-covered table. Today the flowers on it were red roses. "Take a seat over here, Thomas. And be more mannerly."

"I'm being mannerly."

"You're being insensitive."

"Insensitive? What in the bloody devil is that? I'm telling her what she wants to know. You said she'd been looking clear to Durry to learn something of the woman. All I'm doing is saying what she's come to hear."

"Well, you're saying it poorly. A thing like this needs to be broke gentle like."

"Was I lost?"

At Sara's quiet, decidedly hesitant question, the two relatives stopped short. Both glanced to her, but only Kathleen appeared to realize that their bickering was only adding to Sara's anxiety.

"You weren't exactly lost," she said, searching for a delicate way to proceed. "It happens sometimes that . . ."

"You were abandoned," Thomas put in bluntly and sat down as he'd been told, now that a respectable time had passed since the order had been issued.

Refusing to meet his sister's quick scowl, he plunged ahead. It was, after all, his story. "I found you in the woods. It would happen from time to time that a baby would be left in such a way. A pitiful practice to be sure and one certain to long trouble the poor wretched soul so driven. We hadn't a foundling here in the forty-eight years I'd been living up to that time."

"Usually you'd hear of a babe being left closer to Durry," Kathleen cut in. "Most often at the church there. But Thomas said we'd had a band of tinkers staying in the woods not the week before. He suspects that's where you came from."

At the interruption, Thomas glared at his sister. Sara didn't notice.

Abandoned? Tinkers? She understood the words, but what she heard made no sense. "But my grandmother said my father . . . her son," she clarified, "brought me to her to take care of. He'd been gone for a long time and wouldn't say anything about my mother . . ." Her voice trailed off as she tried to fit what she knew with what she was hearing. "How could you have found me?"

"Kathleen said you have a ring. May I see it?"

Sara's hands trembled slightly, making it difficult for her to work the clasp of the chain. When she finally managed to undo it, she slipped the ring off and handed it to Thomas.

Slowly he turned the ring around, holding it up to the lamp on the table between their chairs. A bit of his abrupt manner eased when he looked back at her. Either his memories were mellowing him or he was beginning to realize the effect his news was having on Sara. She looked as pale as the porcelain teacups.

"I don't know what you were told. But if this is what you were given to bring to me, you were the baby I found. I gave you to the old woman who came along just as I was wondering what to do with you. I was cutting wood back where I shouldn't have been, and she startled me so that I nearly dropped you back in the stump you were cradled in. Her name was Fiona Madigan, she told me, and she lived nearby. She was wanting to know what I was doing with a baby and an ax in such an isolated place. It's for certain she thought I was up to no good. But after I explained the predicament, she said she'd take you in. She had no one, she said, and since you didn't, either, handing you over seemed the logical thing to do."

Remembering, he looked back to the ring in his hand. "I gave her this to sell for the gold to help feed you. It was the only thing of value I had, and seemed the least I should do. I was a man with an ailing wife and couldn't take you in myself. But she looked upon it as a kindness. She didn't expect kindness from people from the village."

A frown creased his already furrowed brow, as if he'd just thought of something but wasn't sure of its significance. "She told me that for my generosity, the child would one day return to help the village. I would know the child by the gift I'd given."

It is as I promised, she remembered her grandmother saying.

"The ring was the gift you gave," Kathleen said, realizing what had apparently already occurred to Thomas.

His voice grew a bit quieter. "I paid her no heed. She was one of them, after all. After she told me that, she said I needn't tell anyone that I had spoken with her. I saw no call for it anyway. She was one of the woods people and so was the baby. It was only proper that she be raised with her own. Was no more of my concern."

Undoubtedly he'd been happy to be rid of the problem. And by not mentioning his encounter with Fiona, he didn't have to explain why he'd been so far back in the woods. So many trees had been cut down that the forests were vanishing. Sara'd heard that it had become illegal to cut more.

Those thoughts weren't what forced her silence, though. As she sat with the empty chain folded in her palm, she was trying to accept the idea that her grandmother hadn't been her grandmother at all. Fiona had even lied to her about who she was, who Sara was. Yet Sara couldn't help feeling that beneath the lies was a core of truth. To her, Fiona had been too good a woman, too *kind* a woman, to create such a deception. Or was it kindness that had caused her to cover that truth? Even as Sara muddled over that thought, she had to remember all the times her grandmother had evaded her questions.

Oddly the deception didn't matter to Sara. Not as much as it probably should have. She loved Fiona for the years she'd spent raising her, caring for her. What did matter to her was that the picture she'd had of herself, of Sara Madigan, had been subtly altered. "Then the baby my grandmother—Fiona—left Ireland with wasn't my father. It was me?"

"I'd be inclined to think that the case. When you were nearing three, I'd say it was. She left a note tacked on the door of the church saying she was moving on and anyone who truly needed it was welcome to her cottage and whatever was in it. The hut's no longer there. Washed away it was by the stream when it flooded so badly the following year."

"That was the first time any of us ever heard of Fiona Madigan," Kathleen said. "Except Thomas, of course, but we didn't know at the time he'd come across the woman. We'd see the people from the woods sometimes. Catch glimpses of them now and then. But we never knew them by name. Hers was the first we knew because of her signing her name to her note."

"Then I was born here?"

Thomas merely nodded as he pushed his hand between the side of the chair and its cushion. Smiling, he dug out a small box of matches.

"You know," Kathleen began, sounding quite amazed. "Devon used that very same tone himself when I told him that not two hours ago. I told him I knew there was something about you." Excitement lit her face. "And, Thomas, you just said yourself Fiona told you the baby would come back to help the village...."

"Now don't go starting in on that again, Kathleen," her brother warned as he struck the match. "Sara doesn't look like a leprechaun or a sorceress to me and I'd be doubting very much that if she were she'd be sitting here talking to us. If she were capable of transporting and conjuring or whatever it is spirits do, I doubt she'd have stuck around waiting for me. She could have vaporized herself right to wherever I was. Isn't that right, Sara?"

Sara had no idea what spirits were supposed to do and since she was becoming more bewildered by the moment, Kathleen had ample opportunity to cut right back in.

"I still think there's a difference in him. That difference started coming about with Sara. At least he doesn't walk away from her when she's talking to him as he does with the rest of us." A very smug look flitted across her wrinkles. "You said yourself just before you went trotting off up north that it would take a miracle for anyone to make him listen. You even said you wouldn't be surprised if something didn't start happening to make him see how unreasonable he was being. Could be you had a premonition," she informed him with decisive nod. "'Tis entirely possible you foresaw what was happening here. Such things occur, you know."

Thomas was suddenly very busy with his pipe and his tea and the alignment of the buttons on his sweater. He was particularly concerned about a loose thread on one of them and mentioned to Kathleen that it should be mended before it fell off. Sara would have thought his manner most curious had her mind not already been on overload. So many questions had formed that she scarcely knew where to start.

The most pressing came first. "You've spoke with Devon this morning?"

A thin stream of smoke danced toward the ceiling as Thomas stood. Still inordinately preoccupied with the thread, he began rummaging through the sewing box next to the sofa for scissors.

Kathleen watched him for a moment, shaking her head, then turned back to Sara. "He was here before he went to the mill. Said he wanted us to know about the people who want to buy so much of the cloth. Imagine someone wanting to make their clothes out of nothing but our linen."

"He's still buying the looms," Thomas grumbled. He shook his head, suddenly looking as old as he was and very sad. "Seems there's no stopping him on that score."

"There was no stopping you this morning, either," his sister returned. "I don't agree with what he's doing any more than you, but I'd have thought the two of you would have at least finished your breakfasts before you started in on each other's throats. He came by to greet you back and tell us his news and no sooner are the words from his mouth than you're off and running. It's no wonder he was angry when he left here."

Sara rose, marveling at the composure she managed. They could argue without her. Right now she needed some air. First she needed to thank Thomas for his time and Kathleen for the tea she hadn't touched.

Thomas mumbled, "You're welcome." Kathleen said the same and pocketed the ring her brother had left on the table as Sara started for the door. "He's always misplacing things," she said. "Wouldn't want him to lose it after the trouble you went to bringing it back. You stop by before you leave now."

All Sara could do as she left the cottage was give her a nod and a weak smile.

She had hoped that, somehow, she'd have found a way to ask Thomas if she could have the ring. Buy it from him, perhaps. There was no way she could that. It was Thomas's. It always had been.

That thought crowded in among the others she'd yet to sort through. She felt upended. As if every constant in her life had been destroyed. In effect, she supposed, it had. Yet in reality, everything was still exactly the same.

She was still pondering that dubious logic half an hour later. So preoccupied was she that she didn't realize where she was headed—until she saw the mill.

Postponing the inevitable sounded like a wonderful idea. Knowing she'd only have to face Devon later, knowing, too, that it might be harder if she had time to think about it, she continued on.

She'd walked, but her heart was racing when she stepped through the open side door and into the building's cool interior. The sounds were muffled, but the old, automated machinery could be heard clanking away at the far end of the mill. Following a leaf the breeze blew in, she started toward Devon's office.

To her immediate relief, he wasn't there.

Turning to head back down the hall, she found that relief short-lived.

He'd just rounded the corner. Seeing her, he stopped dead in his tracks.

Sara slowly reached for the doorjamb. "Hi," she said, trying to smile. "Are you still speaking to me?"

His jaw clenched. "Why wouldn't I be?"

A mountain lion would have held more appeal for Sara at that moment. Devon's manner was distant, his expression devoid of anything remotely inviting as he strode past her. "Come on in."

He was all business. The efficiency of his movements indicated he had plenty to do, but that he would suffer the interruption if only to get it over with. Clearly he hadn't forgiven her for what she had said last night.

The trouble was that she didn't know which part of it he was so upset about.

She stepped closer. "I came to give you the information you'll need to contact the designers. I'll be leaving in the morning," she added, hiding the ache accompanying that thought.

His head was bent as he stood behind his desk shuffling through papers. The shuffling slowed, but he didn't look up. "You've finished your business with my uncle?"

She nodded. Then, realizing that he hadn't seen the motion, offered a quiet, "Yes."

"I'm sorry he couldn't tell you anything about your family."

Finally Devon looked up, seeing what he'd been afraid to notice before. She looked tired, as if she'd slept no better than he, and unbearably fragile. The other day after they'd left the priest in Durry, she'd had that same haunted look to her. It had nearly torn him apart then. It wasn't much easier to take now. It couldn't have been easy hearing what she had.

"Babies have been abandoned for centuries," she said, sounding as if she were grasping that rationale. "It just never occurred to me that I had been." She glanced away, no more comfortable than he with silence. "Kathleen said you told her and Thomas about the buyers. Your uncle didn't seem too pleased."

Dragging his fingers through his hair, he moved to the front of the desk and sat down on the edge. She was only a few feet from him now, close enough that he could smell the windflower scent of her hair. He tried not to breathe too deeply. "Some of the people around here are just going to have to get used to the idea that I'm getting the new machinery."

"People like your uncle?" she asked, remembering Thomas's disgruntled attitude about the new looms. Something else nagged at her, too. Something Kathleen had said that had made Thomas suddenly anxious to be out of the conversation.

"Especially my uncle," Devon replied as she tried to remember exactly what that something was. "Just before he left, he was going on about it as if my buying that equipment would bring on the end of the world. I was hoping his being gone for a while would have mellowed him."

As he spoke, Sara recalled what she'd been trying to remember—Kathleen's reference to Thomas's "premonition." He'd said he wouldn't be surprised if something happened to make Devon see how unreasonable he was being.

"When did your uncle leave?"

Devon obviously didn't see what the question had to do with anything, but answered anyway. "Nearly three weeks ago. Why?"

"Is that about when things started happening to the mill? When you found the flax bundles torn apart and the chemicals were stolen?"

"What are you getting at?"

It was crazy. She didn't want to accuse. Yet his uncle's absence seemed awfully coincidental. "I just wondered if he might know about what's been going on here. If he left the village about then and if he was so opposed to what you wanted to do, is it possible he could have had something to do with the vandalism?"

"Uncle Thomas? Not hardly. He's as dedicated to the mill as I am."

That was her point, but she'd already alienated Devon by expressing her perceptions last night. Not caring to make matters between them worse, she chose to say nothing more on the subject. It was entirely possible that she was wrong anyway. She didn't know his uncle at all.

But she knew Devon and she knew when he was agitated. Rubbing at the muscles banding his neck, he pushed himself away from the desk. He took a step closer, looking as if there were something he wanted to say, but didn't know where to begin. Then he met her eyes and she saw the distance in them.

Steeling herself, she waited to hear the goodbye she was sure would haunt her forever. That was what was coming, she knew. Eventually. No matter what else he said between then and now, the end would be the same.

It was the hardest thing she'd ever done, but she made herself smile. Having already experienced his rejection last night, she saw no point in allowing him to do that to her again. She'd leave before he told her to.

"I know you've a lot to do," she told him, pulling a neatly folded piece of paper from her jacket pocket. "So I'll get out of here. I still have to stop by your cousin's and say goodbye to Beth and Mickey and then I have to get back and finish packing."

That task would take all of five minutes, but she wanted to sound busy. Pride could be very strict in its demands.

The edges of the paper quivered slightly when she held it out to him. Wishing he'd hurry up and take it before he realized how hard this was for her, she made the mistake of looking up. No expression marked the hard angles of his face. No emotion betrayed the thoughts behind those piercing blue eyes. "These are the phone numbers you'll need."

Still holding her glance, he took the paper. But Sara was spared his parting words when Mary McMurtry shoved open the door.

Mary's brown curls bounced around her head as she drew to a halt. She was obviously in a hurry, but immediately embarrassed at not finding her boss alone. Clearing her throat, she took a step back, demurely folded her hands in front of her and planted herself in the doorway to wait.

For the moment, Devon ignored her. Tension snaked between him and Sara. It electrified the air, making him edgy and her restive.

"You're leaving in the morning?" she heard him ask.

"So soon?" Mary piped in. "We were just getting used to seeing you around."

The smile Sara managed was faint. "Thank you, Mary. I'm going to miss being here."

She hadn't intended for it to happen, but her glance had returned to Devon as she'd spoken her last words. His eyes flashed with some indefinable emotion, but his face hardened. Giving her one last, long look he turned away.

"What's the problem, Mary?"

"Well, I don't know that it's a problem exactly. Your uncle arrived a bit ago and he's telling us we can take the day off from our weaving. Not an hour ago you said we'd be getting overtime."

Seconds later Devon was out the door. Mary, her hands planted on her ample hips, was right on his heels.

Sara stayed where she was, fighting her impulse to take off after him. Any business between Devon and his uncle was none of her concern. Like two rival bucks, they'd probably butt at each other until one of them backed down. Or, as she suspected could easily happen, they could lock horns and, like real deer who were then unable to break away from each other and died of starvation, destroy what they were fighting over. Devon had already pointed out that it shouldn't matter to her what happened here.

Maybe it shouldn't. But it did. And he mattered. She couldn't leave without letting him know that.

Taking a sheet from a pad on his desk, she quickly wrote out a note. It said only that she would be at the inn tonight and she'd appreciate it very much if he would stop by.

Remembering that he'd once missed the note she'd left him by the phone, she taped this one to the back of his chair where he couldn't miss it.

But he never came.

Devon sat with the note in his hands, running the folded paper between his fingers. The rush of the water over the rocks in the stream shrouded the other night sounds: the hoot of an owl, the rustle of leaves as something furry skittered among them. A nearly full moon shone bright and luminous in the dark sky.

So much had happened in the past day, the past several days actually. And it was taking him a while to assimilate it all.

It was hard to let go. Harder still to admit he'd been wrong. He could scarcely believe that his own uncle had been responsible for the trouble at the mill. He'd even had him followed. Until confronted with it himself today, he'd never have thought it possible. Thomas had been behind everything: the theft of the chemicals and the ledgers, the loss of the load of material. Only the material wasn't lost. Along with everything else, it was in a cave on the other side of the glen. That's where Kevin had met Thomas and stored it all.

Kevin. Devon shook his head when he thought of his friend. The man hadn't been in an easy position. But Devon couldn't blame him for helping his uncle. He supposed he couldn't blame his uncle, either. After fighting the knowledge for hours—denying, blaming, rationalizing— Devon had finally faced the fact that what he'd pushed them to do was his own fault.

He held the note up. Sara had been right about his uncle. She'd been right about many things.

He knew now why he hadn't wanted her to get too close, why she had felt such a threat at times. She saw him too clearly for comfort, made him question himself when he'd rather not explore his motivations too closely. Her insights had frightened him because they'd been so damnably accurate. And because he hadn't wanted to face them, he'd shut her out just as he'd done with everyone else.

A faint howling sounded off in the distance—the plaintive cry of a wolf. Devon listened for an answering howl, but there was none, just the woods' peculiar silence. There was no peace in the silence, though he remembered feeling peace with Sara. The night felt lonely, too. Yet he hadn't realized quite how lonely he had been before she'd come into his life. She'd shown him what was missing and, at the same time, given him so much.

Because of her, he'd had moments where he felt the wonder of simply being, experienced the joy to be found in such simple pleasures as lying in the clover watching the clouds. She had been the one to open his eyes when he'd failed to see the colors right at his own door. And it had been through her that he'd felt something he hadn't felt in a long, long time.

Happiness.

If the man failed to win her heart, she would take his happiness with her and disappear at the full of the moon.

He glanced toward the patch of sky above the clearing. The moon hung above the treetops. It was only a day away from its crest. Sara had told him herself she was leaving tomorrow. Kathleen had mentioned it, too, when she'd come to the mill with the ring Sara had given Thomas. He still thought her eccentric for some of what she'd said to him when she'd made him take it. The woman was incorrigible when it came to her conclusions.

The ring was still in his pocket. Standing up, he absently brushed at his pants, feeling the metal circle when his palm slid over it. Devon knew the similarities between reality and the legend were only coincidence. But he wasn't quite as quick as he once would have been to deny the connection.

Looking up at the moon, he wished it weren't so late. He wanted to talk to Sara. Badly. He needed her—and he would do everything in his power to keep her with him. He had no idea at the moment what he could do that would make her want to stay, but he fervently hoped something would occur to him before he knocked on Mrs. Carrigan's door.

He started toward the path, intent on getting to the inn before the hour grew much later. It was entirely possible that Sara was already asleep, more possible still that she might not want to see him. Avoiding the hurt encroaching at that last thought, he considered only the time. It was nearing midnight. Soon only the night animals would be awake.

One of those animals was nearby. Leaves rustled, then stilled, rustling again as whatever it was moved toward the stream. Drawn by the sounds, Devon slowed, then stopped.

About thirty yards away, a deer stepped from the trees. Its brown coat shown golden in the spectral light, its body instantly alert to the man watching it. Without drinking the cool water, as he was sure it meant to do, it turned gracefully and bolted back into the trees.

Seconds passed while he waited for it to return.

"Devon?"

At the sound of his name, he whirled around, so startled his heart felt as if it had slammed against his ribs. "Sara," he breathed. "You scared the bloody hell out of me."

"I'm sorry." Quickly she stepped back. Already hesitant, her voice grew quieter still. "I shouldn't have come."

She took another step back and started to turn.

"No." He practically leaped forward, grabbing her by the shoulders. His fingers bit into her soft flesh, easing only enough to insure she wouldn't move. "Don't leave. What are you doing out so late?"

"I often walk when I can't sleep."

Had he wished her here? he wondered, knowing even as he did how impossible such an idea was. Still, only moments ago... "You couldn't sleep?"

She shook her head, her hair swaying around her shoulders with the motion. "I couldn't leave without seeing you again."

"How did you know I was here?"

"I didn't. I was just coming through this way." As if unsure of what to say next, she looked from his eyes. "I heard about your uncle. Are you two speaking to each other?"

Devon wasn't quite sure why, but he was afraid to let go of her. Sliding his hand down her arm, he curled his fingers through hers. He left his other hand on her shoulder, his thumb absently brushing her slender neck. "We will be. He can be awfully stubborn."

"So can you."

He made a self-deprecating grimace. "I know. But I'm not irredeemable. You were right about what I wanted to do to the village," he told her, finding it easier to admit to her than it had been to himself. "I presumed too much. I'm still going to make a few changes. I want to use your idea about backing the cottage industries around here, and I'm still modernizing the mill. But I won't do anything obtrusive. I wouldn't want to tamper with the village's soul."

Those had been her words. "I have a big mouth."

"You have a beautiful mouth," he told her and moved his hand to trail his finger over her bottom lip.

The motion of Sara's head was barely perceptible, just enough to break the contact. She wanted him to kiss her. She wanted a lot more than that. But there was something she needed to say first.

It had taken her all her life, but she'd finally realized the kind of love her grandmother—and she would always think of Fiona that way—had once told her she would find. The unconditional kind. The kind that doesn't hold back even though there's a good chance it can't—or won't—be returned. "I love you, Devon," she told him and saw him go utterly still.

She had intended to tell him that she didn't expect him to return her feelings. That she understood that sometimes it just didn't work out that both people felt the same need. The expression in his eyes stopped her. She saw disbelief, then a wariness that matched her own.

There were calluses on his hands. She felt them when he cupped his palm to her cheek. "That must be what I feel for you, too, Sara. Only when I thought of it, it felt more like need. I need you. But I don't know what to do to keep you here."

Her heart leaped. "You want me to stay?"

"You belong here. Even if it wasn't for very long, it was once your home."

That was true. And it was probably why she'd felt such an affinity for the place from the moment she'd arrived. But the place without Devon wouldn't matter nearly so much.

"You could give me a job," she suggested, knowing of one quite perfect for her. She drew a deep breath. "Or you could consider marrying me."

"I don't need to consider it," he told her and gently brushed his lips over hers. She tasted sweet and warm. And her smile when he lifted his head after pulling her to him was the most wonderful thing he'd ever seen.

"I have something that belongs to you." Releasing her, he reached into his pocket and held out his hand. He watched her eyes widen, his thoughts anxious. "It's far too big for you to wear as it is, but we can take it into Cork and have it made smaller. It could be your wedding ring, if you want."

"My grandmother's...Thomas's ring," she corrected. In the moonlight the ring glinted silver. "How did you get it?"

"Kathleen gave it to me. With everything else going on today, she stopped by, insisting that I hang on to it. She said she'd figured out why Fiona had sent you to Brigen Glen with it. According to her, the ring has been for you all along. She thinks that somehow Fiona knew once you got here..."

His voice trailed off as he remembered Kathleen's words—and the jolt of truth that had come with them. "That once you got here," he repeated, folding the ring into her palm, "you'd find the love to go with it."

Sara smiled at the hesitation in his expression. She knew he didn't believe that anyone could predict something like that. But Sara had lived with her grandmother too many years to dismiss Kathleen's conclusion. She'd come to one herself, just as probable and just as likely. By sending her to Brigen Glen, Fiona felt Sara would be in a safe place, where she'd be taken care of, and Sara in turn could take care of the place Fiona had loved so much.

Sara looked up at Devon, her smile luminous. "I believe she's right," she whispered.

Caressed by the love in her eyes, enticed by the lyrical tones of her voice, Devon answered the invitation on her lips. He'd never believed in much of anything before. But he believed in the love he felt for Sara and the future that love opened to him. With her, he felt that anything was possible.

The moon hung directly overhead. It shone on the place where they stood and long after they left the stream to walk hand in hand into the woods, the moon illuminated the footprints they'd made in the damp earth. One set looked like that of a man. The other, where Sara had raised on tiptoe to kiss him, strangely like that of a doe.

* * * * *

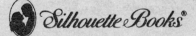

Silhouette Special Edition

This April,
Silhouette *Special Edition* is pleased to present

ONCE IN A LIFETIME
by Ginna Gray

the long-awaited companion volume to her bestselling duo

Fools Rush In (#416)
Where Angels Fear (#468)

Ever since spitfire Erin Blaine and her angelic twin sister Elise stirred up double trouble and entangled their long-suffering brother David in some sticky hide-and-seek scenarios, readers clamored to hear more about dashing, debonair David himself.

Now that time has come, as straitlaced Abigail Stewart manages to invade the secrecy shrouding sardonic David Blaine's bachelor boat—and creates the kind of salty, saucy, swashbuckling romantic adventure that comes along only once in a lifetime!

**Even if you missed the earlier novels,
you won't want to miss**

ONCE IN A LIFETIME #661

Available this April, only in Silhouette *Special Edition*.　OL-1

WRITTEN IN THE STARS

**Star-crossed lovers?
Or a match made in heaven?**

Why are some heroes strong and silent...and others charming and cheerful? The answer is WRITTEN IN THE STARS!

Coming each month in 1991, Silhouette Romance presents you with a special love story written by one of your favorite authors—highlighting the hero's astrological sign! From January's sensible Capricorn to December's disarming Sagittarius, you'll meet a dozen dazzling and distinct heroes.

Twelve heavenly heroes...twelve wonderful Silhouette Romances destined to delight you. Look for one WRITTEN IN THE STARS title every month throughout 1991—only from Silhouette Romance.

STAR

Silhouette Books®

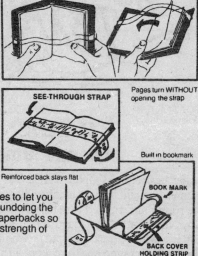

Silhouette Romance®

LONG, TALL TEXANS

HARDEN
Diana Palmer

In her bestselling LONG, TALL TEXANS series, Diana Palmer brought you to Jacobsville and introduced you to the rough and rugged ranchers who call the town home. Now, hot and dusty Jacobsville promises to get even hotter when hard-hearted, woman-hating rancher Harden Tremayne has to reckon with the lovely Miranda Warren.

The LONG, TALL TEXANS series continues! Don't miss HARDEN by Diana Palmer in March...only from Silhouette Romance.

LTT-1